THE DRUMMER'S ROOMMATE

A Spicy Rom Com Novel

From the author of *TIMESHARE BOYFRIEND*

M. K. HALE

FIRST EDITION - Publication Date: August 2, 2024

Cover Design by Meredith Hale

Cover Art Character Illustration © Kayla Planty

M. K. Hale - http://www.mkhale.com

Ebook ASIN: B0D77BPW6Y

Ebook ISBN: 979-8-2279709-2-3

Paperback ISBN: 979-8-9861402-3-0

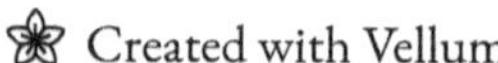 Created with Vellum

Praise for M. K. Hale

"Banter on point! ... Seriously I'm still in a bit of stunned disbelief!"

— RACHEL VAN DYKEN, NYT
BESTSELLING AUTHOR OF THE
WINGMAN SERIES

"Full of charm, wit, and utterly loveable characters... M. K. Hale is a romance writer on the rise."

— LEISA RAYVEN, INTERNATIONAL
BESTSELLING AUTHOR OF BAD
ROMEO

"I love her. Even though she writes sex scenes."

— MOM

To the reader who loves Pride & Prejudice but who also loves bad boys

#DarcyAsAMisunderstoodDrummer

Warning:

Trigger warning: *The female heroine is deaf and experiences some moments of prejudice toward her in this novel.*

Additionally, do not read this novel if you are:
1. Not ready for HEAT. We're talking spicy, people. Get ready for mutual pining, dirty talk, and sizzling sexual tension.

2. Watching a fierce deaf woman shed her people-pleasing ways and demand what she wants in life.

3. Not a fan of reading about a sexy-as-heck man who struggles with self-esteem and the world's perception of him.

The Drummer's Roommate

M. K. HALE

Chapter One

"Unbelievably attractive male seeking roommate. Must be able to tolerate loud drumming and even louder sex. Serious inquiries only."

Thea blinked several times after reading the online advertisement glowing on her phone.

She was supposed to live with the cocky, arrogant man who wrote that ad? Just because she was desperate to find a cheap place to stay in L.A. as soon as possible?

She looked up from her phone and quirked a single dark eyebrow at her closest friend, Mallory. Slowly picking up her large cappuccino cup—trying to exude the calm energy of a confident mob boss and not a woman who lost her job, boyfriend, and place of residence within days of each other—Thea took a long sip, licking foam from her lips.

After placing the cup back onto a table at their favorite local coffee shop, Thea signed, *"Who do you take me for?"*

She would *not* move in with drummer and playboy Draven Maxwell, no matter how desperate she was for a place to stay with cheap rent.

"*Look,*" Mallory signed, "*I know he's a bit of a manwhore, but you're not going to find a cheaper apartment to rent. He cut the original rent to a third of what others cost.*"

"*Because he can't keep a roommate,*" Thea signed back with an expression screaming, "*Duh.*"

"*Only because of the loud drumming, which wouldn't be a problem for you,*" Mallory stressed. "*He is not that bad.*"

Thea's eyebrow somehow curved even higher on her forehead in disbelief. Yes, Mallory dated one of Draven's rock star friends and had been around him in more social settings than Thea, but Thea *knew* Draven.

Maybe she'd never conversed with him, but she knew his type.

The man was the living embodiment of sex. The dirty kind. The taboo kind that involved handcuffs and his thick fingers cupping her throat as he thrust—

Thea! She shook herself.

The first time she saw the drummer at one of the band's gigs, Thea had stared, swallowed the sudden dryness in her mouth, and broken eye contact. Before or after the eye contact, she may or may not have squirmed, fidgeted, and pressed her thighs tightly together when they threatened to spread themselves for the man.

But after her body's tactless reactions, she recognized

him for what he was: a self-centered, selfish player who never slept with the same woman twice.

But the one thing Thea hated the most? Draven Maxwell believed he was better than everyone else. Hell, he described himself in the ad for a roommate as an *"unbelievably attractive male."* Was he honest? Sure.

But would it kill a muscular white man with perfect bone structure to have a little modesty? Damn.

"I hardly know him, and I already dislike him," Thea signed to Mallory. *"If I move in, he will expect me to cook, clean, and do his laundry. I know it."*

To Thea, Draven was the kind of man who grew up having other people do all of his work for him in group projects in school. Meanwhile, Thea worked harder than anyone. The word "overachiever" did not scratch the surface when describing her.

When you are underestimated, you want to be better than everyone in the room. And she had been.

What hard work had Draven ever had to do? Movie star—or more like porn star—good looks. A charming and addicting charisma.

Perfect teeth—had he ever needed braces? Thea had worn braces for six years throughout middle school and high school. *He has probably been allowed to eat popcorn his entire life, yet, his teeth are perfect and white.*

Asshole.

"You don't know that, Thea," Mallory shot back. *"He might offer to do your laundry."*

"Yeah, to fondle my underwear."

Mallory rolled her eyes and laughed. *"Babe, you wear granny panties."*

"High-waisted, full-coverage panties are comfortable, and being sexy is about being comfortable."

That earned Thea another eye roll from her closest friend.

"He is not a bad guy, really. He just probably has too much sex," Mallory signed. *"I already told him not to hit on you, though. I think my exact words were, 'Try to seduce her, and I'll strangle you with Wren's guitar strings.'"*

Thea scoffed. Men like Draven Maxwell—thirty, tattooed, and emanating waves of sinful pleasure—did not go for women like Thea, a twenty-five-year-old deaf woman who wore a strand of pearls and dresses that puffed out at the waist like she walked out of a 1950s film.

"You need a place to stay, Thea," Mal reminded her.

"I know." Swallowing her pride and nearly choking on it, Thea thought, *I need a new place to stay immediately for as little money as possible.*

Within three days, her whole life had fallen apart.

Last week, she had the perfect job, the perfect apartment, and the perfect boyfriend. A few days later, her cheeks were covered in smeared mascara and tears as her long-term boyfriend Alec told her, *"She didn't mean anything. It won't happen again."*

Plus, she got fired from her job in a manner that suggested no flowery, kind-hearted reference would be offered to help her find new employment.

Cheated on and fired. Now, homeless. *You're really living the wild L.A. life now, Thea.*

"*If you still had your finance job, you could think about other apartments, but Draven's is the only thing you can afford right now,*" Mallory added; her hands signed slowly as if she didn't want to offend Thea by driving the point home too harshly.

My only option is a sleazy drummer. Fantastic. "*How irresponsible with money does the guy have to be to need a roommate? Wren is dripping with money from the band. He has you guys set up in a mansion,*" Thea commented.

The band *Medusa's Tears* had started selling out at arenas over the last few years. They would go on an international tour soon. Thea hadn't heard of them—she wasn't a rock kind of girl—but she'd looked them up when Mal said she dated the lead guitarist.

Thea could assume, from her background in finance, that the band members were rolling in some serious cash.

So, why did Draven only have a two-bedroom, one-bathroom apartment in L.A. that he rented to a roommate?

Yes, city real estate was outrageously expensive, and it had to be one of the nicest apartment buildings she would step into without being promptly escorted out, but... *How?*

Did Draven spend all his hefty paychecks on things like beer, condoms, and sports gambling? Thea wanted answers to the financial mystery.

Mal shrugged.

Thea exhaled a lengthy sigh. "*And Draven already*

agreed to it?" she signed. *"He is fine with me moving in so quickly?"*

"A deaf roommate is basically the only kind of roommate a drummer can have," Mal signed back with a grin.

Thea nibbled on her lip and stared into her creamy cappuccino. She wrung her fingers in front of herself before signing, *"Does he know about Alec?"* The whole being-cheated-on-with-a-member-of-her-friend-group was a situation Thea did not want to rehash.

"He knows you're single now," Mal replied. *"But not how it happened."*

Alec had never seemed like a liar. Like someone who would throw away everything he had—they had—for sex. Some men hid it, and some men were like Draven—confident and blatantly honest with their utter lack of morals and commitment.

If she was expected to live with someone like that, she did not want him to know about Alec. She did not want to hear a flimsy excuse of *"Boys will be boys. Better to accept it now."*

Not that she planned on listening to any nuggets of wisdom Draven had to say. She imagined living with him to be like living with a ghost. She planned on interacting with him only to provide the monthly rent payment.

As long as he kept his threesomes in his bedroom and not their shared living room, all would be fine.

It will just be a place to live. Until I'm back on my feet, she thought.

Yes. *Temporary.*

Like all of Draven's hook-ups.

"If you fuck her, I'll kill you," Wren threatened Draven again, tallying the death threats to twice in less than one hour as the two men waited for Wren's fiancé Mallory and her friend Thea to show up and take a look at the apartment.

"Dude, why do you keep saying that?" An aggravated groan rumbled from Draven's lips as he ran a hand through his shoulder-length black hair. "I'm not going to fuck her. Stop acting like I'm some kind of animal."

"You *are* an animal."

"She is her own person. What if *she* fucks *me*, huh?" Draven questioned, gesturing to his chiseled frame.

Wren shook his head. "You are such a gentleman."

Draven grumbled as he continued cleaning the kitchen—with no help from Wren. "Besides, I'm sure she'll be back with that on-again, off-again boyfriend soon anyway. She will probably be gone within two weeks."

"Actually," Wren said in a cautious voice. "I'd say they are one hundred and ten percent done now. I don't see her taking him back."

That piqued Draven's interest. "What did he do?"

Wren shrugged. "I'm not supposed to say."

"Cheated," Draven guessed. "Didn't he?"

Wren frowned and shrugged again, not denying it. Draven's friend had no poker face.

"Asshole," Draven grunted. If a man wanted to play the field, fine. *But then have the balls not to promise exclusivity.*

Draven wasn't all that surprised, though. He had seen Thea two to three times in his life, and in two of those moments, she stood next to her boyfriend *Alrick* or Alex or some dumb name.

He resembled that boring, pompous, trust fund Wall Street type, and he had never even held Thea's hand. At parties where other men lurked and looked at his girl, he didn't touch her at all. Not a hand on her back or an arm around her shoulder.

She had stood, stiff as a board, beside the man. A well-loved woman had some curve to her spine. Thea was constantly stern-faced. Poor girl probably hadn't experienced an orgasm in months. Oh God, what if it had been a year?

What if, after a few weeks under the same roof, she snuck into Draven's bedroom, climbed on top of him, placed his hand to the wet heaven between her legs, and begged him to show her everything she had been missing—

"You're thinking about sleeping with her now that you know she is single, aren't you?" Wren asked in an annoyed, knowing tone.

Draven dismissed the thought. "Never gonna happen."

The few times Draven and Thea had met gazes at various bar gigs or parties, she glared at him with a displeasure that mimicked his third-grade math teacher, Mrs. Scardina.

"She hates me," Draven added, his voice transforming into something softer and more vulnerable than he wanted.

It shouldn't matter what some stranger thought of him, right? She was the opposite of his type. Well, no. He was the opposite of hers.

That constant pearl necklace around her neck that she fooled with—she was practically a stereotype. A future Mrs. Governor of some state.

A year or two down the line, she would marry a preppy, trust fund man with political aspirations. She would pop out two kids in a house with a picket fence and live happily ever after with three golden retrievers and several designer purses to keep her company when her husband was out on "business trips."

And that was fine if that was what she wanted.

But I would want more, Draven thought. Someone to hold and drag on world tours with him. Someone to write songs about. Someone who sang to his soul.

But if he admitted to any of that, his friends would rag on him until Draven's tombstone read, *"Here lies a man who admitted to wanting a woman to 'sing to his soul' in front of his rocker bandmates."*

"I wouldn't say she hates you." Wren tapped a finger to his chin. "She just thinks you toy with women's hearts and do nothing but drink beer and party. And she hates you."

So, she thinks I'm a drunken manwhore. Just like everyone else.

Wren watched as Draven threw empty red plastic cups and beer cans into trash bags and swept crumbs from the floor. The apartment was—in one word—trashed.

This is what I get for being a good friend, Draven thought to himself as a miscellaneous potato chip crunched under his left shoe. *Rock bands and rock groupies are such messy goddamn eaters.*

"How come the afterparties always have to be at my place?" Draven asked.

"Because you are the only member of the band who is single and kid-less."

Not my fault women are only interested in me for one-night stands. Draven kept his thoughts to himself, trying to ignore that rising memory of his ex-girlfriend telling him, *"Look, babe, you fuck a drummer. You don't date one."*

Draven was sure Thea would agree with that ex's opinion. *After all, I'm just a drunken manwhore, right?* A frustrated huff came from him as he tied off another trash bag. "If she sees all of this mess, she will think I caused it," he muttered.

"What do you care what she thinks of you?" Wren asked.

Exactly. Why would he care what Thea thought?
But he did.

For some reason, he cared what she—and her strand of pearls—thought.

He still remembered the first time he saw her standing in a back corner at a local bar where his band played.

He remembered how she closed her eyes and swayed with her friends, able to feel the vibrations of the music. He remembered hitting his drums with more fervor, more force, silently pleading with her to look at him and pay him any attention.

He remembered walking up to her and asking for her name, but she kept her back to him, ignoring him—or, at the time, that was what he thought. He had not realized she could not *hear* him. His dejection had only increased when he realized she had a boyfriend.

She had never shown any interest in Draven.

He had never had a single conversation with her because A) He did not know sign language, and B) She clearly hated him.

But yeah, he stupidly and inexplicably cared what she thought. *I really am a dumbass*, he thought.

The woman who, odds were, grew up being seen as a stereotype, saw him as one. Immature, shallow, untalented man candy—Draven had heard it all from people who believed drummers were only good for a "good time."

Sue him for hoping the owner of those piercing gray-blue eyes would be the first person to make him feel seen.

He bit his inner cheek, opened another trash bag, and shoved more items into their rightful place.

Chapter Two

"It won't happen again. I promise. Thea, come back home. Where are you?"

Thea stared at the text message from her boyfriend—Correction: *cheating ex*-boyfriend, Alec.

"She didn't mean anything. I love you."

She ground her teeth and clenched the phone in her hand.

It did not help matters that her family messaged her, *"Where are you? Alec is worried. Forgive him, Thea. He made a mistake. We are all human. You two are perfect together."*

Perfect together? Was she just supposed to accept him cheating on her because they were both from the same world? Dating in the deaf community—it was a smaller pool. But because she spoke a language that was rarer in the city than others, that was supposed to mean she should accept less love? Hell. No.

There have to be other deaf men in L.A. I haven't met yet. Or maybe hearing men who knew sign language. *The possibilities are endless,* she told herself as she turned her phone screen to black. *You don't need him to not be alone.*

She had friends. She had a pressing new need to find a job. *More important things are happening than* men.

At that moment, while she and Mallory stood outside the apartment, the door swung open to reveal Draven Maxwell: Aka, the most attractive man in California.

God. Damn.

Thea gripped her notepad harder as it threatened to slip right out of her fingers like buttered noodles instead of dry paper. She deserved a gold medal for her self-control in not letting her jaw drop at the sight of him. She had just never been this close before.

Slicked back, shoulder-length black hair flowed out in wisps to frame his face. Prominent, sharp cheekbones cast sinful shadows over his lickable jawline. Tattoos wrapped around his forearms, the ink stretching over veined, thick muscle.

He reminded her of a dark, villainous elven fae—beauty that felt otherworldly.

Every bit of dark clothing he wore stretched over muscle. Black, fitted jeans strained to encase strong thighs.

His black sleeveless shirt dipped at the sides and showed...so much skin. Like *so* much skin. Smooth, tan skin. If he turned to the side and bent over, his entire toned chest and abdomen would be on display through the gaping fabric.

She had seen the all-consuming sight of his abs before —when he threw his shirt off during most of his band's shows.

He played drums, shirtless and sweaty, and thrust those arms, muscles bulging and straining as he slammed his drumsticks down again and again. An endurance and talent that made a woman think about all other contexts where a man could use such a constant rhythm.

But more than anything, his eyes made her heart beat harder in her chest. Those slanted green eyes, narrowed in that sexy fox-like kind of way, always made it seem like he was thinking something indecent. Something shamelessly dirty.

Bright green irises, like Peter Pan's tights. A wicked smile that whispered of sin and sex and more sex. He was the human version of the Cheshire cat from *Alice in Wonderland*. Sly and charming and dangerous. *And all you want to do is pet him.*

"Unbelievably attractive male seeking roommate" was right. Thea couldn't even judge him for writing that in the ad. She thought to herself, *If I looked like him, I'd be a narcissist too.*

Her chin tipped up just to gaze at him. The man was the kind of tall that led to a lot of head injuries and many smitten women.

His sparkling chartreuse-green eyes examined Thea as hers did to him. His gaze paused at her pearl necklace, and he glanced down to where her skirt hit her knees—a professional length.

Was he expecting every woman who passed his doorstep to wear a tight mini-dress? Did he think Thea was some groupie dropping by for a quickie at three o'clock in the afternoon?

She frowned at him. *Look at the guy.* Those mouthwatering muscles. Those sexy tattoos. He was the textbook definition of a player.

He probably wouldn't be able to define the word "monogamy" if he had a gun to his head. Hell, he might spell it 'mahogany' and ask what wood had to do with anything.

Thea's duct-taped heart had no time for that.

Mallory strode inside the apartment to hug her fiancé Wren.

Gut-wrenchingly handsome Draven stepped back, gesturing for Thea to walk inside. To enter his world.

This may be my worst idea yet...

She suspected dirty floors and sticky counters from spilled alcohol and soda. *There's probably a drum set obnoxiously placed in the living room, taking up space.*

Draven's fingers clenched around the doorframe, balancing his forearm just over her as he continued holding it open. The longer she hesitated, the more annoyed the drummer appeared to become. Scrunched eyebrows. Flaring nostrils.

You left Alec, and now you have to deal with the consequences.

For the first time in a long time, she had choices to make. *New home; new job; new life.*

She stepped inside.

"Uh, hi."

Draven Maxwell's heart banged to a harsh, hard rhythm that put his drumming skills to shame.

There she was, dressed like a 50s housewife with her white pearls and her neck-to-knee dress, flaring at the hips, and his body reacted like she wore a thin, silk slip and held up a sign that said, *"I am here to seduce you."*

Thea could wear a trash bag as a dress, and his body would still act like she was a supermodel.

What is it about this girl?

His mouth dried up; an aching in his chest began. He was ready to accuse her of witchcraft because she transformed him back into that awkward teenager who had no idea how to talk to girls.

His body needed a reality check because she looked like she had been groomed her entire life to be a politician's wife. Forbidden. Prim. Proper. Not someone who would have any interest in a drummer from a rock band.

But damn, she was beautiful.

Do not lose yourself in those intelligent, piercing gray-blue eyes, he told himself.

Her hair hung in loose, dark brown waves, and some strange part of him wanted so badly to reach out and touch a strand. Rub it between his fingers. Prove she was real.

She did not seem as transfixed by him. Why did her frown feel like a punch to the jugular?

He gestured for her to come into the apartment. "Come on in."

Her cute little nose wrinkled at him, displaying the judgment he should have expected but hoped not to see.

After what felt like an eternity, she strode inside, glancing around the messy living room. She raised an eyebrow at his large drum set in the corner of the room.

Black trash bags were stacked up against a wall. Alcohol bottles still decorated the coffee tables. Draven had done his best to clean up the place. Still, a little over an hour was not enough time to cover cleaning the kitchen, living room, and shared bathroom after hosting the band's latest afterparty.

"Sorry it's such a mess." Draven grabbed one of the trash bags that tipped toward the ground, ready to spill over. "An afterparty got a bit out of hand."

"Dude," Wren muttered, shaking his head. "She can't hear you."

When Draven looked back over to Thea, she pointed to her notepad, on which she had written, *"I'm deaf."* Her furrowed eyebrows and pursed lips painted a clear expression of, *"Wow, you are stupid."*

Draven had spent most of his life seeing that expression.

"Right. Sorry, um..." Draven mimicked drinking from

an invisible cup, shimmied his body like an odd snake dance, and mouthed, "Party."

She nodded grimly, her regal eyebrows furrowing even more as she watched him.

"We'll leave you two to get acquainted," Wren said, pulling Mallory after him as they left Draven's apartment.

Mallory waved goodbye to Thea and made a threatening hand gesture at Draven to make herself clear: Thea was to be protected and treated with respect. It really pissed Draven off that they expected him *not* to do that—what he believed to be the bare minimum of human interaction.

When the door closed, leaving Thea and Draven alone, he shifted his weight onto his opposite foot and awkwardly tapped a palm against the side of his leg. "So..." he began.

Seeing his lips move, she uncapped her pen again and underlined the *"I am deaf"* on her notepad. She then turned to a new page in her notepad and wrote something. She showed it to him. *"How often do you throw parties?"*

Right. She thought he was a party animal. "Not often."

She looked at him like he was dumb again, then she turned back to show him her original note.

Right. He walked to his kitchen and found a pack of blue Post-it notes and a black pen. *"I don't throw parties often."* He showed her his note. *"Promise."*

Her gaze fell from the note to his black nail-polished fingernails. Her nose wrinkled again.

Right. Fighting off annoyance and hurt, Draven

gestured for her to sit on the couch across from him so they could talk.

She took her time sitting, fanning out the skirt of her dress and checking for crumbs in the cushions before allowing her full weight to settle. She then stiffened and jolted to the side of the couch.

Her hand dipped between two cushions and yanked out a red lace bra that had poked her.

Her expression twisted into one of disgust as she held the crimson lingerie. She then dove her hand right back down between the cushions. She pulled out *another* bra—clearly a different size from another woman.

"Goddamn, are you a great fisher or something?" Draven couldn't even recall hooking up with someone on his couch. It was entirely possible someone *else* had hooked up on his couch after he had gone to his bedroom to sleep post-afterparty.

But now, Thea thought her new roommate was the manwhore of L.A.

Shit.

She hastily jotted down another note, and he held his breath while waiting for what she had to say next.

When she held up the notepad, he read her words, "*I need a place to stay, but I just want to be clear: I'd like to limit our interactions with each other. I think it is clear we are two very different people, and I don't think we need to be more than cohabitors.*"

Was it just him, or had a cannonball ripped through his chest and left a gaping hole?

If she wants to judge me without even knowing me, fine, he thought to himself.

Her gray-blue eyes seemed to stare through people, but apparently, she couldn't see him, just the archetype box he had been thrown in. *Just like everybody else.*

His ex-girlfriend's words again speared through him, "*You fuck a drummer. You don't* date *one.*"

If Thea wanted to think of him as nothing but the dumb, sex-addict drummer—fine.

He would be the biggest manwhore she had ever seen.

Chapter Three

He had filled every kitchen drawer with condoms.

Thea pinched the bridge of her nose and released a deep sigh of what had to be only fifty percent carbon dioxide and fifty percent annoyance.

Just the night before, he had made out with a woman in their living room as if to purposefully vex Thea.

He had been shirtless—because, of course. And as aggravated at her new roommate's immaturity and blatant sexual blasé as she was, she was also pissed at herself for the pang of jealousy at watching all that potent masculine energy focused on the stranger and not her.

Yes, she found him immature and annoying, but she did not know lips could *move* like that. *This apartment is going to mess with my mind.*

Disoriented by the astonishing feeling of envy and overwhelmed by her own feelings of loneliness and lack of normalcy, Thea flipped out. She speedily signed words at

Draven that he did not understand as he made eye contact with Thea and continued kissing the woman's neck.

"How immature are you? Do you have no respect for others? No, you probably don't have a single thought about anyone but yourself."

She swore he sang a jolly tune of, "I can't hear you."

But something particularly mind-boggling occurred when Thea tiptoed behind the living room to get to the kitchen later that night.

She had expected to see them still dry humping each other on the couch. Instead, Draven kept his hands to himself and sat straight and stiff beside the woman, trying to watch something on the TV. He looked almost uncomfortable.

When the woman placed her hand on Draven's upper thigh, he grimaced at it like she had just randomly spread tuna salad on his leg.

Confused, Thea stutter-stepped and must have made enough noise that Draven's gaze swung over to her, and in the next second, he'd crashed his lips to the woman's and acted like they were seconds away from stripping off their clothes and having sex on the couch.

So, he was doing it on purpose just to upset Thea.

It triggered two thoughts:

"Why does he care what I think about him?"

"This is a man of limited maturity and must be handled with an equal amount of immaturity." Obviously.

Thus, it began. They became enemies under the same roof.

It was an unspoken battle. Passive aggressive notes left all over the apartment.

"Because you're single, I have to go without sex?" He had written her his version of an apology on a Post-it note and left it on the bathroom mirror for her to see the next morning.

She had clicked her pen and written on the bottom of the note. *"You couldn't go without sex for a week if you tried."*

His jaw fell to the tiled floor when he saw her note later that day. *"You don't even know me."*

To which she wrote back on a new pink Post-it, *"I know your type."*

When she entered the bathroom to brush her teeth the next morning, his blue Post-it hung proudly in the center of the mirror.

He had written, *"One week without sex. Challenge accepted. Just don't judge me for any unmanageable erections you see in the next few days."*

"I'm sure you can take care of them yourself," she had impulsively written and rushed out.

After half an hour of searching online for job postings in the privacy of her new bedroom, she ran back to their shared bathroom to take down her note. It seemed too... flirty, seeming to suggest she *imagined* him "taking care" of himself. And, of course, she did.

She just did not need *him* to know that. To know that late last night, she imagined walking in on him pleasuring himself in their shared bathroom. His head thrown back as he fisted his cock and stroked—

Shoot. She gaped at the mirror. Her note was gone. He had kept it.

And he had written back, "*Oh, I plan to take care of myself a lot this week. Nothing like a little self-love. Maybe you should try it?*"

That was flirty, wasn't it? Telling her that maybe she should touch herself.

She was definitely tempted.

He walked around the apartment *shirtless.* All the time. He glistened like his skin produced a light coating of liquid gold and sweat at all times to create an alluring shine.

Later that morning, when she ate cereal at the kitchen island, she could do nothing but stare as he strode into the kitchen wearing only a pair of modest boxers.

As he turned and opened the fridge, grabbing *her* almond milk, his muscular back and slim hips were on complete display before her. *My God.*

Yes, she would have expected a drummer to have muscles; he would have to be fit and full of stamina to voraciously hit those drums all night. But... *Wow.* Alec had never been a toned, muscular man; she never thought muscles were all that attractive, but on Draven... Everything about him was provocative. Arousing.

Thea finally understood the term "animal magnetism."

When Draven finished making his bowl of cereal, he

turned and faced her, his chest only three feet from her. When he caught her drooling over the ropes of his chiseled abs, he chuckled and smirked at her.

To which, she wrote on her notepad, *"Do you have something against shirts?"*

He grinned at her, stealing her pad. He grabbed a Sharpie from a kitchen cup of pens and *bit* off the cap in a tantalizing manner that made Thea's thighs clench.

The black cap twitched between his sinful lips as he wrote back on her notepad. *"I'm anti-establishment, baby. Plus, I've found that you glare at me less when I'm shirtless. Just trying to keep my new roommate happy."*

She pursed her lips at his words. Had she glared at him that much? She had only been living there three days and mostly hid in her bedroom. Draven tended to sleep in late, fumble into the kitchen for breakfast, then stumble out of the apartment to head to his band practices, the recording studio, or wherever he went.

He was not a struggling artist; the man was a drummer in a well-known, successful rock band called *Medusa's Tears*. Thea knew Mallory was excited to join Wren on their world tour in a few months.

So, the question Thea had was: *how irresponsible with money does Draven have to be to need a roommate?* Was it gambling? He did not seem like someone who did drugs. *His vice is sex*, she thought to herself, remembering the lingerie she found between the couch cushions. *But he'd never have to pay for it.*

Knowing Wren's wealth, Thea strived to understand

how much Draven had to spend to *not* have his own apartment—maybe one with two bathrooms instead of a shared one. Though, maybe that was her financial brain tingling to solve a money management issue.

She tsked her thoughts. Other women might look at bad boy Draven and think, "*I can change him.*" Thea thought, "*I can save his finances.*"

Thea took her notepad back from him and jotted down another note. She spun it so he could see. "*That's my almond milk, you know,*" she told him.

His lips moved, but she didn't know what he said. After years in public school where hearing students expected her to read lips, she still failed at it. Only about thirty-five percent of the English language could be read on the lips.

It did not help that Draven's lips were particularly distracting. He just always licked them. Suggestively. He flashed that seductive tongue at her and expelled all other thoughts from her brain.

Even now, as he lifted his spoon of cereal to his mouth, she swallowed and watched with wide, fascinated eyes as his cupid's bow lips moved together, and his jaw flexed with each chew. She should have been annoyed that he used her almond milk. Instead, she shifted on the barstool and crossed her legs, suddenly very aware of a tingling occurring between them.

Those lips.

She blinked and glanced down at her notepad where

he had written back, "*Check your facts. That's my almond milk.*"

She frowned, looking back up at where he loomed over her. Even as she sat on the high barstool, he was so *tall* in front of her. The island counter between them blocked the view of anything below that lickable, defined V at his hips.

"*That's* my *almond milk,*" she wrote back, underlining "my."

He read it and shook his head. He took another bite of almond-milk-soaked cereal.

She nodded her head. *Mine.*

He shook his.

Nod. Shake. Glare.

"*Using the groceries of your jobless cohabitor is not a good look,*" she wrote.

He did not seem to like that at all. His jaw clenched. His eyes narrowed angrily at her note. His shoulder blades drew up in a defensive manner.

Oh geez, you've pissed off the drummer now, Thea.

"*I bought that milk, princess,*" he wrote. "*I'm sure you are used to your Wall Street man supplying all your food for you, but I'm not him.*"

She made a hand gesture as her expression screamed, "*Obviously.*"

Alec and Draven were polar opposites. Alec once said he didn't like the texture of pumpkin pie on his tongue. Thea was fairly certain Draven had his tongue *pierced.*

Oh God, what if his cock was pierced too? Some men did that, right? The metal piercing was meant to increase male and female pleasure during sex. Not that she, uh, read up on it or anything. She certainly had not *not* stayed up late reading about such a thing.

Draven's bad boy, rocker image messed with her mind.

What if he is pierced? What would that even feel like?

Her gaze fell to the countertop, which blocked his crotch.

Draven put his bowl down and clapped, gathering back her attention. He then said something and pointed to his face. She assumed he said something along the lines of, "*My eyes are up here.*"

His Sharpie rapidly moved over the notepad. "*If you're going to tell me to put a shirt on, maybe try not to leer at me so much,*" he wrote.

She blinked. The drummer had just used the word "leer." Regaining herself, she wrote, "*You must be cold, walking around half-naked all the time.*"

He smirked and dragged a hand down his left bare pec. *Do not drool, Thea.* That sinful tongue dove out again, wetting his lips. He wrote back, "*Oh, I always run hot.*"

She *felt* hot whenever he was around. The man emitted radioactive warmth.

Draven turned, opened the fridge, and wrote "Draven's" in marker on *her* almond milk.

This means war.

Always run hot, huh? As the day passed, Thea lowered the thermostat by two degrees every hour. Draven played his drums in the living room, shirtless and shivering once the apartment reached sixty-three degrees. Still, he never added another layer of clothing.

In fact, the next time Thea went to the thermostat, she saw it was lowered two degrees more than what she had left it.

The temperature was now a battle.

They went back and forth that evening, lowering it until Draven shivered and wrapped a blanket around himself as he drummed—still shirtless.

Thea wore her puffy winter coat as she poured herself a glass of almond milk in the kitchen.

From his spot in the corner of the living room, he glared at her.

And as cold as the apartment was, she felt especially warm.

Chapter Four

"She keeps drinking my goddamn almond milk," Draven complained to Wren and a few of his other bandmates after they finished up practice at the studio, and they asked him how his new roomie situation was going.

Wren snorted. "You do realize you're almost thirty and whining about milk."

"It's *my* milk," Draven stressed. He would have been fine with sharing if she had not accused *him* of stealing *her* milk. Was she so used to having everything paid for her? Was she so spoiled that she truly believed she had bought his milk? "She's crazy."

"Dude," Yin, the band's bassist, said in a warning tone. "Men don't call women crazy."

"But...my milk," Draven repeated.

She wrongly believed she owned his milk. She had fooled with the damn thermostat to try to freeze him to death. Yeah, she was crazy hot when she got that smug, stubborn *I win* expression, but come on!

"Thirty. Years. Old," Wren repeated as if Draven was the one being immature.

Was he already planning another thermostat war as retribution? Yes. But he wasn't about to share his battle plan with his traitor bandmates. Odds were, Wren would run to his fiancé Mallory, who would communicate the plan of attack to her friend, thus eliminating the crucial element of surprise.

"I'm just glad you are not trying to sleep with her," Wren said.

Because that was all anybody thought Draven was good for nowadays. *Nice,* he grumbled to himself.

Draven raked his hands over his face. "Why does everyone seem to think I'm only capable of sex?" He was two out of seven days through his "no sex" challenge with Thea. He would sooner die than lose that. *I hate the way she looks at me.*

"Dude, we once walked in on you screwing that one groupie in our *shared* dressing room."

"When I was twenty-two years old," Draven shot back. His bandmates shrugged. *God forbid anyone sees me as more than the sexed-up, irresponsible rock star drummer.* "Dicks."

"Drave, we're about to go on tour in two months," the lead singer, Tomi, said. "Let the apartment go. Hell, how do you not have enough money from the band to pay for a two-bedroom and one bath apartment yourself *without* a roommate? Where is your money going?"

My money is going everywhere. Draven was paying for his two younger siblings to go to college while also paying for his grandmother's expensive as heck nursing home.

Not to mention, he had put a bunch of his money into stocks, thinking he could invest in his future and not be a washed-up has-been with no money in twenty years, but the stock market had dropped, destroying that hope and the bulk of his savings for now.

The men shook their heads at Draven, most likely assuming the drummer spent most of his earnings on beer, porn, and anything else seemingly immature. Had there been a time when that assumption had been true? Maybe in college, when their "boy band" became popular and videos went viral overnight. But Draven was approaching thirty years old, along with his other bandmates. He was not the same stupid kid he once was.

"You really need to start thinking more like an adult, man," Wren chastised him. None of the bandmates knew about Draven's family expenses, and Draven wanted to keep it that way.

"What's your new roomie up to today?" Yin asked, flipping his bleached hair.

"She is out doing some job interviews," Draven replied. He kept to himself that she looked cute as hell leaving their apartment in her black and white polka dot dress and pearl necklace. "Hopefully, she gets something, so she can pay for her own damn milk."

Wren palmed his face with a groan. "Thirty. Years. Old."

Nobody wants me. Thea trudged into the apartment after a long day of unsuccessful interviews with financial firms. No one had acted interested in her, and she could hardly blame them after one interviewer asked, "*Where do you see yourself in five years?*" and she struggled to respond.

Thea had worked in finance since she graduated college four years ago. It was ridiculous that her old financial firm would not give her a professional reference. *All because of a stupid, impulsive note.*

She participated in office gossip. Once.

While other hearing people could huddle around the coffee machine and say whatever they wanted about the boss, Thea had to write down her complaints about her leadership's incompetency to join in with her coworkers. And since everyone else's words weren't *written down*, she was the only one to lose her job over it. She had only complained to feel like more of a member of the team. *It's not fair.*

As Thea walked into the living room, a wave of heat slammed into her.

Literal heat. *My God*, it had to be over eighty degrees in the apartment.

Draven, she grumbled silently to herself.

Was this the start of their new and improved thermostat war? Was she supposed to strip down to her undies to not perish from heat exhaustion—all due to her pride of not wanting to admit defeat?

But I feel defeated.

Arms spread wide along the back of the couch, Draven sat in front of the television, lounging in nothing but boxers again and looking too damn sexy for this earth. *He has probably never been rejected from a job. Probably never been rejected in general. Hate that. Hate him.*

In a moment of hurt, anger, and frustration, she stripped her jacket and threw it to the living room floor, stomped over, and threw herself down on the couch cushion beside him.

His lips curled at her dramatic display of annoyance. He lifted the remote and hit a button. When Thea glanced at the TV, she noticed he had turned on subtitles. Without her even asking.

Blinking in surprise and sudden warmth, she looked back at him. Even her parents occasionally forgot to turn them on when she visited them.

He leaned over to the coffee table on his left and lifted a notepad. On it, in his handwriting, was: "*How did the job hunt go?*" As if he had written it hours ago in preparation for when she returned home.

She blinked again. He handed her the notepad and an uncapped pen. He *wanted* to hear about her day?

She swallowed the emotions rising to the back of her

throat and wrote back to him. *"Fine. Nothing yet, but I'll find something. There are always finance jobs."*

That was why she went into finance in the first place. A stable and steady job meant a stable and steady life. *Oh, really? How is that working out for you, Thea?* She frowned at herself.

Draven nodded at her message, writing back, *"I don't trust people who find math fun."*

"It isn't fun. It's a job," she wrote.

His lips curved downward as he jotted, *"I find my job fun."*

"Yeah, all you do is hit a drum set and sleep with women." She joked and smirked at him, surprised to find herself trying to tease him.

But he did not take it as a soft, playful jest.

Draven's nostrils flared. His jaw ticked. His once at-ease body stiffened on the couch. The drummer's light green eyes were like clear pools of pond water, reflecting every ripple of emotion he felt. Anger. Hurt.

He furiously wrote back, *"At least I'm following my dream and not selling out for a 401k."*

Jerkily, as if having to find his footing, he stood from the couch and strode down the hall to his bedroom.

Thea had...hurt his feelings? The playboy drummer had feelings to hurt? Her front teeth sank into her bottom lip.

"At least I'm following my dream." Draven's words echoed in her head, bouncing around her skull in an annoying zig-zagging way that told her maybe he was right.

She had chosen finance because it was safe.

She had chosen Alec because he felt safe.

But what did *she* want?

What was her dream?

And why did she suddenly feel the need to apologize to Draven freaking Maxwell?

Chapter Five

"Yeah, all you do is hit a drum set and sleep with women."

That was what Thea thought of him. Screw. That. As he laid back on his bed and closed his eyes, the image of her smirking at him after she wrote that *burned* in his mind. And suddenly, lyrics flowed out of him.

He grabbed his pen and the new notepad he bought to interact with his new roommate. His every breath rushed out of him as words poured from every stroke of the pen.

"Piercing eyes I hoped would see me.
Cactus skin I hoped would bleed me.
I'll be the poison apple to your fairytale lips.
Bite me, devour me, send in your warships.
Give me that mutual destruction, that killer seduction.
Make me sheer; see me here."

Stupid. Draven ripped the paper out and crumpled it into a ball. He threw it to the floor and groaned. Draven The Drummer did not write songs. He played the beats his friends told him to play. He suggested some changes here and there. But writing music? Writing lyrics? About *her*?

Unacceptable.

When he felt like this, dejected and raw and vulnerable, he typically distracted himself with sex. *When I can't do anything else right, I do the one thing I know I'm the best at.* Aka, give women multiple screaming orgasms.

But due to having to prove a Little Miss wrong—*oh, one-week sex-ban, how I loathe you*—all he could think to do was stomp back into the kitchen and grab a beer. *Should probably put the thermostat back to normal too.* Now, a temperature war with Thea sounded a lot less fun.

The second he stepped into the hallway, he fanned his face. Yeah, he was shirtless and rocking only boxers and sweatpants, but damn, it was hot. *I may have gone overboard with the heat.* But, he supposed, all was fair in love and war. Not that it had anything to do with love. Obviously.

More like every time I look at her, my skin feels too tight, like my soul wants to freaking hop out and wrap around her, but she thinks I'm the worst, so...

He strode to the fridge, hankering for a beer and hoping Thea had gone back to her room for the rest of the night. It was six o'clock, but she had never "hung out" in their shared space over the last few days of living together.

She hides from me. His shoulders sank inward, and he opened the fridge and grabbed a silver can. Cracking it open, he turned and faced the open space. His direct line of sight aligned with the living room, where Thea touched his drum set.

She touched his drums while wearing a pair of hot pink short-shorts.

He did not know what was more infuriating: that she dared to touch his drums or that his body lit on fire and his cock twitched between his legs at the sight of her in shorts. *Goddamn, those legs...*

He had only ever seen her in knee-length dresses. The vision of Thea in shorts was too much for his nearly thirty-year-old heart to take. It thudded dangerously fast behind his rib cage; tingles ran up and down his skin. *Is that what she wears to bed?*

"What are you doing?" he shouted over to her, which, of course, she did not hear.

He grabbed a grocery list from one of the fridge magnets and turned it over for a blank side. He wrote, "*Why are you touching my drums?*"

When she noticed him walking up behind her, she jumped and landed a hand on her chest. *Such a perfect chest. No!* Those curves belonged to a crazy woman who lied about buying milk.

She read his note and stepped away from the drum set. She grabbed her notepad and wrote back, "*I was just looking at them.*"

"*You were touching them. Why?*" Was she thinking of doing some enemy-roommate prank on his drums?

She scowled at his response. She underlined her previous note of "*looking at them.*"

"This is looking," Draven said aloud, gesturing to his eyes. He demonstrated dragging his gaze over her body from head to toe. "This is touching." He took her hand and pressed it to his warm, hard pectoral muscle. "See the difference?"

She blinked those gray-blues at him, staring at where he placed her hand over his taut skin. Could she feel how hard and fast his heart beat? *It has been like that since you moved in.*

Draven pointed to his previous note. "*Why were you touching my drums?*"

She hesitantly dropped her hand from his chest, squeezing her fingers into a fist, releasing them, and stretching out the digits. He tried to ignore the lingering tingles of where her skin had touched his.

She took her time writing a response. "*I'm trying to figure out my dream. How did you know music was yours?*"

Draven sipped in an uneven breath. It had been years since someone asked him that.

When his college boy band became popular, everyone coined him as the player, drummer "bad boy." They asked people like Wren or Yin about their musical influences or song writing process. Reporters tended to ask Draven about what female musicians he had hooked up with and left brokenhearted.

No one asked Draven about music. His reply to her question felt especially important, like she might finally see him if he answered correctly.

He wrote, "*Music chose me, but I chose to get good at it.*

Does that make sense? Sometimes, a passion will overwhelm you, and you want to master it. You want to be the best and have others see how good you are. There's adoration to be had. Pride in what you do. A creative outlet." Damn, he wished he was better with words. *"There's a peace. When I play the drums, the whole world feels quiet."*

Thea stared hard at his note. Particularly the word *quiet*. His whole world felt quiet when he played the drums? He played loud *rock*. Yet, he described pursuing his dream as a peaceful quiet. That resonated with Thea more than if he had described it any other way.

She also understood wanting to be the best at something—needing to be the best. As the only deaf daughter to parents of other hearing siblings, as the deaf girl in hearing classrooms growing up, she had always strived to be the best. To be noticed. To be seen as something more than a label or an inconvenience or the "odd one."

Adoration, Draven had written. An answering tug occurred behind her ribcage. If there was anything Thea could understand, it was the need to be loved. *I just never thought a man like Draven would feel that need too.*

As she stared into those light green eyes, she saw a reflection of pain she felt in herself. But, of course, such a thing was ridiculous. How could a heartthrob drummer ever feel the same loneliness she did? *He is adored by everyone.*

She bit her lip as her gaze fell to examine his mouth. It

was almost eye level, after all. Well, not really. *He is just so tall.*

He inched closer, as if pulled by that same invisible force that yanked her toward him. His bare chest—because he was *still* shirtless—rose and fell in front of her. She wanted to touch it again. To feel those hot muscles twitch beneath her fingers. To feel his heartbeat again. Strong and demanding.

His scent tickled her nose—linen and citrus bergamot oil. The rocker smelled like clean sheets and looked like he could spend all night doing dirty, dirty things in them. Limbs entangled. Heavy breathing. His lips slanted on hers.

She watched his mouth move as he asked her something, but she couldn't make out the words. Her pulse skipped and thrummed in her throat as she watched his tongue dab out and lick those full lips.

Oh damn, I want to kiss him.

Danger!

She blinked several times, trying to clear her thoughts. He frowned at her now, concern and confusion lighting up those hypnotic eyes.

He wrote, "*What do you like to do, Thea?*"

Right. He was helping her figure out her dream. Wait, *he* was helping her figure out her dream? More traitor warmth settled and swirled in her lower stomach.

She stared at his note. Because she didn't know what she liked to do. And how pitiful was that?

Finance had never been fun to her. It had only ever

been easy. She needed to find her passion that made the world fade away around her. After so long of suppressing any artistic inklings, she worried nothing would rise to the surface.

She knew what she needed to do.

She hastily wrote to Draven, *"Can I have my friends over tomorrow night?"*

He shot her an offended *"Of course. I'm not your keeper"* expression.

She added, *"Do you promise not to flirt with them?"*

This time, real offense—not the playful kind—poured over his emotive face. Shaking his head, he wrote, *"I'm not interested in anyone else."*

She blinked. *Anyone else?* What did *that* mean? That he was interested in...her?

He examined her surprised expression, looked back at what he had written, and quickly crossed it out. He scribbled over it again and again until it was illegible, then wrote, *"I mean, I won't flirt with them. I'd never try to make any of your friends uncomfortable."*

So much to unpack there. She had meant she did not want him flirting with them because, well, she didn't like the idea of one of her friends flirting right back with him. She had not meant her request to be taken like she thought he would leer at them.

Draven would never be crude or cringey enough to make them uncomfortable. He was...Draven. *If anything, some might try to seduce him.*

She shook her head and wrote, "*I know you wouldn't. You're not a bad person. I'm sorry about what I said before.*"

His eyes widened, so big and dramatic, her lips nearly quirked into a smile. He made a big show of fanning himself. He glanced around like he looked for TV cameras on a *Punk'd* show. He wrote, "*Thea Gullybil apologizing? To ME?*" He even drew an open-mouthed, gaping stick figure.

He was such a brat, and she kind of liked it. He had the rare type of smile that made everyone who saw it want to mirror it right back to him.

"*Now, are you going to apologize for drinking my milk?*" he wrote, raising an eyebrow.

Just because he was hot and funny, he thought he could charm her into forgetting she was the one who bought the almond milk?

"*No, I bought that milk,*" she replied, adamant.

His scowl was back.

Chapter Six

"Baby, I see those thighs trembling for me. I think I know what you need, Roomie. Why don't you lay back and let me show you how good I am with my tongue?"

Thea jolted awake, sweat clinging to her skin as she realized it had been a dream. She also discovered her pesky hand slipped between her legs during the night. *No wonder it felt so real.* Her body was a traitor.

She hadn't had a sex dream in, well, forever. *I knew living under the same roof as him would cause something like this.* If he would only wear a freaking shirt.

As Thea sleepily rubbed her eyes and walked to the kitchen, Draven's presence surprised her. He typically slept till close to eleven. Granted, he had not had a show last night. And due to the one-week sex ban, he was not hooking up at all hours of the night.

Draven stood by the coffee maker and held up a blue Post-it. *"Coffee?"*

Tempting. The hot liquid smelled as delicious as the man making it. She shook her head and wrote, "*Too much caffeine in the morning can make my ears ring.*"

He tilted his head as he read that and nodded.

The kitchen was not tight, but his presence was massive. As a tall, broad-shouldered man, he blocked the main cabinets and drawers she needed to get into for her cereal bowl and spoon.

And damn, the view of his naked back left her breathless and horny again. The lines and ridges of his muscular back snared all of her half-awake attention. *I need a cold shower.*

She stepped forward to reach over his shoulder for the upper cabinet.

She misjudged his height, and her arm brushed over his right shoulder as he stood in front of the coffee maker. At the minimal touch, her breath caught in her throat, and the memory of the sex dream seared itself into the frontal lobe of her brain.

Her smooth forearm glided over his toned shoulder again as she pulled a bowl from the cabinet. Goosebumps raced to claim her skin. Awareness crackled through her with its intense electricity.

Dang it, she cursed her body for how reactive it was for him.

His back stiffened at her slight touch, muscles clenching and on complete display due to his shirtless-ness. The ridges making up his tantalizing back were nearly enough to make her sleepy-self swoon.

Were the jumping movements of his muscles signs that he felt the same electric hyperawareness around her too? His hands bunched into fists on the counter as if he fought himself to not touch her.

I still need a spoon.

When she moved to reach around his waist to get to the silverware drawer, he spun around. He accidentally aligned his crotch directly with where her hand extended.

She gasped, but the movement happened so quickly that there was no way to stop it.

Her fingers brushed lightly over the crotch of his sweatpants, landing there.

Landing on something hard.

Both of them froze. Wide-eyed, they stared at each other, neither moving—neither breathing.

Her hand was on his cock.

Well, directly over it. A thin, thin layer of light gray sweatpants separated Thea's fingers from Draven's hardening dick. The fabric was thin enough for her to tell that he was not wearing boxers. And he was, uh, *growing.*

Thick, hazy lust wrapped a firm hand around her throat and throttled her.

She should have removed her fingers from him the second they touched. She knew every second that ticked by of keeping her hand there was inappropriate. *You don't want him thinking you're trying to hook up with him, do you?* she chided herself. *Step. Away.*

She couldn't. Her lungs wrung every ounce of oxygen

from her, leaving her so breathless that thinking felt like too much of a sport.

Glancing up from where her hand still laid over his crotch, she met his gaze. Her body could have melted to the floor in desire.

His eyes *blazed*. They did not burn; they destroyed—like a forest fire of need. The lust-drunk expression on his face was nearly violent. Like he wanted to scoop her up in his arms, throw her onto the closest soft surface, and fuck the life out of her.

Or maybe she was just projecting that. After all, surely the drummer only knew how to have rough, earth-shattering sex.

Breathe, Thea.

His lips moved, saying something.

She would have killed to know what he said at that moment.

Had he asked her to release his stiffening cock from his sweatpants? To touch him, stroke him? Did he want her as much as she wanted him?

Even though it shouldn't have, the idea of this punk rock star on a sex-ban, full of pent-up passion that all got focused on her... *Mmm*, it made her shiver.

She was sure a psychologist would inform her that, after losing her long-term boyfriend to infidelity, her attraction and desire for Draven was somehow an act of lashing out to prove her sex appeal. If Draven, a sex-god, who could have literally anyone he wanted, but he wanted her, then, yeah, she would feel better about herself. *Who wouldn't?*

But was that all it was?

His tongue dabbed out to suggestively lick those plush lips again. Nostrils flaring, he reached down to wrap his fingers around her delicate wrist, but he did not remove her hand from him. He did not insistently push her fingers firmer against him either. He just held her wrist and stared her down with fierce, narrowed eyes.

She stared intently at his lips as he spoke again. He seemed to be repeating a phrase. She cursed herself for her lack of talent for reading lips. *Say it again, Draven. Maybe I'll get it this time.*

He repeated whatever it was again, and both of them seemed to peak in their frustration.

Thea had always preferred her silent, peaceful world. But in this moment, she wished she could have heard him. She wished he knew sign language. She wished...

This time, Draven did pull her hand away, but not before his cock thickened and jerked behind the thin material, rubbing against and seeking her fingers.

She swallowed as his strong jaw visibly ticked. He dropped her wrist to reach in front of himself and realign his erection to a more comfortable state.

Big erection. She swallowed again.

He said something and pointed toward the bathroom. Shower. He stiffly spun and walked briskly away from her.

She palmed her reddening face. *I just groped a rock star,*

and he got hard under my hand. She opened her mouth and let out a silent scream.

If Mallory found out... Mal would think Draven "seduced" Thea and possibly murder him. Meanwhile, Thea felt ready to be the seducer.

The way he looked at me. A vibrating volcano about to blow. Her core tightened and ached between her legs. Her nipples pushed against the front of her sleep shirt in tiny peaks. She had loved Alec, but she had never in her life felt raw, carnal attraction like this.

When Draven held her wrist and stared at her with a dominating order shining in his eyes of "*Do something about it,*" she had wanted to fall to her knees, pull his straining erection free, and take him into her mouth. She wanted to challenge him. She wanted to see the sex god's eyes roll into the back of his head *because of her*.

She needed to cool down.

But wait, could Draven be going to shower or to "take care" of himself? The mere thought of the drummer touching himself had her thighs clenching together as another rush of lust rippled through her.

Considering Draven reemerged after less than ten minutes without wet hair, Thea's question was answered. *What did he imagine when he came?* She couldn't let the moment drop.

Some annoying and self-sabotaging part of her wrote on her notepad and showed him, "*Did you really just jerk off?*"

With a tense jaw and lips pressed thinly together, Draven read her note and nodded.

Heat overwhelmed Thea. It was worse than when he messed with the thermostat. Her clit pulsed between her legs with every beat of her heart.

He took her notebook from her, stole her pen right from her trembling fingers, and wrote, *"This will be my fourth day in a row without sex, you wore shorts last night, and you touched my dick this morning. The big guy needed some lovin'."*

Her mouth fell open. First, he called his dick "big guy." Second, one of the reasons he listed was because he had seen her in shorts. A man who had women flash him at shows had gotten aroused by *her* in shorts? Warmth spread over her chest.

"Any other questions about my jacking off, or can I make myself some breakfast?" he wrote.

She held her breath as he moved in front of the kitchen island, where she sat on a barstool and ate her cereal. He grabbed a bowl and a spoon. When he reached for his cereal box sitting on top of the fridge, his back muscles rippled, and Thea let out a little, breathy sigh—which he must have heard because he stiffened for a moment.

He poured a large amount of cereal into his bowl, then he turned to the refrigerator and pulled out the half-gallon carton of almond milk. He froze as he closed the fridge door.

Thea swallowed again, her body tensing as it sensed his displeasure.

He shook the light blue carton, weighing it in his large hand and making it painfully obvious that the container was *much* emptier than he expected.

Great, he's going to accuse me of stealing his milk again. Thea lifted another spoonful of cereal to her mouth and crunched loudly. *I bought that damn milk.*

Draven's fiery eyes narrowed on her and her full bowl of cereal as he placed his bowl in front of her. Maintaining eye contact with her, he slowly tipped the almond milk, but it let out a thin trickle of liquid, hardly enough for the big bowl of cereal he poured himself.

Uh, oh.

With a clenched, frustrated jaw, he pointed to the milk, then slapped a hand onto his chest, over his heart.

Thea accidentally dropped her spoon into her bowl.

Because unbeknownst to him, his gesture had just been very close to using sign language. Close to communicating, "*My milk.*"

Thea still sat with wide eyes, shocked at his attempt to communicate with her without paper notes. Hearing people never attempted to sign to her. *Too much effort*, she thought grimly.

Thinking she did not understand him, Draven made the same move again. He pointed to the milk and thumped his flat hand over his chest. *Milk. Mine.* His angry smolder scorched through the space between them and caressed down her arms, leaving little flames in its wake.

So hot.

Her body would not freaking shut up about how hot she found him. How hot he made her *feel*. Her nipples were tight little beads behind her shirt, pebbling to peaks. Could he see them? Could he tell?

And then he... He actually signed. He used the real hand motions to sign in American Sign Language. "*My milk.*"

Thea's jaw dropped.

He learned how to sign...for me? Yes, he learned a specific two-word phrase to be passive-aggressive and pick a fight with her, but... *He learned to really sign for this interaction with me.* Maybe he didn't realize how jaw-dropping that was to her.

Everyone assumed Thea should conform to understand them. People assumed she could read their lips. People used pen and paper to communicate—all in structured English, her second language.

People had never cared to try to sign for her. They had simply assumed she would try for them.

But at that moment, Draven cared so much about communicating with her that he had *learned* to speak in her language.

My milk.

And the way he stared at her, with such pulsating rage —that made no sense, considering it was just a carton of milk—stunned her. It ignited something inside her.

Growing flustered and under the guard of the kitchen island, she crossed her legs, pressing them together to ease some of the prominent ache occurring between them.

I've never been turned on by anger, she thought. But Draven's anger was a lot like the rest of him. Never scary, but still dark, dramatic, and drop-dead sexy.

She signed back, mimicking his motions because he had made them perfectly, "*My milk.*"

A vein pulsed in his forehead as his lips flattened.

The room's temperature rose to match a greenhouse where radiation and heat of pure sunlight penetrated her.

They were about to have...a conversation. Without pen and paper.

Had she ever been so turned on?

He pointed to the milk, rubbed his fingers together—the international sign for money—and he palmed his chest again. Basically, he signed, without knowing the official way to sign, "*I bought it.*"

Thea made the same gesture back to him. Because *she* had bought it.

He shook his head, his expression screaming, "*Liar.*"

She shook her head back. It was her milk. It was not her problem if he had to go to a store and buy his own or risk calcium deficiency. It was called being responsible, which was clearly foreign to this drummer.

His lips curled back, revealing perfect white teeth. She could not be sure, but it looked like he was growling.

God, he was just such an *animal*.

Thea shifted on the kitchen island barstool once more, pressing her legs together harder as that ache continued to swirl around her lower abdomen. Her clit tingled for him, begging for pressure. For *touch*.

She grabbed her pen and pad of paper and quickly wrote, "*Look, we both know I bought the milk. Now, do I need to pull out a receipt, or are we done here? Please gently place the milk back in the refrigerator. —Your respectful roommate.*"

She showed him her note. It was like a dam broke open.

Draven's lips separated on a curse as he gripped the milk to his body. For a moment, Thea couldn't help but be jealous of the inanimate milk carton, which was lucky enough to be up close and personal with his hard body. As it was, her brain fought to ignore the persistent throbbing between her legs at his unbreakable attention on her.

Draven did the unthinkable.

He uncapped the milk and raised the bottle to his lips. Just when he appeared ready to guzzle its contents, instead, he slid his tongue around the rim. That pink fleshy tongue grazed over the circled rim, claiming it in strong, controlled strokes that had Thea's heart racing in response. The way he curled and flattened his tongue... The way he licked it...

Was this porn? It had to qualify as some kind of porn.

Because the sight of Draven doing something so wickedly inappropriate with his tongue to a milk carton fueled the kind of fantasies and desires Thea did not realize were inside her. *He really is talented with the ladies, huh?*

After the tongue-lashing show of a lifetime and some insane jealousy over a dairy product, Thea watched in silent shock as Draven twisted the cap back onto the milk, which was practically empty, and threw it back into the fridge.

Isn't that what he does with all his conquests? Thea reminded herself. Tastes them, ruins them, then casts them aside?

Draven hostilely stole her pen and jotted down a response to her note before dropping it onto the counter in front of her and strutting back to his room like he knew exactly how good he looked walking away.

His note read, *"If I lick it, it's mine."*

Beholden to an odd, inexplicable instinct, Thea slid the note into her pajama pants pocket and kept it.

Panties damp and body overheating, she tried not to wonder what it would mean for him to lick her. What that strong, skillful tongue would feel like dragging against her quivering body. *If I lick it, it's mine.*

What would it be like to be claimed in such a possessive way?

What would it be like to be his?

Chapter Seven

"See me, hear me.

    Never leave me.

    Want to stick us in a maze

    and pretend I don't know the way.

    Get lost in you."

Draven crumpled up the paper and threw it to his bedroom floor again. He just couldn't stop thinking up lyrics, even if they were dumb and amateur and nothing his bandmates would use in a song.

Thankfully, his phone rang, distracting him from his pity party.

"Drave!" His twenty-year-old sister's voice pierced through the phone. "I got in! I got into the cellist summer program."

Draven's two thoughts of *"I'm so proud of her"* and *"Shit, that's going to be expensive"* bashed through his brain.

"You should have seen Margo's face," Summer squealed with excitement. "She hates me so much right now."

Amusement tickled the edges of his lips. "Don't act too smug around your understudy, Summer."

His younger sister snorted. "It's called being second chair to *my* first chair. Not 'understudy.' And geez, Drave, she's not gonna to break my fingers in a dark alley or something. You watch too many soap operas with Mimi."

Draven rolled his eyes but grinned. His grandmother, Mimi, had gotten him hooked on soap operas as a kid. When he visited her in the nursing home, they watched episodes nonstop.

Damn, that reminded him: *I need to make sure Mimi's care is all paid up for the year before I go on tour in a few months.*

It also sounded like Summer's new cellist program would have a hefty price tag. Draven made a lot of money and saved a lot by living in a two-bedroom one-bath apartment with a roommate. But, he had also bought his parents a mansion, paid for Mimi's swanky nursing home, and footed the bill for his two younger siblings' college degrees.

Maybe money-savvy Thea could give him some financial advice.

Money was...tight. And he definitely could *not* ask Thea to chip in more for rent.

He sighed. His manager had tried for ages to talk him into doing an underwear modeling shoot. Maybe it was time to swallow his pride and distaste for being nothing but a sex symbol and accept that big paycheck.

Everybody sells a partial nude to pay for his grandmother's care and his siblings' college at some point, right?

"Hello?" Summer asked. "Are you listening to me, Draven? Scream with excitement, dammit," his wild little sister ordered.

Draven goofily shrieked, "*Oh my Goddddd.*"

The sound of his sister's laugh warmly wrapped around him. She asked, "Will we see you for Thanksgiving?"

Draven scoffed. "Of course, why ask me that?"

"Because we know you're busy getting ready for your next world tour. I mean, the packing alone would take me months."

"*Months* to pack?" he echoed.

"A day to pack for each day of the trip. Isn't that how math works?" Summer cackled at her own joke.

He loved his little sister. With scientists as parents, Summer was the one who, while growing up, shared Draven's love for music and eccentrics. His grandmother, Mimi, was the same.

Summer and Draven had an almost ten-year age gap; he would never forget the loneliness before she was born. Geo, his nineteen-year-old brother—*because I guess Mom and Dad were handsy that year after Summer was born*—was also dear to him, even though Geo followed the medical school track instead of music.

"Hey, could I visit you in a few days?" she asked. "I need a place to crash on Wednesday, near L.A."

"Sure, I just, uh, I have a roommate again, so you can sleep in my room. I'll take the couch for the night."

"Bro, be honest, that roommate could move out by next Wednesday." She snickered to herself. "When have you kept someone there longer than three weeks?"

"I don't think she'll be moving out; she doesn't care about my midnight drumming."

"What? Is she deaf?" Summer joked.

"Yes," Draven replied.

Summer paused. "Oh, shit, I'm sorry, that was insensitive. How do you guys talk, then? Are you learning sign language?"

"I've watched a few videos. It's intimidating to try it. Like speaking French for the first time in front of a native, you know?"

"Draven Maxwell, the famous drummer of *Medusa's Tears*, is intimidated by his new female roommate?" Summer performed an exaggerated gasp. "I must meet her and proclaim my love."

"She's straight, Summer."

"Eh." Summer's shrug was audible through the phone. "Some women don't realize they are gay until they figure out that only another woman knows exactly how to touch another woman."

"Stop implying you could seduce my roommate, Summer."

"Sorry, sorry." She whisper-shouted, *"But I could, though!"*

Draven chuckled, but a vexing thought drifted through his mind. *"You'll have to get in line."*

Thea aimlessly floundered around the living room, waiting for her group of friends to arrive. They all wanted to see Thea's new digs and confirm she was doing okay after her breakup with Alec. She had, of course, not invited the girl in her friend group who had slept with Alec.

Draven strode from his bedroom and walked to the kitchen as Thea rearranged the couch pillows for the fourth time. He grabbed a water bottle from the fridge and turned to face her.

She nervously lifted her hand in a wave to him. *A wave? Stop making it so obvious that you're lusting after him!* Why didn't she just flash him her underwear while she was at it?

Draven nodded in greeting at her, smiling in that seductive, sinful way that made her insides turn to goo.

He is a player. You were just cheated on. Be smart, Thea.

He wrote on a Post-it note and handed it to her. *"You okay?"*

Why did he have to act like he cared? It was so confusing. Thea nodded and flashed him a quirky thumbs-up. She motioned to his shirt and gave him a double thumbs-up. Her meaning was clear: *Nice job not being shirtless for when my friends come over.*

Amused, he rolled his gleaming light green eyes with a smile. Wasn't he still mad at her for the milk? He seemed to realize it at the same moment because he frowned and shifted his weight between his feet.

Draven opened his mouth to say something but looked over at the door. Could he hear someone outside? Thea glanced at her phone and saw two of her friends messaged, "*Here!*"

Before she could stop him, Draven walked to open the door. She sprinted after him and bit her lip when her friends saw the drummer letting them inside the apartment.

Elisa and Fifi gaped at him, elbowing each other, as they entered.

Thea blushed at their obvious gawking. Real-life men did not look like Draven. It took getting used to. What was she thinking? She was far from used to it.

Thea moved forward to sign to her friends but paused when Draven moved. Draven swung his arm outward and back to his torso, flattened a hand to his chest, and then moved the hand from the side of his chin to his ear.

Thea's heart stopped.

Draven had just signed, "*Welcome to my home.*" It was a bit shaky but clear. "*Let me know if you need anything,*" he added.

Her friends frantically started signing to him. Elise

signed something along the lines of: "*I need a piece of you, please and thank you.*"

Thea stared at Draven. He had learned sign language to interact with her friends? To welcome them and offer his help with anything? A thick, dry swallow fought its way down her throat. This man was a player? Had she been...wrong?

Once Elise and Fifi quickly signed to him, he lost most of his confidence. His front teeth sank into his bottom lip. They noticed his discomfort, paused, and watched him.

He jerkily put a hand on his chest again, then held one hand out flat, palm facing the ceiling. He used his other hand to make a pinching motion over his palm and moved those fingers to his head.

He signed, "*I learn.*" But the women knew what he meant. He was learning sign language.

Thea was fairly certain her heart had just fallen out of her chest and tumbled its way to his feet.

Chapter Eight

"*Damn, girl, your roommate is hot as Hell,*" Fifi signed to Thea.

Thea shook her head, replying, "*No one needs abs like that. They could grate cheese.*"

"*Did you see his eyes?*" Elise signed. "*They penetrate you. To the point that you can't help but think about other ways he could penetrate you. Like his dick. I'm talking about his dick.*"

Thea shook her head again at her friends, blushing a deep, hot red.

"*Have you accidentally seen him naked yet?*" Fifi signed. "*Please sign 'yes.'*"

"*No!*"

"*You are living together. There must be a moment where one of you accidentally drops your towel after leaving the shower. It is roommate law.*"

Thea giggled, feeling lighter and more at home than she had since leaving Alec. She had missed her friends. It was always awkward when breaking up with someone inside your friend group. She had worried some of them would take sides.

"*Thank you guys for coming,*" Thea signed to them.

They waved off her comment with "*of course*" and "*duh.*"

Mallory showed up a few minutes later, hugging everyone. When she didn't see Draven, she joked to Thea, "*Is he out at the bar finding his next hookup?*"

Thea's lips curled down into a frown. That was what she had thought about Draven in the beginning too. "*No, he is in his bedroom.*"

Mallory noticed her frown and blinked in surprise. "*What's wrong? Is he being nice to you?*"

Too nice. "*Draven's fine.*" Other than being delusional about having bought her almond milk.

"*Very fine,*" Elise signed. "*How come he doesn't own a three-bedroom apartment? I'd move in tonight.*"

Fifi laughed. "*Elise, you're married.*"

After enjoying snacks and making frozen margaritas, Mallory signed, "*So, how are you doing with everything? Have you found any possible jobs yet?*"

Thea scooted to the edge of the couch cushion as she nervously signed, "*Actually, I've been thinking about doing something different.*"

"*Different?*"

"*I don't like finance. I mean, it's fine, but this could be my turning point, you know? The moment I find what I really want to do with my life. Hitting rock bottom—"*

"*You have not hit rock bottom.*" Mallory patted her shoulder. "*An asshole cheated on you and lost his amazing girlfriend. He hit rock bottom.*"

"*And I was fired,*" Thea reminded her. "*Rock bottom.*"

"*What are you interested in doing instead?*" Fifi signed.

"*Well, that's the thing. I have been working toward a job in finance after my parents pushed it on me since freshman year of college. I don't really know—I mean, I need help coming up with a dream.*"

The women glanced at each other.

"*We need a brainstorming chart and more alcohol for this,*" Mallory, the genius of the group, signed.

So, they got drunk. Well, they got *Thea* drunk, since she was the one not having to drive home. Plying her with margaritas and shots, they asked her rapid-fire questions, trying to see what type of career fit her best.

Finally, when Thea started "slurring" her words, meaning she signed slower and more exaggerated, repeating motions at different moments, it came out that Thea used to love makeup.

"*Like being a makeup artist for brides and stuff?*" Elise asked.

"*No,*" Thea signed. "*Movie makeup. Horror movie makeup. With monsters and zombies.*" She sighed and hiccuped. "*Grandpa used to show me all these silent horror movies, and I used to paint my dolls' faces to look like* monsters. *Mom hated it. One day, she switched all my dolls with math textbooks.*"

"*Oh my God,*" Mallory signed. "*You live in L.A. Doing movie makeup is the perfect job.*"

The alcohol may or may not have contributed to the blasé manner in which they regarded Thea entering the highly competitive and skilled career path of a movie makeup artist.

Fifi's eyes lit up. "*I have a friend who does costume design,*" she signed. "*I bet she could help you get a job as a makeup assistant or something!*"

"*Do my makeup right now, Thea,*" Mallory demanded. "*Make me look super creepy. I want to scare Wren when I get home.*"

"*What if his six-year-old daughter sees you?*" Mallory was engaged to Wren, but truly she was marrying into his family: a young deaf daughter Mal used to nanny.

"*Psh, that girl fears nothing,*" Mallory signed back.

By the time the women left, Thea felt better. Floating on clouds. Swaying. *Ooof!* She cupped her face after having walked into a wall. *Wow, I drank a lot.*

Draven was *sooooo* nice earlier. *He is learning sign language. For me?*

She fumbled to her bedroom, unzipped her dress, and climbed into bed in nothing but panties. Not being as curvy as her friends came with one major perk: she rarely needed to wear a bra.

Instant comfort. She covered herself in cool, smooth sheets and passed out.

A shift in weight shook the bed, jolting Thea awake.

Groaning from a significant hangover migraine from Hell, Thea opened her eyes, leaning up from where she slept on her stomach.

A shirtless Draven laid beside her on the bed, balancing himself up on an elbow. His mouth hung open as if he saw her and screamed in alarm, which she mimicked as she screamed at seeing him in her bed.

Wait. This was not her bedroom.

Draven's lips moved wildly, shrieking something that was probably, "*What are you doing in my bed?*"

She winced, her throat sore with thirst and her headache killing her. *Too much to take in all at once.* Draven was beside her in bed wearing nothing but boxers, which did nothing to hide his massive, straining erection.

Massive. Straining. Erection.

He leaned toward her, shooting forward, and for a moment, she thought he might mount her or something. Instead, he reached over her naked back to grab something from his nightstand. A notepad.

He wrote, "*Thea, why are you in my bed?*"

He shoved the pad and pen to her, but she groaned. *Too much effort.*

She mimed drinking a lot and pain in her forehead.

His mouth remained open, gaping at her the entire

time. "*You got drunk last night and climbed into my bed?*" he wrote.

She shot him an expression that screamed, "*It seems that way.*"

"*Why are you naked?*" His gaze drifted down her body, everything below the waist hidden behind the sheet as she laid on her stomach.

Great question. She took his pen and pad this time to write, "*I'm not naked. I am wearing panties.*"

Chapter Nine

He stared at her note. *"I'm not naked. I am wearing panties."*

What was he supposed to say to that?

She buried her face into his pillow, still lying on her stomach and hiding those beautiful breasts from him. But this was *Thea*. Even her bare back was enough to make him hard.

Shit, he was so hard for her.

The second he realized she was in his bed and not some stalker groupie who broke in, he ran a hand through his dark locks and cursed.

Had she drunkenly climbed into his bed by mistake or had Drunk Thea subconsciously chosen to sleep close to him? He pouted to himself. *I wish I'd gotten to meet Drunk Thea*. He wanted to know every side of her. Wanted to meet every version.

She shuddered in the bed, pulling the sheet up to her

neck before she turned on her back to face him. The thin bedsheet did little to hide the stiff peaks of her nipples.

His cock thickened and pulsed violently. "Fuck, what are you doing to me?" he asked her, but she didn't understand him.

She wrote, "*Wow, you are very hard.*"

He shot her a "*duh*" expression.

"*Are you going to go take care of that monster or what?*" She gestured to his engorged crotch.

He took the pen and paper. "*You're in my bed, baby. Unless you want to stick around to watch, I suggest you leave so I can 'take care' of this monster dick.*"

She rolled her eyes and smirked at his use of "monster dick." "*Go take a cold shower,*" she wrote.

"*Today is number five of no sex,*" he reminded her. "*You're lying in my bed practically naked. I can see your nipples poking through the sheet. A cold shower is not going to fix this issue. So, I repeat, unless you want to watch, please leave my bed.*"

He waited for her to wrap the sheet around herself and run for her bedroom, but she shocked him by staying exactly where she was.

She breathily inhaled and exhaled and *stayed.*

Fuck. His cock throbbed between his legs, the pressure distracting. "I'm serious," he said.

Her gaze clung to the last thing he wrote on the page. *Unless you want to watch, please leave my bed.*

And she licked her goddamn lips.

His hand drifted down his bare chest; her eyes tracked

the movement. When his fingers fell to his lower stomach and fingered the waistband of his boxers, she let out a little gasp.

"*Baby, unless you want to watch me jerk off until I come, you need to leave,*" he wrote.

She. Did Not. Move.

His breaths came out in rapid pants. Surely, she did not plan to stay and watch him jerk off. Was she bluffing? *For what reason would she bluff?*

Lust dilated her pupils. Her fingernails dug into the sheets, bunching the material. Her gaze locked onto his hand, positioned over his lower abdomen.

She did not touch him, yet, Draven was more turned on than ever before in his life. Just the idea of Thea naked beneath that sheet, clamping her thighs together as her pussy grew slick for him, as she watched him stroke his cock up and down for her.

Watching her cool and calm demeanor melt away for him and only him...

Unable to stop himself, his hand slipped under the waistband of his boxers and wrapped around his pulsing dick behind the fabric. He gave a single, slow stroke, holding his breath to see her reaction.

A shaky breath vibrated her chest as she fidgeted on the mattress. She audibly gulped.

He stared at her plush pink lips as he groaned and gave his hard cock one more stroke.

Damn it. *I don't want this with her.* Well, he did, but he didn't want to only be good for lust. For sex. He wanted to be good enough for everything else. Good enough for love.

I want the woman in pearls to hold my hand when we go grocery shopping for almond milk.

He tore his hand from his boxers, the material fighting to hold back his lengthy, aching erection. He wrote, "*Go get dressed and meet me in the kitchen. I'll make us breakfast.*"

She sucked in a breath, her disappointed eyes wide as she stared into his. She looked back down to the tent in his boxers. She motioned toward it.

He sat up on the bed and shook his head, motioning for her to leave. *I don't want her to think of me as the sex-obsessed drummer.*

Stunned, she hesitated but twirled herself into the bedsheet, like she was a cotton candy stick going round and round to cover herself in a sticky pink and blue barrier. When the wrapped sheet sufficiently covered her, she rose and quickly made her way to leave. But she stumbled over two crumpled-up pieces of paper.

The song lyrics he had written.

About her.

She paused, frowned, and crouched down to pick up the closest ball of paper at her feet.

Draven did the only thing that came to mind. He *dove* for the balls of paper, securing them all in his arms before she could get to any.

Her frown deepened, and she stared at him like he was crazy.

He was.

She left his bedroom.

This hangover is killing me. Thea cursed her friends for getting her so drunk. She was certain she was still a little drunk. After all, she had almost *watched Draven mastur-bate in bed beside her.* She slapped her hands over her face and silently screamed.

Why? Why had she not sprinted out of there?

Because it was the hottest experience of my life.

Just watching his hand dip beneath his boxers and seeing the bulge and muscles flexing in his arm as he stroked made her panties a certified wet zone. Her stomach clenched with sensual heat.

However, now that the tantalizing high was wearing off and Draven had not given her the show she expected, her hangover migraine banged on the interior walls of her skull.

When she shuffled into the kitchen, after taking her time to get dressed, Thea noticed Draven cracking eggs into a medium-sized mixing bowl. He pressed his lips together, suppressing a smile, as she tottered into the kitchen and sat at a barstool in front of where he prepped breakfast.

She dramatically collapsed her face and arms onto the

granite countertop of the kitchen island. After a full minute, she lifted her head.

Smiling to himself, he wrote her a note on a blue Post-it and handed it to her. *"Someone got drunk and irresponsible last night."* He grinned. Evilly.

She smacked a hand over her face. Called irresponsible by Draven the drummer? *Is this rock bottom?* She shot him an expression of, *"Must you torture me? This hangover should be torture enough."*

He chuckled. The quaking of his chest and the shining in his eyes momentarily stunned Thea. *I like making him laugh.*

One side of her that she hadn't revealed in a while—due to her life going up in smoke—was her goofiness.

Thea was the over emotive friend who joked and played and made everyone smile—or at least, she tried.

When she lost a game of charades against her friends, she dropped to the floor, flailed, and played dead. When her friends went out dancing, she felt the vibrations. She choreographed the perfect shopping cart, sprinkler, Cleopatra, and any other cringe-y, quirky dance move imaginable.

She may not have been a "class clown," but she spent most of her life trying to make others happy. To a hearing crowd, Thea seemed like a wallflower. To her crowd, Thea was an outgoing comic relief. *I think Draven would like my goofy side.*

He cracked one more egg into the bowl, washed his

hands, and wrote her a new note. *"You realize I will hold this over you for years to come?"*

Years? Thea blinked and tried to calm her accelerating heartbeat. She blanked her expression, feigning complete innocence and motioned a thumb to herself as if to say, *"Who? Me?"*

He smiled, leaning down again to jot something else. *"Drunk Thea crawled into my bed. Naked. And you thought I would be the inappropriate roommate."*

She rolled her eyes and snorted, pointing to him and signing, *"You are the inappropriate roommate."*

Draven used context clues to understand her. He feigned an innocent expression to match hers from a moment ago, gestured to his crotch, and pointed his thumb at himself as if to say, *"Who? Me? The guy who had the huge erection?"*

Thea shook with amusement and giddiness. This interaction with him felt like...glee. Like a childhood crush —but with more erections and sexy threats of voyeurism.

He motioned to the coffee maker behind him and quirked an eyebrow.

She shook her head.

He turned, opened a cabinet door, and showed her a package of decaffeinated coffee grounds. She pursed her lips in surprise and intrigue.

She signed, *"Did you buy that?"* She made a little money gesture by rubbing her fingers together the way he did before, so he would understand.

He nodded.

She wrote, "*Why?*"

He frowned at her notepad, then he gestured to her ears.

She sipped in a breath. He remembered that she said caffeine made her ears ring?

She watched him closely as he whipped the eggs and poured them into a pan on the stove. He cut up green peppers and tomatoes and added shredded cheddar cheese.

Watching the sexy bedhead-haired drummer make her breakfast, she thought to herself, *I may be in trouble.*

Chapter Ten

Draven's heartbeat refused to keep a consistent rhythm in his chest as Thea bit her lip and stared at him from across the kitchen island as he stirred their eggs. Maybe the hangover was altering her brain chemistry because it sure seemed like she liked him this morning.

She watched him with a twinkle of amusement and appreciation in those piercing gray eyes, rather than the distaste he got used to seeing in her expressions. *Maybe making her breakfast was the key all along.* The key was certainly not fighting over almond milk.

"*Why the eggs this morning?*" she wrote.

"*Someone—*" He underlined the word and gestured to the empty blue and white half-gallon beside the microwave. "*—used up all the milk, so no cereal for breakfast.*"

She shrugged and wrote back, "*Must have been the milk fairy.*"

She is so damn cute. He put down the spatula and wrote, *"A veggie omelet should help with your hangover. Not that I would know what it's like to have a hangover or be an irresponsible partier like Thea Gullybil."*

She smirked and took back her notepad. She twirled her pen in her fingers as he mixed in the cut-up vegetables with the whisked eggs. She pressed the end of the pen between her lips, tapping it again and again against her mouth, drawing his attention to it.

She is contemplating writing something. But what? What would she hesitate to say to him? Maybe *"I was wrong about you?"*

He finished cooking their cheesy veggie scrambled eggs —because, damn, flipping an omelet is hard—and placed her plate in front of her first. He used to love cooking for Summer and Geo when his parents were off on brainiac scientific work trips. At sixteen, he often took over household chores like prepping his younger siblings' lunches for school and cooking dinner.

Draven's grandmother, Mimi, taught him different meals, priding herself on passed-down recipes. As her memory began to slip, the recipes were some of the first things to go. She started putting out five random ingredients for him, telling him to "make it work" and create something. It worked out since Mimi was obsessed with the *Food Network* TV show *Chopped*.

I want Thea to like my food. I want her to look at me with those big, soulful eyes and smile and see that I'm...good at something.

Draven's mind skipped with lyrics.

"Make me feel whole,

and I'll feed your soul.

I'll give you everything you need.

Baby, just hunger for me."

He shook his head. *You're a drummer, remember?* Not a songwriter. In some people's eyes, he was not even an artist.

He held his breath as Thea lifted a forkful to her mouth, taking a bite. She groaned as she chewed, and the throaty sound of it reverberated in Draven's body. *She likes it.*

His cock woke up, twitching at the sound she made. The pesky body part seemed particularly awake this morning. Draven tried *not* to think about how Thea had been naked in his bed.

They ate quietly, chewing, swallowing, and smiling at each other. Thea *inhaled* the eggs, and Draven recognized a similar hunger in himself. *Just not for food.*

She showed him her notepad, *"I'm almost jealous of your hookups."*

His eyebrows rose so high that they nearly broke off into his hairline.

She quickly jotted down, *"Because they would wake up to breakfast, I mean. These eggs are amazing. That's what I meant."*

He swallowed thick emotion down his throat, the vulnerability choking him. *"Women don't tend to stay for breakfast,"* he slowly wrote back.

She rolled her eyes. "*Please tell me you don't kick them out when you're done with them.*"

More like they run off once they're done with me. Draven shook his head furiously at her words. "*Not at all.*" To tell her or not to tell her. To be vulnerable or to be comfortable. Draven watched her clean the rest of her plate, scraping any melted cheese that still clung to the glass onto her fork.

He wrote, "*My 'hookups,' as you so sophisticatedly referred to them, tend to be a bam, wham, thank you, ma'am.*"

She blinked at his message, frowning.

He clarified, "*A 'one, done, thanks, hun.' You know. 'A down and dirty, then scurry.'*"

She rolled her eyes and wrote, "*A 'have sex, then off to the next?'*"

Grinning, he nodded. "*Intercourse, then make like a racehorse.*"

Grinning back, she added, "*A pump and dump.*"

"*A classic 'penetrate and skate.'*"

She laughed, the sound louder than the average person's chuckle. *Because she can't hear herself*, Draven realized. The sound was so free and pure and good-natured. *I love music, but damn, her laugh could be one of my favorite melodies.*

He wanted to keep making her laugh. But she grew serious and wrote, "*I thought that was what men preferred? A one-night stand. A hookup, then never having to see or talk to that person again.*"

He wrote, "*There is hooking up with someone, and then there is rushing out and making the person feel like abandoned, dirty trash.*"

Her frown reappeared. *Shit. Said too much,* he thought. "*What do you mean?*" she asked.

Draven sighed. "*I once asked a woman to stay for breakfast, and she looked at me like I was stupid for suggesting it.*"

As she read, Thea's dark brows furrowed, and he wanted to soothe them and stop talking about this. She wrote, "*Was she on a diet or something? Maybe you accidentally offered a vegan some bacon.*"

Oh, Thea. Draven shook his head and shot her a sad smile. "*Women only want me for one thing. And once I give them their wild oats-sowing night, they hightail it out of here like I have cooties.*"

"*Draven, all men have cooties,*" Thea wrote back, trying to lighten the mood and make him feel better. "*They're men,*" she underlined, then she feigned a cringe. "*Ick.*"

Ignoring the tightness in his chest, he revealed, "*Women hook up with drummers. They don't want to have breakfast together or watch a movie or date. So yeah, none of them stay for breakfast. They get their 'experience,' and they leave.*"

Her expression turned pouty, the pitiful statement shining in her eyes, "*Oh, Draven.*"

"*It's fine; it's not like I say no to the sex. It's not like it is not fun for the both of us,*" he wrote, tapping his pen to the page a few times. "*But I'd like to eat breakfast with someone once in a while, you know?*"

I like eating breakfast with you, he thought.

She bit her lip, her eyes freaking *watering* as if she could feel the pain he felt, as if she saw right through him. She wrote, "*Draven, them skipping breakfast has nothing to do with you.*"

He rolled his eyes and scoffed.

"*You're worth more than just a one-time fling. Anyone would be lucky to spend a lazy morning with you, even if it's just cold cereal in front of some cartoons. No eggs or extra effort required.*"

He exhaled sharply. She had basically painted the exact picture he imagined with her. And those words... *You're worth more than just a one-time fling.* He wanted her simple, beautiful words to overwrite the memory of his ex saying, "*You fuck a drummer. You don't date one.*"

"*I'm sure they don't rush out because of you,*" she stressed, reaching out and touching his hand.

A light touch. Like she originally planned to squeeze the back of his hand in solidarity but hesitated and ended up pausing just when the skin of her palm hovered over his flesh.

At that mere touch, little flames ran down Draven's back. His spinal cord was a poured line of gasoline, igniting every nerve ending for her. "Tingles" and "sparks" did nothing to describe the sensation.

Feel it too, Thea. I beg you. I dare you. Feel it too.

She pulled away. She bent her head down as she jotted

a new message. When she looked up, she grinned and flashed him an utterly goofy expression as she showed him the note.

"*They probably rush out on you because you're horrible at sex.*"

Chapter Eleven

"They probably rush out on you because you're horrible at sex."

She tried to lighten the mood with a little joke. Instead, at reading her comment, Draven's eyes narrowed and darkened, radiating an intensity she had not expected. An intensity for which her body was not prepared.

At that challenging, sultry, and sinful look in his eyes, Thea's nipples tightened. Her lips separated, seeming to pucker for him of their own volition.

Her body *hummed*.

He placed his fork down on his plate, stood to his full swoon-worthy height, and walked around the kitchen island to stand behind where she balanced on the barstool. Her mouth went dry at his proximity.

His scent of lime, mint, and *man* swam through her brain, drugging her thoughts.

Once he stood behind her, his chest heating her back

through the thin T-shirt, he slid her plate away from her, flattening his hands to the granite, his arms on either side of her.

He trapped her against the kitchen island counter, his body a warm, hard cage. *Dear God, those forearms...*

She swallowed—unsure if it came out as an audible, nervous gulp.

Leaning his hard, muscular chest into her back, he took her pen from her shaky fingers and wrote directly onto the notepad in front of her. *"Baby, you don't want to know how good I am at sex."*

Gulp.

He was saying something out loud. She couldn't hear him, but she felt his lips moving against her hair, then the back of her neck. The warm puffs of air coming from that active mouth caressed the sensitive skin of her cheek and chin. What was he saying?

She could imagine.

Dirty words. Dirty promises. Dirty threats.

I can see your hard little nipples poking through your shirt. You want me to suck them, Thea?

I'd make you beg for it. Take my time. Your pussy would be dripping for me by the time I got to it. A pink, wet little mess. Soaked for me. Clit swollen and throbbing.

I'd spread your legs wide open. Admire what I made so slick.

Then, I'd devour you like a tray of warm cookies.

Had Thea moaned? She was not sure. Her mind blanked as the fantasy speared through her—spearing between her legs at the same time. Heat coiled low in her abdomen. Twisting and curling.

He dragged his lips down the edge of her jaw as he moved her hand to rest on the notepad. He pressed her finger down to where he had written a new note while she zoned out in sexual fantasy.

He had written, "*The thing about drummers is that we have an incredible sense of rhythm and stamina. I've got steady hands, sure. But, baby, the way I can move my hips, the way I'd ride you... You have no idea.*"

Well, she had *some* idea, considering that morning sex dream.

He wrote, "*I could be deep inside you, and I'd still hold that rhythm, that beat. Pounding between your pretty thighs would become a song.*"

She wanted it. She wanted him. Her breaths escaped in huffy pants, which he was sure to hear with his face grazing the side of hers.

His palms slid down the countertop before her; she felt the motion, the invisible touch of those hands, gliding over the tops of her thighs. The *inner* tops of her thighs.

"*When I woke up and realized you were the one lying next to me, I got so hard.*" As he wrote the new note, the chords of his muscular arms flexed. The sight made her shift on the barstool. Her legs clenched together as a pulsing began in her core.

His left hand drifted toward her, moving off the counter and rising to delicately drag his fingertips over her throat in a tender yet dominating touch.

She exhaled all of the oxygen in her lungs. Her body blazed and ached for him.

He gently cupped her throat like a collar as he moved his lips over her hair from his stance behind her. With his right hand, he wrote, "*What are you doing to me, Thea?*"

With a shaky breath and a trembling hand, she wrote, "*I think the seven-day sex ban is starting to get to you.*"

He released her throat but did not move away from her. His hard chest burned into her back. "*I promise you, it's not that,*" he wrote.

Did that mean his desire for her was more than pent-up arousal? Would he feel this way about her in three months? In two weeks?

Thea, you've been used and discarded before. You have been dropped by friends who felt it was too much effort to learn how to sign. This man would be just like the rest. Yet, somehow, she knew he would manage to break her heart worse than the others.

He said he wanted someone to eat breakfast with.

And his *body*—his presence—overwhelmed her senses. She felt like a tuning fork, vibrating with sound. The *air* changed when he entered a room. Oxygen molecules shook until everything had a hazy, wavy shimmer like a desert mirage.

Thirsty. She was thirsty.

She jolted up in her seat, trying to snap out of the over-whelming fog of lust. Shuffling to get around him, she signed, "*Drink.*"

He reluctantly uncaged her, and she fumbled to the

refrigerator. She dug around, rooting at the very back of the fridge for her special lime waters. She shifted items around, so she could get to the back, and froze.

When she pulled out a full, now close to expiration date, almond milk—the exact same brand as the empty carton beside the microwave—she locked gazes with Draven.

His mouth hung open.

There had never been *one* milk. They had each bought the *same* carton and assumed the other was using it. The cluttered fridge caused an entirely unnecessary and dramatic roommate tiff.

Thea's giggle rose from the depths of her soul at the ridiculousness. Draven's chest shook with laughter.

They could not stop laughing and snickering like first graders at the park who shared a sacred secret. Thea wiped at her eyes as she laughed harder than she had in years. Both of them bent over, wheezing for breath.

Laughing has never felt like this, she thought. She was a grown woman, yet those overwhelming giddy hormones of a mindless middle school crush ran through her veins like pure adrenaline.

Draven's grin didn't cause butterflies. It caused woodpeckers, leaving permanent damage and chipping away at the surface to leave a newly carved masterpiece.

"Stop smiling," Wren told Draven as his band sat on Draven's living room couch. Draven sat on the seat of his drum set as they all brainstormed the band's next album.

The men had all been deep in discussion while Draven grinned at the kitchen behind them.

The men always met up at Draven's apartment to practice anything that wasn't "studio-ready." Since Thea now lived with him, Wren's fiancé Mallory and his daughter Armie joined Thea in the kitchen to bake cookies. Considering Mallory, Armie, and Thea were all deaf, they had no problem hanging out while the band strummed some chords and exchanged some curses.

Draven, however, was utterly distracted by Thea's presence. She wore a bright yellow, to-the-knee dress, sporting her classic pearl necklace. A Belle from *Beauty and the Beast* reimagined as a 50s housewife.

"Looks like a flower,
but she's got teeth.
Venus fly trap,
promise to consume me."
Lyrics flowed through Draven.
"Looking like a politician's wife.
Baby, I'll give you a stance.
Hands on the desk; let's make the journalists happy.
Be my scandal, my everything."
Thea glanced up from the mixing bowl and connected gazes with Draven from across the rooms. There must have been something powerful in Draven's expression because her hand moved up. Her fingers toyed

with her pearl necklace as she nervously broke eye contact.

"That's right, baby, clutch your pearls.
Would Mr. Trust Fund touch you like me?
Pull that hair?
Kiss you like a religion?
It's not up for debate.
I'd give you what you need."

"Draven, stop grinning like a damn idiot. What has you so high right now? Did you smoke something?" Wren asked. "I swear to God, if my daughter is in a house with drugs in it—"

Draven frowned, the insult wiping away his giddiness. *Drugs?* Did he not know Draven at all? "Dude, I'm clean. You know I don't mess with anything."

"What's got you so happy? It is freaking all of us out."

"Can't a man smile at one o'clock in the afternoon and not be questioned by his friends?"

Wren's eyes narrowed suspiciously at him, then he followed Draven's line of sight to the three girls in the kitchen. Wren's head spun back to stare at Draven. His narrowed eyes became little slits.

Uh, oh. Draven quickly jumped into the album conversation, "I say we go for a few more love songs in the new album. The audience loves those."

"The *female* audience loves those," Yin replied.

"The female audience makes up eighty percent of our fanbase," Draven replied.

"Yeah, because you keep doing shows shirtless."

Draven huffed. "I get hot when I drum."

"*Sure*, you do." Yin rolled his eyes but grinned at his friend.

Wren still stared at Draven, glaring.

"Maybe we could play a new song at the Halloween bash?" Tomi, the lead singer, suggested.

Draven's band, *Medusa's Tears*, had been instructed to play the Halloween party at the home of the owner of their record label. No one said no to Judas Maximo of *Maximillian Records*. The man was a god when it came to music careers. He had the Midas touch for turning records to platinum and gold.

The same man who Draven had approached to ask for a raise/loan due to his siblings' college and his grandmother's nursing home expenses.

Ice-cold Judas Maximo had replied, "*Draven, you're a drummer who doesn't write music. Easily replaceable. If you want more money, do something to earn it.*" Because saying a simple "no" was below Judas Maximo's standards. *Has to hit you where it hurts.*

After more of a brainstorming and songwriting session, and the dominating smell of chocolate chip cookies tainted the air of Draven's kitchen and living room, the band called it quits for the day.

Draven moved to join Thea—and those delicious-smelling cookies—in the kitchen, but Wren's hand flattened onto his chest and held him back. Draven flashed him a distressed expression of: "*What the heck, dude? There are warm cookies at stake.*"

"What's going on with you, Draven?"

"What do you mean?" Draven watched from over Wren's shoulder as Tomi and Yin greeted Thea and Mallory and ate the warm, fresh cookies.

"I mean, you were smiling like a crazy person when we got here. Then, you were suggesting lyrics for a love song. A love song, Draven. You. *Lyrics.*"

"You make it sound like the world is ending."

Wren shifted to move his face in Draven's line of vision of the kitchen, securing his attention. "Is it?" Wren asked. Shaking his head, he accused, "You're lusting after Thea."

Draven blinked and focused his full attention on Wren. Why did he have to accuse him of "lusting" after Thea. Why not "liking" her? It was one thing for his new roommate to think of him as shallow and sex-obsessed, but his closest bandmate? Someone he had known for over ten years... It was a special kind of hurtful.

"So?" Draven countered. "Is this the part where you threaten me to stay away, so I don't break your future wife's best friend's heart?"

Shocking Draven, Wren shrugged. *Shrugged.* "I'm not worried about it."

What the hell did that mean?

Wren let his words dangle there until Draven snapped, "Elaborate."

Wren sighed. "I know you, Draven. You need someone to stroke your ego. You would never date a woman who couldn't hear your music and spew compliments all over you."

He's wrong, Draven thought. But was he?

Draven knew he needed reassurance; he knew he was needy. It probably had something to do with having barely-present parents who had only ever been disappointed that he didn't go into science or law or mathematics or basically anything but music. Hell, they might have been happier if he had been an English major. *Always a disappointment.*

"Dude, you're making me sound like an egomaniac douchebag," Draven shot back, the hurt ringing in his voice like the lingering sounds of smashing metal cymbals.

"I don't mean it like that. I just—look, you two aren't a good match, and I don't want my future wife having to pick up the pieces of her friend's heart when you get tired of the chase." Wren crossed his arms and shifted out of Draven's way. "I don't know why I was worried, sorry, man," Wren said. "She might be getting back with her ex soon anyway."

"WHAT?" Draven shouted. His bandmates, who were currently enjoying hot chocolate chip cookies, glanced over at where Wren and Draven spoke in the living room.

"Mal said he keeps texting Thea to 'talk' and that Thea's been 'thinking about it.' You know how off and on they've been. Plus, her parents are pushing for them to get back together, so who knows?"

Draven's mind was a mess of lightning-speed thoughts and rising dread. Thea deserved better than Alex or Alric or whatever the heck his name was. "But he cheated on her. How can her parents want them together?"

Wren shrugged again. He calmly moved his shoulders up and down while Draven's heart beat out of his chest. "Apparently, her parents love the guy. You know he's making serious money. Mal said Thea's parents are hearing, so maybe they think a rich deaf dude is the best choice for her."

"He *cheated* on her," Draven repeated, spitting out the words with such disgust that Wren's eyebrows rose. "And what's the deal with them assuming she has to be with a deaf guy? You hear, and you and Mal are together."

"I got fluent in sign language for Armie," Wren replied slowly, his eyes narrowing again. "You don't actually *like* Thea, do you?"

Tense and impatient for this conversation to end, Draven said, "Wren, there are semi-warm chocolate chip cookies in my kitchen right now, growing colder and colder as you warn me away from my roommate."

Wren snorted and stepped out of Draven's way, gesturing for him to go to the kitchen.

Draven strode over, nodded hello to everyone, and grabbed a warm cookie. He wanted to shove it in his mouth and block any potentially dangerous thoughts from boiling over. He wanted to scream.

Why do you not think I'm capable or deserving of anything more than lust?

Why do you think I'm not good enough for her? Why assume I would break her heart?

The chocolate chips melted into his mouth as he stood beside Thea in the tiny kitchen area where his band dominated the space. Thea bit into a cookie at the same time, looking up at him and watching as he swallowed and licked the chocolate from his lips. She did the same, her tongue dabbing out in slow motion to slick those perfect pink lips.

Wren warned from beside him, "Careful not to burn yourself, Draven. Or anyone else."

<h1 style="text-align:center">Chapter Twelve</h1>

"You can't actually like him, Thea. He's Draven," Mallory stressed to Thea when she visited earlier that day. *"I think you're just confusing lust for like. You were in a relationship for a long time. I'm sure your attraction to him is linked to some desire to sow your wild oats."*

Wild oats. That had been the same thing Draven said. That women only wanted him for a hookup, to sow their wild oats, and then never speak to him again.

Mallory is wrong about him.

In the beginning of living with Draven, Thea often spent her nights in her bedroom. But tonight, feeling at home and high on the sugar rush of too many cookies, Thea remained in the living room. In their shared space.

She stretched out on the couch in front of the TV and found a new horror movie to stream that she had not seen before—which was difficult to accomplish since she loved them and watched them as soon as they came out. Alec

97

never liked horror movies, so she would go with a group of friends to see them in theaters or stay up late and watch them by herself after he went to bed.

She cuddled into Draven's obnoxiously soft, fuzzy blanket. The man had good taste in blankets. Even his bedsheets had felt like silk against her bare skin.

Nope! She needed to *not* think about her blip of waking up next to him, naked and hesitating to leave, when he threatened to start touching his hard cock right in front of her. She may or may not have been disappointed that he didn't follow through on that.

Her phone vibrated against her hip, and she picked it up. Alec. *"Babe, answer my texts! This is getting ridiculous. You're going to throw everything we have away over something so meaningless? It was meaningless, Thea. I promise you."*

He wanted to say *she* was throwing away their relationship over something *meaningless?* Hypocritical asshole.

Her phone lit up again, this time with a message from her parents. *"Have you talked everything through with Alec yet?"*

Thea turned her phone screen to black as she wondered if anyone trusted her sense and judgment.

She pressed play on the movie, settling into her bundle of blankets and pillows on the couch, creating a little nest of comfort.

The couch cushion dipped from where her feet laid at the other end, stealing her attention from the screen.

Draven sank, sitting at the end of the couch and holding two bowls of popcorn.

Had he seen her getting set up in front of the TV and popped some? Was this the part where he stole the remote and put on something else because it was "his" apartment?

He handed her a bowl of popcorn and a Post-it that said, "*What are we watching?*"

Hyperaware that her bare toes brushed against the side of his thigh, she paused the movie and showed him the title.

He feigned a gasp and horrified look, mouthing, "*Horror?*"

Do not giggle at the sexy, over-emotive man, Thea. She nodded, mouthing back, "*Horror.*"

He put his popcorn bowl on his lap and wrote on a notepad. With wide, gleaming eyes and a gaping mouth, he showed her, "*But you wear pearls,*" with the word "pearls" underlined.

She rolled her eyes and snorted, writing back, "*I love horror movies. Horror and action movies tend to be less subtitle-y and more, um, BOOM. You know? Wow, I'm really bad at describing this right now.*"

She tapped the pen to her chin and wrote, "*Growing up, sometimes my family didn't like to use subtitles. I like horror and action because they're easier to follow without subtitles; they're sentimental to me. They're compelling and fun. Dramas and romance bore me.*"

Slack-jawed, he wrote, "*Horror is fun?*"

"Is Draven Maxwell, drummer of 'Medusa's Tears,' a scared-y cat?"

He read her note, puffed out his chest, then comically deflated as he nodded rapidly. Major scared-y cat. He flashed her a pantie-melting smile.

She clucked her tongue and wrote, *"We can watch something else?"* She hoped he said no. She *really* wanted to watch this one.

He waved off her offer and gestured for her to hit play on the movie.

She exhaled in relief and excitement as she resumed the film. The beginning credits faded as the movie began.

On screen, there was a couple having sex.

Graphic sex. *Hello, nudity.*

The woman's breasts were on full display, moving against a man's naked chest. The man's sweat dripped down his forehead as he thrust into her, his expression one of tortured euphoria.

Thea held her breath, waiting for the horny couple to be found in their cabin in the woods and brutally murdered—as was the trend in horror movies. Sex equaled imminent death. A metaphor for Thea's current crush or lust or whatever it was she started feeling for Draven.

Sex with Draven would mean a death. Death to her old life. An end to her ever finding a better lover—so she assumed, based on the rumors.

She swallowed and stiffened in her seat beside Draven as the couple on screen kept grinding onto each other.

Humping. Thrusting. The subtitle literally read: "*Moaning. Sex sounds. Grunting.*"

Slowly, she shifted on the couch, moving from a lying down position to sitting up, until the two of them sat on opposite sides of the piece of furniture—like an awkward first date.

When it felt like the sex scene droned on, passing the two-minute mark, Thea dared a glance at Draven, who stared back at her.

His dark eyebrows quirked.

She shrugged, tossing him an uncomfortable yet accepting expression of "*Welp.*"

They both burst into awkward laughter, vibrating the couch.

"*See?*" Thea wrote. "*Horror movies aren't so bad.*"

Draven pointed to the screen of graphic sex and wrote, "*I am learning so much about you.*"

She fought off a grin as she rolled her eyes. "*You're the one obsessed with sex.*"

"*I'll have you know, this is my fifth day in a row without any sexual relations.*"

"*Do you want an award?*"

"*I expect to wake up on the seventh day with a blue, first-place ribbon hanging from my dick. Blue to match my blue balls, if that wasn't clear.*"

She tossed her head back and laughed, throwing a piece of popcorn at him. He bent his head, trying to catch the piece in his mouth. When he accomplished it, astonishing them both, they threw their arms up in the air in unison as if they were watching a soccer game and someone scored a pivotal goal.

Draven grinned at her like no one else—like he saw right through her. Like they were best friends growing up and knew everything about each other.

In two days, once the sex ban is over, will he bring home a band groupie? Imagining him bringing home a random girl...hurt.

Damn it, Thea. She tore her gaze from him and refocused on the screen. *You cannot* like *Draven Maxwell.* He was the opposite of her type—the opposite of what her family expected.

Draven was a dream; he symbolized the artistic career someone wanted as a child. She needed reality. The grown-up adult reality.

But wasn't she trying to follow her dreams for the first time in her life? She had been watching movie makeup tutorials for the last few days. She had looked up any possible apprenticeships, sending out *"Are you hiring? Pretty please?"* emails.

Thea zoned out, lost in her thoughts, until the first murder occurred on screen, a jump scare followed by blood spraying everywhere. Draven lurched and covered his eyes with his hands. *Darn it, how is this sexy man allowed to also be adorable?* There had to be some law broken by his mere perfect existence.

When she finished her popcorn, he scooped some of his remaining buttery goodness into her empty bowl, sacrificing his own kernels.

He is feeding me. First, breakfast. Now, popcorn.

I want him.

Mallory's words played through Thea's head again. How different the two of them were, how Draven would never settle down, etc.

After about fifteen minutes into the movie, Draven shifted closer to her on the couch. He slid her a note. *"If you get scared, feel free to climb into my lap."*

How did she like this? Draven marveled at her as he suppressed his own fear. *She is grinning as people get murdered.* During certain moments, when the characters made dumb choices leading to their deaths, Thea aggressively signed at the TV and groaned.

Meanwhile, Draven was attempting *not* to jump at each scare. Or hide his eyes.

Why couldn't she be into comedies?

When he initially joined her, he thought he would fake a yawn and stretch his arm and lay it behind her shoulders on the couch like a smooth high schooler. Instead, he was freaking the heck out.

He did not like ghosts. Or buckets of blood. A gory action movie was one thing, but possessed people attacking others with knives? *Not* his jam.

"Ahh!" He jerked on the couch when a shadow took over the screen, showing that the ghost was about to find the main characters in their hiding spots.

Thea giggled, clearly enjoying his fear. She wiggled her eyebrows at him in a challenge, her eyes silently teasing him, "*Aw, is poor Draven scared?*"

He shook his head. "You're a little bit twisted, aren't you?" he asked aloud, unable to keep his lips from curling at the edges.

Two minutes later, he jumped again.

Her eyes laughed at him.

"It came out of nowhere," Draven defended himself.

Ten minutes later, he sat right next to her. *Right* next to her. For comfort. To comfort her, of course. Since the movie was scary. Poor girl.

Another ten minutes passed, and Draven was under her blanket. Specifically, the fuzzy material covered their legs and Draven's face when he slouched and hid under it. Thea snickered beside him, but he couldn't find it in himself to watch the terrifying screen, even if she thought he was a weakling.

The third time Draven lifted the blanket to cover his eyes, Thea dropped a hand onto his head and tussled his long, black locks of hair. She patted his head as if he were an amusing child.

Goddamn it, I'm losing all sex appeal, he grumbled.

She moved closer to him; the side of her warm thigh pressed firmly against his. His thick arm brushed hers. Terrifying and exhilarating lightning coursed through his veins, threatening to burn him to a crisp. Being this close to her...

She smelled like grapefruit. He had noticed the scent from their shared bathroom and saw her pink grapefruit body wash in the shower. But knowing *why* she smelled like grapefruit didn't lessen the primal desire to splay her legs open, squeeze her to him, and lick up her juices.

The movie scared him. Her presence aroused him. Thus, his body was confused.

Her little head pats to comfort him—and the way she kept her fingers in his hair, stroking and massaging his scalp—made his cock harden and lengthen beneath his sweatpants.

She held onto him, rubbing the wavy strands between her fingers. He ever so slowly tilted his head, giving her easier access as he burrowed his face onto her shoulder.

Inhale. Shiver. Groan.

She smelled so damn good—buttery from the popcorn, and sweet and tart from her body wash. *Want to devour her.*

Want to kiss her.

Another possessed person abruptly came on screen, and Draven dug his face into the crook of her neck and shoulder even further. Her scent overwhelmed his senses, his body on fire for her, cock thick and pulsing.

Do not kiss her neck, Draven told himself.

But it was right there.

Don't.

But she smelled so good.

No.

Thea tapped his shoulder and showed him a note when he reluctantly lifted his head. She mocked him by shooting his earlier words back at him. *"If you get scared, feel free to climb into my lap."*

Chapter Thirteen

Could Draven hear her erratic heartbeats? His face practically laid against the pulse in her neck as he hid his gaze from the TV. She should not have found his adorable fear sexy, but she did.

His body heat radiated into her from where he cuddled up against her. His mouth kept grazing her throat. The proximity of his lips caused a tantalizing warmth to swirl in her lower torso, her abdomen tightening under the blanket.

His breath blew out just below her ear. Each puff of warm air turned her on even more.

She showed him her note to try to break through the sexual tension. *"If you get scared, feel free to climb into my lap,"* she teased.

He pursed his lips and wrote, *"Don't think I won't."*

She gestured to her open lap and taunted him with a pesky smile.

So, he pulled the blanket from both of them and claimed her lap. But instead of sitting on it, he stretched out on the couch and rested his face on it.

Snuggling into her, he wrapped his right arm between her back and the couch, securing it around her waist. He lowered his head to balance on the top of her thighs. As he faced the screen, his cheek rubbed the skirt of her dress, bunching up the fabric until the hem sat mid-thigh.

His left hand settled onto her bare knee, ready to hide his face if another scary moment occurred in the film.

He must have made some type of humming noise because his cheek vibrated against Thea's thigh. Those vibrations traveled up, up, under her dress, reverberating between her legs.

She blew out a slow breath as a fantasy slammed through her mind. One where Draven dug his face into her skirt, bunching it up further and further until his lips were mere centimeters from her quivering sex.

"I'm hungry for more than popcorn tonight, Thea," he would tell her. *"Let me between those silky thighs."*

"D-Draven—"

Fantasy Draven stared up at her with an intense yearning that shook her to her core. *"You'd deny a starving man?"*

Meanwhile, Real-life Draven laid his head peacefully over her lap. His hand curved around the top of one of her thighs. His fingers stretched out over her flesh, his thumb stroking back and forth like he used her skin as a fidget spinner to calm his nerves.

Back and forth, his thumb dragged across her sensitive thigh. Back and forth. He used such a precise rhythm, she couldn't help imagining that same consistent, swiping touch between her legs. Right over her throbbing clit. Back and forth.

Something happened on the screen again, and Draven hid his face in her lap. The bridge of his nose fit perfectly between her legs. He shook his face; the motion caused her thighs to separate by an inch or two.

All the while, his thumb continued those persistent strokes on her tender thigh, the skin there tingling.

She fanned her face when he was not looking.

With her free hand, she kept her fingers in his hair, suppressing the instinct to tangle them in his wavy locks and pull his face firmly against the junction of her thighs.

He probably doesn't even realize how he is touching you, she told herself. The possessive arm around the back of her waist. The sensual strokes on her thighs.

The skirt of her dress bunched up higher, revealing more of her skin.

Thea swallowed her lust and refocused on the movie.

But Draven's hand crept up her leg. His thumb slid up her inner thigh as he shifted on her lap.

Her breath hitched—surely, he heard it because he paused and turned his head to look up at her.

Draven was so hot for her. Boiling. His heart pounded harder than any drum. His hard cock throbbed with each beat. The back of his head now nestled perfectly into her lap as he stared up at her.

Stunning woman. Her dark chestnut hair hung down from a messy bun, her brown eyes wide and pupils dilated.

"You're that scared?" She wrote to him, showing him the notepad with shaky hands.

Draven was more than scared. He was terrified—of Thea. Of how much he wanted her. Of how much he wanted her to want him. Was it the curse of forbidden fruit? Knowing Wren said she was off-limits? Was it her prim and proper exterior yet goofy and feisty personality?

What if she goes back to her ex after this? Women "escaped" with Draven, then they left him and returned to their real lives.

Reverting back to his flirty defense mechanism, Draven wrote, *"Maybe we should sleep in the same bed again tonight. In case I have nightmares."*

She snorted and rolled her eyes. Somehow, that reaction sparked unadulterated glee in his chest. *When I amuse her, it feels better than thousands of fans screaming my name in a concert hall.*

Working on nothing but dangerous instinct, he reached up and touched a piece of her hair, sifting it through his fingers. Soft. Silky. Pretty. *Why did she have to be so freaking pretty?*

Her lips parted on a sudden exhale. Her eyelids dropped to half-mast at his touch.

"I am scared, Thea," he said, knowing she wouldn't understand him.

She inquisitively tilted her head and stared at his mouth—because she was trying to read his lips, not because she wanted to kiss him. Of course.

Draven sighed.

After a minute of peering down at him, she wrote something else.

"*I'll protect you.*"

A promise no one had ever made to Draven.

Not when he was a little kid, taking care of his siblings. Not when fans grabbed at his clothing and body parts as he was ushered to the car from venues.

She promised to protect him.

And it happened again. Draven's heart shot right out of his chest and into Thea's hands.

He liked her.

He really did.

Shit.

"*Next, use the blue eyeshadow...*" Thea read the subtitle on the makeup tutorial. Each day, she attempted to master a new type of movie makeup.

For today's lesson, she set out to conquer the *down-on-his-luck action star*—meaning bruises, a split lip, and a bloody gash coming from somewhere on the face. Forehead or cheek, she had not yet decided.

She dabbed more blue and purple around her eye.

"The trick is to make the black eye look like you've tried to cover it up with normal makeup."

She nodded at the tutorial. So far, she had mastered the "glam" and the natural "woke up like this" makeup—because Hollywood did not go for a natural look without some hacks.

She had also attempted a "skeleton" skull makeup of grays and whites to make her face look made up of shadow and bone. She washed it away before Draven saw her and had a heart attack. *Poor guy is a scared-y cat.* She smirked.

As she finished with the split lip and black eye, she took a few photos and sent them off to her friends with the context of: *"No Thea was harmed in the making of these photos. Look at how good at this I'm getting!"*

A sense of giddy pride overrode her system—personal finance had never made her feel like this. Like she created art.

Even though she looked beat up to a pulp in the mirror, she felt like an absolute masterpiece.

Readying to wash the makeup off, she realized she left her face towel in her bedroom. Needing to grab it, she opened the bathroom door to exit.

She walked right into Draven, who stood just outside the door. Her chest slammed into his, and his arms shot out to help her rebalance as she catapulted off the hard muscles of his abs.

Her palms slapped onto his taut pecs, seeming to super glue themselves there when her hands realized who and where they touched. *We're good right here,* her palms said. *No need to remove us.*

She gasped at his firm hold on her hips, their fronts pressing together as he steadied her to his toned chest. There was something about being sweetly hugged by a man like Draven—aka, one with tattoos, an all-black wardrobe, and a penchant for smirking.

His fingers wrapped tightly around her like she was the edge of a cliff from which he dangled. Like she was the one thing in the world that could wipe his classic self-assured smirk off his face.

She breathed in his scent and shuddered as the sensual tingles she had grown familiar with over the last few days rose to the surface.

Then, he started shaking her.

Fiercely shaking her.

Her gaze fell to his lips, which moved at the speed of light. Honestly, a person could fly to Mars in a day with the speed at which Draven said something to her. There was no chance she could read those speedy lips.

Now, he backtracked her, walking her back into the bathroom. His height and broad shoulders melted her body into submission as it mindlessly took any and all of his direction. He steered her until both of them stood in front of the mirror in the bathroom.

He kept speaking aloud, and she frowned at his lips, having no idea what he was yelling at her.

Because he appeared to be yelling.

Face turning red, breaths shallow, Draven slapped at his chest and said something. Even though he appeared to repeat the same phrase again and again, she couldn't decipher it.

Impatient and frustrated as hell, Draven glanced at the bathroom sink, grabbed a tube of her expensive lipstick, popped it open, and *wrote* on the mirror with it.

Thea's jaw dropped.

"*WHO DID THIS TO YOU?*" he wrote in smeared red lipstick on the mirror.

Stunned, she blinked several times, absorbing what was happening. Absorbing the waste of forty-dollar ever-lasting plum-apple lip stain on the mirror.

So.

Draven thought the black eye and split lip were real.

Two thoughts shot through her at once:

1. Wow, she really did that good of a job on the makeup?

2. He was terrified during the horror movie last night, but now he looked ready to chop someone up with a chainsaw for her.

Playful, goofy, smirky Draven evaporated from exis-tence as this hulking, dominating man *shook* with pent-up rage at the idea of someone hurting her. He *trembled* before her.

When she didn't instantly respond, he underlined his message on the mirror, using her lipstick again.

She made a noise at him, reaching for her lipstick.

Avoiding her outstretched hands, he shouted the same phrase he had written on the mirror. "Who did this to you?" This time, due to the context, she understood those plush, sinful lips.

She shook her head, wondering how to explain when her brain was distracted by the hypnotic way his chest heaved up and down. The way he stared at her was like he wouldn't just burn the world for her but would give it a good ole pummeling beforehand.

Like he would make the sky itself bleed. For her.

Her dazed reaction did not appease him because he used her lipstick on the mirror *again* to add two question marks after his plum-red note.

She waved her hands in the air and signed, *"Stop! Calm down."*

He rushed to write more on the mirror in her lipstick, *not* calming down. *"Why do you have bruises on your face?"*

She fought with him to take back her lipstick, and he eventually released it. She pressed her lips together and tried not to weep as she wrote under his note in maroon, *"Stop writing on the mirror!"*

His eyebrows went into his hairline as he shot her a look of disbelief. He then gestured to her and the new note on the mirror as if to say, *"You just did it too."*

She rolled her eyes.

He moved forward, caging her to the sink as he lifted a hand to her cheek. Just before he touched her, he paused, hovering, then ever so gently stroked a thumb down her cheek. He hissed, staring at her bruises.

She swallowed at the intensity he emitted in the small bathroom. She touched the hand he held at the side of her face and shook her head. She directed his gaze to the random eyeshadow containers and the blue and purple tinted makeup brushes.

Those dark eyebrows furrowed. Taking in a shuddering breath, Draven pointed to the makeup and then to her face.

She nodded and mimicked putting it on around her eyes.

His chest concaved. His fingers on her cheek slipped around to cup the back of her neck as he leaned forward and pressed his forehead to hers. Even if she couldn't hear his deep sigh, his relief was ear-piercing.

He stole the tube of lipstick from her grip once more and wrote, "*WHY?*" on the mirror.

She slapped at his chest and slammed a hand next to her original note of "*Stop writing on the mirror.*"

She mimed needing something to write with to explain to him. He swiftly turned, grabbed her hand, and walked her to the kitchen, where he handed her the notepad and pen they kept there.

Her palm and fingers cried at the loss of his hold on her. When was the last time someone held her hand like that? *I can't remember*, she thought.

A memory that would never fade from her mind was the way Draven clutched at his heart when he saw the bruises on her face. Or the way he had tenderly pressed his forehead to hers.

As she explained that she was now pursuing her dream of being a makeup artist for movie sets, Draven nodded. The tension in his shoulders slackened as he nodded along.

"I'm practicing each day. Applying to jobs each day. I know Hollywood is all about who you know, but I think I can do it. I'll find some internship or something..."

Thea painted her goals onto the notepad for Draven's eyes, something that might have bored anyone else. Still, he nodded to everything she wrote, engaged and present.

When he read her, *"I think I can do it,"* Thea swore his lips moved and said, "I know you can do it," but that could have been her imagination.

After letting her babble about her hopes and dreams, Draven wrote back something that made her heart stop and restart.

"My band needs a makeup artist for a Halloween gig. Would you be available for hire tomorrow night?"

Chapter Fourteen

He's paying me. He believes in me. Thea had never felt quite like this.

People said happiness was like walking on water, but she felt like she walked inside the gooey, warm bubbles of a lava lamp. Or maybe that was just the sensation of a part of her melting.

The self-doubt part of her heard her parents repeatedly tell her to "be realistic" in what she asked for in life so she wouldn't be "disappointed." Funny how she—the deaf daughter—was the only child in the family to receive that logical speech.

Draven thinks I can do it. Draven wants to help *me do it.*

She floated around the apartment, packing up makeup that she bought from the store in preparation for tonight's Halloween show.

"Wait, you mean the Halloween concert at Judas Maxi-

mo's mansion?" Mallory texted in her friend group chat after Thea typed out her recent exciting news.

"*Judas Maximo of Maximillian Records?!?*" Fifi messaged back.

Wait, what? Thea's breath caught in her throat. She thought Draven's band was just performing a nonchalant "gig" at one of his favorite bars the way the band sometimes did between world tours. A no-pressure, "for fun" gig.

She was going to do horror monster makeup on the famous band *Medusa's Tears* of Maximillian Records in front of the infamous Judas Maximo and all of his A-lister guests? Wasn't Judas Maximo friends with Hollywood's most renowned, well-known directors, producers, actors and actresses?

Shit, she cursed to herself. *I totally cheaped out on the Halloween makeup.*

"*I didn't realize that was what it was.*" Thea texted, "*Guys, I'm not ready for this. Oh God, I'm going to crash and burn.*"

"*Stop, you'll do great!*" Elisa texted.

"*Elisa*," Thea messaged back. "*You only use exclamation points when you're lying about something.*"

"*I do not!*"

Thea dropped her face into her palms and groaned.

Mallory tried to comfort her. "*Thea, you are a natural artist. Remember all those paintings you did in college? You want to do this because you're good at it. It's more than a passion you're trying to pick up. You already have the talent."*

"It's been inside you the whole time!" Elisa added.

Mallory texted, *"Elisa, stop using exclamation points. You're freaking out Thea."*

"Sorry!"

"Dude, calm down," Fifi messaged. *"At minimum, just put some eyeliner on the guys. At most, cover their sexy faces until they are completely unrecognizable and look like freaky badass monsters."*

"What if I accidentally poke one of them in the eye with eyeliner? And then they lose sight and quit the band forever?" Thea texted.

"Oh geez, she's spiraling," Mallory replied. *"Thea, this will be amazing exposure. You could meet someone important in the movie industry tonight and literally show them your talent!"*

"Yeah!" Elisa added.

"Elisa, what did I say about the exclamation points?" Mallory wrote. *"Thea, offering to do Halloween makeup on the guys for this show was a genius idea."*

"Draven's the one who offered. He hired me."

Elisa texted, *"Yeah, he did!"*

"Elisa!"

Thea put her phone down and gazed longingly at Draven's bedroom door. He had been in there for nearly two hours without coming out. She sat on the couch in the living room, trying to act like she wasn't waiting to see him and absorb more of his self-confidence and faith in her.

She blinked at her sudden realization. *He makes me feel good about myself.*

After five more minutes of nerves and daydreams of Judas Maximo kicking her out of his mansion after she accidentally ruined the entire Halloween party, Thea strode to Draven's bedroom and knocked.

The door opened to reveal a smooth, chiseled chest near eye level. Draven had not been his usual shirtless self around the apartment over the last two days. Her retinas had missed this magnificent sight. She nearly wept at the tantalizing beauty before her.

He smirked at her, shaking out his shoulder-length black hair and running a hand through it. The tattoo under his upper arm flexed and called out to Thea.

Delicious man.

Draven pointed to her, then he flattened his hands to his chest and made upward circular motions, signing, "*Are you excited?*"

Her heart pittered and pattered all over the place. *He is still learning sign language.* She signed, "*I'm nervous.*"

He watched her hands and expression closely, nodding like he understood her. *How much more sign language does he plan to learn?* She wanted to know.

He turned to grab a notepad and a pen from his bed stand to write, "*Thea, you'll do great. Those bruises you did yesterday gave me nightmares.*"

She scoffed out an awkward, nervous laugh. He

handed her the pad and pen. "*That's because you're a scared-y cat,*" she shot back with a grin so playful that it felt like a time portal to elementary school recess.

Instead of appearing amused, a sad smile curved his mouth as he reached out and dragged his thumb over the middle of her chin. She exhaled, her lungs clocking out for their lunch break as she struggled to breathe under his touch.

He let his arm drop, and he took the pad and pen to write. "*When I thought you were really hurt, I was terrified.*" Then, he added, "*And so damn pissed, I could have murdered anyone who dared to touch you.*"

There goes my heart, she thought. *Pitter pattering. Melting and slacking on its vital function of simply pumping blood.* The man was affecting her crucial organs.

"*I know you're nervous about tonight, but it'll be great. Don't worry,*" he wrote.

She took the notepad from him, holding it in one shaky hand as she hastily wrote, "*What if I stab one of you guys in the eye with eyeliner or something? What if I make you all look ridiculous? What if—*"

He pulled the pad from her, shaking his head. She hugged herself as the self-doubt wrung her stomach.

Draven ushered her forward, wrapping his arms around her and holding her to his chest. His wide, warm palm rubbed circles on her back, soothing her and turning her on simultaneously. *His smell.* Pure man.

She assumed he cooed to her, *shh*ing her concerns because she felt his breath fluttering pieces of hair against the side of her neck. Those lips brushed the spot she wished he would kiss.

He pressed their foreheads together once more, blanking her thoughts, before he wrote, *"You really think you'll stab one of them in the eye?"*

She bit her lip, hoping the band had good optical insurance.

He tsked her nerves and patted her head to comfort her as he wrote, *"You'll do Wren's makeup first."*

"What the Hell? I did not agree to this," Tomi griped as Thea brushed more black and white liquid over his jawline and mouth.

"Shut up, you're going to look badass," Draven replied.

His annoyance spiked as his band members did not sit down with utter enthusiasm for Thea to paint their faces. *If these assholes make her question whether she is doing a good job, I will kill them.*

Draven added, "She is making our lead singer have stitched lips. It's ironic and awesome. She is a freaking genius."

Wren, Tomi, and Yin all stared at Draven as Thea jittered around, perfecting each line she created like the artist she was. Unable to hear the griping, Thea was completely ignorant to the fact that the band whined about Draven agreeing to cover their faces in makeup for the Halloween show.

"She's going to make me look like Sally from *The Nightmare Before Christmas*," Tomi complained.

"Yeah, and you're going to fucking like it," Draven said.

Wren pointed to his face. "She gave me diamond clown eyes."

"So?"

"So, she knows Mal is terrified of clowns! The second she sees me, she might burst into tears."

Draven's eyes widened before he burst into laughter. His chest shook with it. Warmth and amusement tainted his airways until all he could do when he caught his breath was stupidly grin at Thea like she was the best thing he had ever seen. "God, she is hilarious."

When he refocused on his band, they all stared at him again in that *"what the hell is going on"* way.

"I don't care what you say, Draven," Yin remarked. "She will not—I repeat—she will not put eyeliner on me."

"You assholes are lucky she can't hear you," Draven said, his tone sharp enough to be lethal. "If any of you make her frown tonight, I will draw a dick on your face in permanent marker and record you having to explain to your wife and kids why your face looks like genitalia. I will then play that recording at your funeral."

Yin pointed out, "Drave, the only reason you're not complaining too is because she made you look like a badass tiger."

Draven pursed his lips but couldn't deny it.

On the drive to Maximo's mansion for the party, Thea had sketched ideas for each band member on her notepad and written to him, "*You're going to be a tiger.*" When he asked why, she had blown out a breath and written, "*Because you remind me of a tiger.*" What the heck did that mean? Hopefully, something good.

He had asked aloud, "Do you find tigers sexy, you Lion-King-loving minx?" Even though she could not hear him, she smiled at him as if she trusted, based on his lips moving, that he had said something fun. Something playful. He wanted to say something downright dirty when she kept staring at his lips.

Like telling her how good she looked in her Halloween costume.

Tight black leggings cased her legs and looked like fake leather pants. Her upper arm sported a fake tattoo. She wore a T-shirt that had a printed graphic of muscular, masculine abs down her torso. Her dark hair was slicked back into a ponytail, but from the neck down, she was supposed to be "Draven the drummer."

Gone were her modest, pastel dresses. Thea was dressed as Draven in faux black leather pants.

Upon first seeing her, Draven's chest felt like a tight balloon without the capacity for more air. Could anything else fill him up more than watching her giggle to herself as she modeled the costume and attempted to copy Draven's well-known smirk?

Playful and sexy. The combination that brought a man

like Draven to his knees—or maybe just kicked his legs right out from under him until he laid, stunned, on his back.

"Great, he zoned out, staring at her leather pants again," one of the guys said, causing Draven to blink and refocus on his current surroundings.

"They're *fake* leather," Draven replied, giving a good, long look at the way the fabric clung to her thighs and ass as she bent over Tomi while she worked. "Because she cares about animals and the environment," he added proudly.

Tomi rolled his eyes. Thea caught this and stepped back, pausing in her task. She glanced around the group of men, and everyone flashed her fake, wide smiles, full of teeth. She nodded politely, smiling to herself, and went back to applying makeup to Tomi.

"What part of off-limits do you not understand, Draven?" Wren growled from his seat next to Yin. "Stop staring at her ass."

"How am I supposed to not stare at an ass that perfect?" Draven snorted but became serious. "But if I catch any of you staring at her perfect ass, I'll poke out your eyes with her eyeliner."

Wren shook his head and warned, "We talked about this. She was supposed to live with you, and you would *not* try to hook up with her. You promised."

"I had two fingers crossed behind my back when I promised that."

Red-faced and frustrated, Wren threw his arms up in the air.

Tomi came to Draven's defense. "In all fairness, you should know by now to check his back when he makes promises."

"Draven," Wren continued, "You aren't her type. And she's not your type."

Yin snorted.

"What?" Wren asked.

"Does no one remember Serene Santiago from college?" Yin asked the group. "The girl with two binders for each class, five pens, wore sundresses, and pearl earrings? Draven drooled over her for three years."

"So?"

"So, Thea is exactly Draven's type," Yin stated.

Wren frowned. "What? Prim and proper? The good girl stereotype he can corrupt?"

Yin's eyebrows furrowed and his lips curved down as he addressed Wren. "No. Serene Santiago was more than just prim and proper. Women have *layers*. She was in a comedy club, did improv and standup, and was hilarious. Draven's type is a good girl in the worksheets, an absolute goofball on the streets, and I would assume a freak in the sheets, but that's more for Draven to clarify."

"Thea is my future wife's best friend," Wren grated. "Even if he actually liked her, we all know how it would end. In tears and heartbreak. And Mallory would murder anyone who hurt Thea."

"What if I didn't hurt her?" Draven asked.

Wren scoffed. "What if? Great choice of words, man." Wren stood to approach Draven, who also stood from his seat. Wren over-punctuated each word as he said, "Don't. Fuck. This. Woman."

"I wouldn't do anything she didn't want me to do."

Wren snarled. "If you hurt her in any way, I'm going to have to choose."

Pain. An emotional sucker punch. "What the hell does that mean?" Draven asked, voice wavering. "If Mal asks you to kick me out of the band, you will?"

A little too calmly, Wren crossed his arms and stared at Draven. "Tell me right now if you think Thea is the one. Tell me you know for sure that your attraction to her isn't just because I told you she's off-limits."

"You can't kick me out of the band over a woman," Draven shouted, caught up in the feeling of betrayal.

"Wrong answer." Wren's words turned everything around them to stone as he said, "Judas told me you were asking for more money. Why? Is it drugs, Draven? Are you hooked on something?"

Draven's mind blew into a nuclear mushroom cloud. "Ex-*fucking*-cuse me?" His friend found out Draven asked for a raise, and his first thought was *drugs*?

It's like they don't even know me anymore. Like I'm a caricature to them.

Wren stabbed a finger to Draven's chest. "Stay away from Thea. She doesn't need to get her heart broken by some drummer who can't survive a year off the last million he made on tour."

Without waiting to hear Draven out, Wren stomped out of the room and into the hall, where he was sure to be mobbed by celebrities who were obsessed with his music and maybe even some groupies, depending on how well Maximo's security team was.

Draven silently gaped, opening and closing his mouth for several seconds. He turned to Tomi and Yin. "You guys know I don't do drugs, right?"

Yin waved off his concern. "We know."

"What did I do that made Wren crawl up my ass these last few years?"

"I'd say it's the hookups," Tomi said. "Once he had Armie and he saw what a manwhore you were, he started getting on your case. Having a daughter changes a man."

"I sleep around just as much as you guys did before you found your wives."

"Look, we're not judging you, Draven, but you've never actually had a long-term, serious relationship," Tomi said. "Even if you like Thea, the fact that she is Wren's soon-to-be wife's best friend means you should keep your distance."

Draven ran his fingers through his hair, roughly gripping and pulling the strands. "He threatened to kick me out of the band. A band I helped *build*."

"Judas has been whispering in his ear the last few years," Yin shared.

Judas Maximo. Owning his band was not enough for the bastard; he had to control it, too. *That asshole thinks of everyone as his personal puppets.*

"Apparently, Maximo's newest kick is telling Wren

about how he could find a more 'manageable' drummer for Medusa's Tears."

Draven's mouth opened so wide, a fist could have fit into it. It already felt like he was choking around one. "Maximo hates me that much?"

"You shouldn't have slept with his assistant, dude," Tomi said, shaking his head, which caused Thea to tsk and flick his cheek, making him stay still for her to do the finishing touches on the makeup.

Draven remarked, "I didn't know she was his assistant!"

"I'm just saying, make sure you don't cross the line with Thea. You two can be friends, but if you sleep with her—if she cries to Mal about you—God help you."

Yin added, "Wren has been a groomzilla planning this wedding. You've never seen a man more anxious to get a marriage certificate and gold ring on a woman. Any minor thing that could mess with Mal and him might make him blow."

"What if she wants me? I'm supposed to just tell her no?"

Tomi rolled his eyes again. "Yes, Draven. If she—for some reason—decides to sleep with you, you keep your dick in your pants and say '*no*.'"

Wide-eyed, Draven stared at Tomi and Yin, shocked that both felt so strongly about the subject. Then, he looked back at Thea, who pushed a stray lock of chestnut hair behind her ear. She licked her red lips as she worked, seeming to zone everything else out.

He liked that about her. The intensity and passion of granting one hundred percent of her focus on one thing at a time. He liked it when that potent attention was on him.

Just friends. Right.

Unable to stop himself, his gaze fell back down to her perfect, black legging-sculpted ass.

One of his bandmates grunted. "He's screwed."

Chapter Fifteen

"They look amazing; you did such a good job!" Mal signed to Thea as they leaned against the wall of the packed room.

Judas Maximo had a living room with a damn *stage*.

The band's instruments were all set up, and people dressed in Halloween costumes, ranging from skimpy to artistic to humorous to scary, packed the large room. Thea wanted to warn scared-y cat Draven not to look at the snake woman with horrifying serpentine eye contacts who lingered by a green, smoking punch bowl.

Judas Maximo knew how to throw a party. Halloween decorations and themed foods were everywhere, some set up at stations and others carried around by servers wearing black and orange.

Thea's heart jumped as she spotted some celebrities in the crowd. Actors, comedians, musicians, athletes... *Wow, I am totally out of my comfort zone here.* Medusa's Tears would have had its pick of makeup artists for tonight. Did they even typically use makeup artists? Pride and nerves battled inside her.

But mostly pride. Because damn, she did *good*, son.

She knew Wren was upset with the clown eyes she gave him, but he didn't have to know that she did it on purpose. Wren had kept glaring at Draven, and Thea's protective instincts flared, making her choose the one thing she knew Mallory feared the most—clowns. Thankfully, her best friend forgave her for turning her fiancé into her biggest fear.

"Maybe it'll be like immersion therapy," Thea signed to her. *"Maybe you'll have a clown kink by the end of the night,"* she joked.

Mallory rolled her eyes and elbowed her, which Thea dodged, laughing.

To be honest, Thea might have a tiger kink by the end of the night. Not for the actual animal, of course. And maybe not for the male actors in the Musical *Lion King*.

It's Draven. He made even tiger makeup sexy.

Confident, calm, collected, and predatory. He moved like a sly, lithe panther, slinking through the crowd, exuding danger and power.

The black and white streaks around his narrowed eyes brought out the bright green-colored irises.

He scanned the crowd with those mischievous and sexy predator eyes, stopping when he saw her standing in the corner with Mallory. His orange and black striped face came across as primal and striking.

The only thing better than that smolder was his smile. When he shot one right at her, Thea's panties evaporated.

Mal nudged Thea's arm, almost causing her to break eye contact with Draven as his band members stood on stage and picked up their instruments. Draven sank onto his drummer seat and lifted his sticks over his head. He banged them once, twice, thrice, before Mal pulled on Thea's arm again, stealing her attention.

"*Are you still lusting after Draven?*" Mal signed to her.

Thea pointed to him on stage—shirtless, because that was how he always performed—and shot a "*Duh*" expression to Mallory.

Mal's front teeth sank into her bottom lip, and Thea wanted to roll her eyes. Sure, Draven had been on a sex ban for a week, but Thea had only ever seen good things from him. Other than their childish, passive-aggressive tendencies in the beginning.

Now, we share almond milk. Like real adults.

"*You are delicate right now,*" Mallory signed. "*After what Alec did, I just don't want you to make a mistake and get hurt even worse.*"

Thea didn't want to be seen as "delicate," and who said Draven would be a mistake? The man sacrificed popcorn from his bowl to fill her empty one—*good* popcorn. Not just the small kernels.

He found out about her makeup dream and hired her for the greatest networking opportunity she could ever ask for. He even drove her to a store that could quickly print out some business cards for her to hand out to people tonight. He came up with a tagline: "*Deaf makeup artist with talent that will make you scream.*"

She wiggled as warmth prickled through her body just thinking about it.

"*Are you just wanting to hook up with him, or do you like him?*" Mallory signed.

"*What's wrong with both?*"

"*How about the fact that you just got out of an on-and-off relationship with a guy you thought you would marry, but he cheated on you?*"

Thea glared at her. "*I didn't ask you for a reality check.*"

Mallory was the "mother" of the friend group long before she became an acting mother to Wren's daughter, Armie. Mal was quirky and fun, sure, but she had the temper and protective instincts of a bear. Hurt someone she cared about? And that person would find themselves clawed to death by perfectly manicured nails.

"*What if I just want to hook up?*" Thea signed. "*Other people do one-night stands. I deserve some fun.*"

"*I know you, and you would not find a lack of commitment fun, no matter how many orgasms he gave you.*" Mal squeezed Thea's arm before signing, "*You need attention, acceptance, and intensity.*" Ever the unsolicited therapist, that was Mal.

Thea's lips thinned into an agitated line. "*I knew I shouldn't have told you about my childhood.*"

"*Knowing what you need in a relationship is important.*"

Just as Mal signed that, the floor vibrated. The pulse of the song's beat reverberated in the air. Though she couldn't hear it, she felt it. Thea felt the sound wrap around her and demand she feel every beat.

Mal gestured to the side of her head, signaling to Thea that she planned to turn on her cochlear implant, allowing her to hear sound. Mal often preferred to keep it off, but since she started dating a musician, she listened to his music.

Some of Thea's friends were able to get cochlear implants, some didn't want them, and then there was Thea, whose version of deafness did not align with a cochlear implant. She preferred the peaceful silence but did enjoy dancing to the vibrations of music. She loved dancing.

She swayed to the beat, her hips swinging back and forth as she nodded to the vibrations. A glance at the stage stopped her dancing.

Draven stared right at her as he beat his sticks against the drums, viciously attacking them to create the beat she enjoyed. He was a god creating magic with his hands. His head banged along to the same beat as his muscled arms moved with a speed that awed her.

She had never noticed before, but drumming was in every inch of his body. The act of it jerked him from head to toe, possessing him, consuming him. The strength and stamina that took... The hard-earned talent...

Thea glanced at Mallory, who danced beside her and mouthed the words to the song.

Thea had never cared about lyrics, unable to make them out. She cared about a fast, mesmerizing, and catchy beat. Something to overpower her limbs until they flailed along to the rhythm.

Under Draven's heated gaze from across the room, she churned her hips and dragged her hands up her sides.

He leaned closer to his drums and hit them harder as he watched her. She licked her lips and sensually undulated her hips. Was this what he wanted? A seductress?

Ha! She threw her arms up in the air and dramatically wiggled and flailed her limbs, goofily gyrating and jumping to the music.

The room was full of scantily clad women—some famous actresses and pop stars—all grinding and shaking their booties while making goo-goo eyes at the band on stage.

Meanwhile, Draven stared right at the crazy woman in the corner doing the can-can, miming throwing pizza dough up in the air and spinning it, and, of course, her signature dance move.

She leaned down and swung her arm, mimicking pulling the chord on a lawn mower, before pushing the invisible mower around with swinging hips.

His grin lit up the entire room.

And she suddenly understood the sensation of having swallowed a swarm of butterflies, ladybugs, and—honestly—hornets. Because she felt each sting in her gut as a woman in the front row flung her black lace thong at Draven's drums.

The thing about Thea frowning was that it made Draven's skin crawl. As powerful as her playful smiles or her giggles at her own jokes were, her *lack* of a smile kicked him in the gut.

She moved through the crowd after the first two songs his band played, and he eventually lost sight of her and glared at Mallory for not going with her friend. This place was packed. What if she got kidnapped? Or lost? She needed a protector, dammit.

Mallory flashed him a "*What gives?*" gesture when she noticed his glare from across the room. Wren, staring at his fiancé like the obsessed man he was, turned to look at Draven with an inquisitive and judgmental "*What did you do now?*" expression.

As the band played their biggest hit—the dirtiest, most sexual one as well—the crowd went wild for them. Typically, Draven would gobble up the attention and praise, but instead, he wanted to know where Thea went and if she was feeling okay.

Tomi sang into the mic, "*Baby, you turn me to stone, so hard for you. Medusa, baby, what more can I do? I don't care about your snakes; bite me in two. Your venom feels like heaven.*"

Beginning to sweat, Draven finally saw a chestnut-colored ponytail emerging in the crowd, moving back toward Mallory. But then, she stopped mid-way. Talking to someone.

Draven squinted, trying to see who it was.

His knuckles went white as he held his drumsticks in a death grip.

Judas *goddamn* Maximo was talking to Thea.

In sign language.

Chapter Sixteen

The Judas Maximo stood in front of Thea and *signed* to her. She quickly closed her stunned, open mouth as she blushed.

"*How are you doing tonight?*" he signed.

She had seen Judas once before at one of the bar gigs she attended with Mallory. He was the man in a thousand-dollar suit who ordered the most expensive scotch available, took two sips from it, nodded a greeting to Wren, and left.

She had no idea he knew she existed or knew sign language, for Pete's sake.

She nervously signed back, "*I'm great. You know ASL?*"

"*My grandmother was deaf,*" he replied. "*I heard you did the band's makeup tonight.*"

Uh, oh. Was this where he sued her for damages?

"*They look great,*" he signed. "*You are very talented.*"

Her blush deepened. "*Thank you.*"

This was the part where she gave him a business card or told him to tell all his Hollywood connections about her. But instead, she clasped her elbow and shifted on nervous legs as she fought to "network" for the first time in her life. Damn it, why couldn't she be better at this?

She was an outgoing powerhouse with her friends, but put her out of her element and with someone she didn't know but who knew everyone else in the room, and Thea got shy. So, sue her! No, please, don't sue her.

"Draven said you're trying to get into the movie makeup business."

"Yes." Here it was—her ticket to market herself and her future. *You want to go for your dream? All you have to do is* do *it.* And no, Nike did not sponsor her inspiring thought to herself.

Just as she prepared to pull out her business cards, the music calmed to a stop. Judas' head shot over to look at the band as if somebody had called his name. Thea glanced over and saw everyone had stopped dancing.

The crowd stared at Draven who now stood beside Tomi, speaking into the microphone and looking right at her.

Draven then pointed right at her, and everyone in the room moved their gazes to her.

Her blood pressure spiked under the attention.

Draven's lips kept moving as he pointed her out to the crowd and spoke into the microphone. Her cheeks burned.

What was he saying? She touched Judas' arm and asked.

Judas quickly signed, *"He is telling everyone how you did their makeup tonight. How you're looking for some jobs on movie sets and that any film would be lucky to have you."*

Thea looked back to Draven, who winked at her and handed the mic back to Tomi. A group of people crowded around Thea, and she divvied up her business cards, handing them out and running out of them by the end of the night.

Is this what it's like to have a cheerleader?

Thea had only one question.

Was she allowed to throw her panties at Draven too?

Just friends, Draven repeated to himself. *Just friends.*

Thea was in the shower, getting ready to go to bed for the night, but he was too awake, too *alive* for sleep. Having Wren threaten to kick him out of the band. Watching Thea dance. Watching Judas sign to her.

Draven's emotions had been up and down all night, a rollercoaster with a laundry list of lawsuits after the neck-breaking and stomach warping falls and turns.

He opened the fridge to grab a beer, closed the door, and saw a pink Post-it hanging on it. Thea had written, *"You did a great job tonight. Thank you for inviting me. You make a sexy tiger."*

His fingers folded over his heart.

Just friends. Just friends.

He slipped the pink square of paper into the pocket of his jeans, wondering if there was a store that framed two-by-two-inch-sized notes. Because people framed notes from friends. Obviously.

Just friends.

Draven settled down onto the couch, stretching out his legs. Sitting up and facing the bathroom door, he sipped his beer. He forbade his mind to think about how Thea stood naked and dripping, water flowing down her body right now, in his apartment.

Her dark brown hair probably looked black when it was wet. Like city streets on a rainy night.

He closed his eyes and tried *not* to listen to the sound of the shower. The rushing water brought up images of her lathering her smooth neck and supple breasts, fingers trailing down her stomach. He grunted and put down his beer.

Maybe getting a buzz was not the best idea when his cock already wanted to overrule his brain when it came to his roommate.

He picked up the notepad from the coffee table as lyrics flooded him.

"She is no wallflower.
She is lethal ivy,
clinging to every piece of me.
A gun with a silencer,
shooting round after round at me.

So quietly.
Those eyes are cannons,
tearing my sails.
Be my anchor.
Siren and savior.
Drown with me."

Dumb. He balled up the piece of paper and jammed it into his other jean pocket—not the one with her precious note.

Why the hell was everyone so convinced Draven would end up hurting Thea anyway? Thinking he would break her heart? As if she would even *give* him her heart.

Wren was right. Draven was not her type. He was nothing like her tie-wearing, snooty ex. Draven had tattoos. He sometimes painted his nails black—mostly when his younger sister Summer visited him and demanded it.

We will just be friends, he told himself, nodding at the thought.

Then, the bathroom door creaked open, and a wet, dripping Thea scuttered out, wearing nothing but a small, pale-pink towel.

Even her bath towels are pastel.

From several feet away, Draven could make out the pink flush across her cheeks and chest from the steam of the shower. The dark tresses of her hair slicked back. Thick beads of moisture dripped onto her chest and the towel and the floor.

The little pings against the hardwood sounded like,

"*Haha, no chance you stay just friends with her, you bastard! She is your dream girl, and you are lusting after her hard, bro.*" Stupid opinionated droplets.

She stood there, staring at him as if *he* were Medusa turning her to stone. Didn't she realize the power she held over him?

More droplets fell to the floor.

She did not move.

Awareness nicked the back of his neck, an invisible needle injecting him with pure adrenaline-spiked anticipation.

Draven slowly rose from the couch, staring right back at her with what he hoped was not an intense expression that revealed his inner thoughts of, "*Baby, I'd fuck you so good, you'd never think about your cheating ex again.*"

From the distance, he could not read her expression. Just felt the *click* as their gazes locked. A bomb could have gone off, and Draven didn't think himself capable of flinching or blinking. Blinking meant a second of not seeing her, not seeing this sudden show of interest and vulnerability from her.

Why is she just standing there? What does she want from me?

"Are you okay?" he asked as he stepped around the couch, hesitantly moving toward where she stood.

She tilted her head and peered at him. Her mouthwatering grapefruit scent slammed into him the closer he got to her.

I want to lick her.

"*Are you okay?*" he signed.

Her eyes widened just a bit at his signing. Her pink tongue dabbed out to wet her lips, slicking them and securing all of his attention.

Just friends. The thing about Thea was that when she opened up, when she got silly and goofy with Draven, it made him feel like her partner in crime. Like best friends.

But he also wanted to kiss every centimeter of her body. Kiss, lick, suck, bite.

He wanted to leave so many hickeys on her neck that, to cover them, she had to wear a scarf or ten sets of pearl necklaces. He wanted to sit her on the couch and set up a wine tasting, where she had different glasses to sip from, and he had his own tasting where he splayed open her thighs and dove his face between them, devouring her. He wanted to hear her whimpers and watch her face twist with ecstasy as she came.

She gripped the side of her towel.

"Baby, are you trying to seduce me right now?" Draven asked in wonderment. He had no idea what was going on in her pretty, talented head. "Because it's working."

Not understanding him, she pursed her lips and exhaled.

"Or are you just trying to ruin my floors by dripping there?"

She bit her lip, and her gaze flicked down his body as he prowled closer.

"Thea, Wren will kill me if I touch you," he muttered to himself, knowing she couldn't hear him. He sucked his top lip into his mouth, perusing her damp bare legs and thighs beneath the towel.

Groaning, he asked in a tortured voice, "Do you know what it's like to want someone so bad you don't fear death?" His feet stopped just in front of her. With his height, he towered over her.

He leaned down so he could look into those piercing gray eyes, little mirrors reflecting his soul. Or maybe trapping his soul? The woman was obsessed with horror movies; she probably practiced witchcraft at some point in her life, even if it was just buying crystals or bespelled candles.

"Little witch, I'd burn at the stake
for a touch. Burn for a touch.
She took my eyes that very first day.
She cast a spell.
Now all I see is her,
but they tell me one touch will take me to Hell."

Draven shushed the lyrics in his head. "Thea, you standing naked in that towel in front of me is giving me ideas I really should *not* be having right now." *Friends. Friends.* Chandler, Monica, Rachel, Ross...

Her fingers tightened around the towel; her chest moved up and down more noticeably. She licked her lips again.

Draven was close to panting. Because she still stood there—like an invitation he wanted to RSVP and stamp and lick the envelope closed.

His cock tingled and hardened behind his slacks,

clearly enjoying this teaser, whether it was a mind game or not.

"Fuck, baby, I can see your pretty nipples poking through that towel." Draven ran a hand over his mouth and chin. "Do you know what that does to me? I should win the Nobel Prize for self-control right now."

She blinked slowly.

"Don't act all innocent, Thea. Do you know how hard you're making me right now? There's a thing called blue balls, and I've had it since you moved in and started leaving pink Post-it notes all over the apartment."

She reached toward him, and his breath caught when he thought for a moment that she reached for his waistband. Instead, she grabbed his hand and pulled him into the steam-filled bathroom.

"Not making me any less hard, babe," Draven mumbled.

She turned to position him in front of the mirror. Leaning forward, she grabbed a container of makeup wipes and pulled a few white towelettes out. She scrubbed his face with them, taking off the tiger makeup.

"This was not where I thought this was going," Draven said sourly as she roughly rubbed the wipes over his cheeks, jaw, nose, and forehead. "Can you at least accidentally drop your towel? Make a man's dream come true?"

She paused her vicious scrubbing and narrowed her eyes as if she heard his comment. Or maybe she just saw right through him and knew he would say something indecent and provocative like that. She resumed removing the makeup.

"So, that's a 'no' to the towel dropping?"

She shoved his head downward so she could get to his forehead. This new position forced his line of sight directly onto her breasts—breasts barely covered by the thin, damp towel.

Yup, those were definitely hard nipples poking through the fabric. *Hello there, darlings. Would you like a kiss? I promise to use tongue.*

The sweet, sour, lush scent of grapefruit clouded his brain as he breathed her in. His dick thickened faster, getting threateningly close to a full-on erection.

Draven clenched his eyes shut and mentally screamed, *JUST FRIENDS.*

When Thea finished, she dropped the dirtied wipes into the trashcan and crossed her arms in front of her, nodding at her job well done.

"Be honest," he joked. "You liked me in that makeup, but I'm a masterpiece au naturel too."

He swore she could hear him because her lips curled at the edges as if she fought off a smile.

Friends.

But then, she leaned forward, yanking down his head and turning it to the side to press her plush lips tenderly to his cheek. The graze of her lips and the resulting waft of grapefruit bliss had Draven's heart wringing itself in his chest, as if the organ was clearing house to make room for something new.

She kissed his cheek, spun around, and left the bathroom.

She left him, stunned, at the sink.

Staring into the mirror as he swallowed the rising, irrevocable truth.

I want to sleep with my friend.

Chapter Seventeen

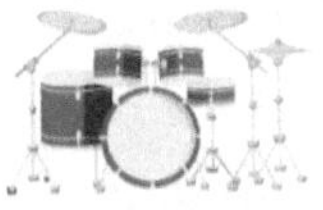

Why the hell had Draven not jumped her bones? Not thrown her onto his bed and had his wicked, bad boy way with her?

She had stood in nothing but a towel in front of him for the span of *minutes*. Too shy to let the towel fall or make the first move with the known playboy, she had begged him with her eyes to touch her. And. He. Did. Nothing.

Was she not his usual groupie type? Sure. But why had he not made a move? Lust had *burned* in his gaze on her. All hooded eyes and parted lips. Flaring nostrils.

Had her standing there in a towel not been a strong enough seduction for the playboy drummer? *Fine, I'll kick it up a notch.*

The following day, Thea changed into short-shorts and set up her yoga mat in the middle of the living room as part of a feminine revenge kick. *A perfect way to start the morning.*

She had never been someone who did yoga, but Alec always said it would be smart to pick up some kind of exercise or sport. Specifically, he mentioned that maybe yoga could help with her "flexibility." *Cringe.* She had bought a yoga mat, flashing it at him on weekend mornings, then met her friends for coffee and bagels instead. She always *meant* to go to a yoga class.

She searched "beginner yoga poses" online and stumbled across an interesting article called: "*The ten sexiest yoga poses to get your partner horny as hell.*"

Was the title a little on the nose? Sure. But at least it was not called: "*Seductive yoga stances to get your sexy roommate to want to touch you.*"

After the first three minutes of random poses, she thought, *I do not like this. How is this for beginners?* After a bit more straining of muscles, Thea sighed, and her gaze caught movement in the kitchen behind her.

Peering upside down, between her legs, she saw Draven pause and gape at her round backside from his spot in the kitchen. He spotted her just in time for his morning appearance of prepping a bowl of cereal and a cup of coffee for himself.

The show is starting, ladies and gentlemen; please take your seats.

Thea moved into a downward dog, a wide-legged folded position, with her ass pointed up in the air and directly at the kitchen. With her legs spread, she could see

Draven between them as he shakily opened a cabinet, eyes glued to her body, and blindly fumbled around for a mug.

Feminine power surged through her as she leaned back on her feet, arching her back. Her tight, pink spandex short-shorts revealed a slight sliver of the curve of her backside. She shivered at the cool air on her hot skin.

See that, Draven?

She hid her smirk as his lips parted; his throat bobbed from a thick swallow. He nearly dropped the glass mug he held before placing it safely down onto the counter.

He turned his back to her as he opened the fridge, and she smothered her giggle as he stuck his entire head into the chilled refrigerator. *Trying to cool down, Draven? I don't think so.*

She lowered herself to her hands and knees into a cat-cow pose, flexing her ass out as much as she could. Her legs quivered as the muscles stretched and the coiling of heat in her abdomen traveled lower.

When she glanced over her shoulder to look at him, he was pouring milk into his bowl, not focusing on how much he added. *I like the way when I have his attention, I have all of it.*

She wanted the bowl to overflow, spill milk, and prove that he couldn't concentrate on anything but her.

His gaze on her felt like a real caress, a large, hot palm curving over the swells of her ass cheeks and down her trembling thighs. Squeezing. Kneading.

From between her legs, his intense eyes penetrated her,

and an answering ache blossomed deep inside her because no one had ever stared at Thea like *that*.

Feeling hot and dizzy at his tantalizing attention, she lowered herself into a cobra position, arched her back, and peeked over her shoulder.

He was no longer looking at her; he was cleaning.

Her mouth fell open. He wasn't watching her with lust? A single look from him made her body quiver with need, yet, her short-shorts and hot yoga positions came second to cleaning? She wanted his gaze back on her.

Her lips thinned as she bent forward and spread her legs as far as they would go. *Look at me. Want me like I want you.*

Finally, he glanced back at her, their eyes meeting. All that fire and sensual heat in his gaze speared right through her. His perusal of her body felt like pinpricks of darts dipped in an aphrodisiac sex potion.

As much as her spike in arousal made her weak, his obvious desire for her filled her with power she had never known. The kind of sensation other women got when they heard Shania Twain sing, *"Man, I feel like a woman... Doo, doo, doodoo, doo, doodoo, let's go girls."*

Suppressing the need to preen, she spread her legs a bit wider, splaying herself for him. He rubbed paper towels on the counter when she glanced back at him. Had he spilled the milk?

His jaw clenched; he glared at her body as if it offended him that her ass was right in front of him, and he wasn't touching it.

Clearly, he needs a stronger message to touch me.

She turned on her back and sat up, facing the kitchen on her mat. Supporting her weight on her back arms, she lifted into a yoga crab position but spread her legs *much* wider.

Draven stumbled, carrying his bowl of cereal over to sit on the couch several feet away from her.

Yes, grab your front-row seat, Draven. He sank onto the sofa and jerkily waved at her as he balanced his bowl on his lap. He wore thin black sweatpants today and, of course, no shirt.

She swallowed her whimper as her gaze licked up the toned muscles, flat stomach, and tantalizing happy trail. Why had she scolded him to wear a shirt when she moved in again? Silly, silly, Thea-of-the-past.

She mentally reminded herself to keep her tongue in her mouth.

Draven smirked at her ogling, and she quickly blanked her expression. This was not about him knowing she wanted him; this was about making Draven drool over her and show her every one of her dirtiest fantasies.

If everyone thinks he'll break my heart, I'll just settle for a hookup. I would take any piece of him as a keepsake.

As she moved to her back, she stretched into what the yoga article called a "Happy Baby pose." Though the title was not very sexy, the position certainly was, as she lifted her legs and spread herself for his hungry gaze. The pose should have been called "Wide Open."

She tried to keep her breathing even as a fantasy

speared through her mind of Draven crawling over her while she was in this position, aligning his hips between her legs, and grinding his hard, insistent bulge against her most sensitive flesh. His lips on her neck. Her fingers raking down his taut, bare back.

Her panties grew slick as a slight pulsing began between her legs.

Thea looked up at Draven, who sat on the couch. Choking.

He was legitimately choking.

She dropped the pose and sat up in a rush. Raw concern threw ice water into her veins.

Draven waved off her concern as he coughed around a bite of his cereal. He placed the bowl onto the coffee table and rose from his seat. When he shuffled around the couch to get to the kitchen, Thea gasped at the sight of the firm bulge pressing forward in the crotch of his sweatpants.

A *big* bulge. A *poke your eye out with that thing* bulge. Was he wearing underwear? Because she swore, the buoyant trajectory of his erection was held down by nothing but that thin layer of black cotton fabric.

She... Oh God, she witnessed it *bounce* as he moved, and her pussy throbbed in response.

Standing on shaky legs, she trailed after him. He opened the fridge door, grabbed a water bottle, and guzzled from it. He threw a hand up to warn her away as she approached him.

She stopped at the kitchen island counter. The stretch

of granite separated them and blocked her view of his arousal.

He grabbed a notepad and permanent marker from the counter. He wrote something on a piece of paper. Ripping the paper free, he grabbed a piece of tape, and without sparing her another glance, he trudged to his bedroom, slapped the note onto his door, and escaped inside it.

She hugged herself and fought to catch her breath. Hot desire pumped through her veins, mixing with her blood until the sensual pining engrained in her DNA. Slowly, she stepped toward his bedroom door to read the note he taped outside of it.

It read, "*Do NOT open this door, Thea.*"

She sucked in a weak breath. What kind of note was that?

It was like something that warned her not to touch wet paint. That obviously just made her want to touch it more. The second the Beast said Belle was forbidden to enter the West Wing, Thea knew Belle would, at some point, enter the West Wing.

Her head dropped as she stared down at the doorknob. If he really didn't want her to enter, he would have locked the door, right? She swallowed and pressed her forehead to the smooth, white door.

Was he touching himself? Was that why he warned her not to enter?

She had seen the tortured look of desire in his eyes when he saw her pink short shorts. Her body had caused him to *choke* on the most chewable, kid-friendly cereal around. So, why didn't he jump on her?

The image of *it*—the large, distended erection prodding the front crotch of his pants—stapled itself to her brain, threatening to cling to her mind forever. Her heartbeat thundered, hard and fast, behind her ribs; her body overheated with lust.

He ran to his room. To do what?

Slide his fingers around his cock to jerk off?

Squeeze the red, frustrated tip to keep himself from coming too soon?

All while picturing her yoga positions?

Does he not realize I want him too?

Breathless, her panties wet and pussy pulsing, she flattened a hand onto the door.

I want to go in.

Chapter Eighteen

God. Dammit.

He had just been minding his business, readying to eat a semi-nutritious breakfast, when he saw Thea's perfect, round ass straining behind tight, tiny pink shorts.

Her toned legs were tanned, heavenly temptations, splayed slightly ajar, her feet hip-width apart. He wanted to push them wide open and feast between them until she came all over his face. His cock lengthened at the fantasy.

He repeated to himself, *"Do not get an erection in the kitchen while she does yoga. Do not get an erection. Stop getting hard, dammit!"*

He tore his gaze away from the show-stopping view in his living room.

His socks were wet due to the pool of milk he spilled after seeing Thea. *Great.* Grabbing paper towels, he soaked up the milk, washed the spot, and disposed of any evidence that the sight of a woman in shorts unraveled him in such a way.

Busying himself in the kitchen, he knew he was lingering. *She is a goddamn magnet, and I'm supposed to stay away?* He glanced back over at the bendy woman practicing sex positions in his living room. *She will never be yours, Draven. She wears pearls.*

With pouty lips and eyebrows drawn into a forlorn expression, he let his gaze run over her one last time. Then, he saw it.

Head bent down between her legs, she stared right at him.

Their eyes met. And the pretty vixen *smirked.*

Less than ten minutes later, Draven slammed his bedroom door shut, shoved his black sweatpants down his legs, and fisted his hard, aching dick. *She drives me wild.*

Her bending over with her ass up in the air, barely contained in those tiny pink shorts, would fuel his fantasies for the years to come.

Just friends? Impossible.

He threw open his bedside drawer, pulled out a bottle of coconut oil, and drizzled the lubricant onto his hand. Clenching his shaft in a tight grip, he stroked up and down, groaning like he had been starved for touch for days. Like he dabbled in tease torture or edging for the past month.

My sexual torture is named Thea.

Pants halfway down his legs and hand firmly wrapped around his full cock, he threw his left palm onto his bedroom wall and jacked off. He couldn't stop long enough to lay back on his bed.

Lust fried his brain. He was so aroused that the fast, slick sounds of his strokes matched each of his panted breaths.

You shouldn't be thinking of her like this. Off-limits.

He pumped into his palm harder, faster, thrusting his hips. Desperate at the thought of her spreading her legs for him on that yoga mat. Of that little smirk on her face.

Had she been trying to seduce him? For what purpose? He shook his head and prepared to let loose all of his pent-up desire for her.

A low, deep groan clawed through him as he twisted his grip; his abdomen and balls tightened accordingly. The tip of his cock glistened with precum, hinting at the release he so badly needed.

He fucked his palm with ragged breaths just as he heard the subtle creak of his bedroom door opening.

Oh, fuck. Shit.

Thea was spying on him. He clenched his eyes closed, not allowing himself to see her. Not allowing himself to see her chest move up and down with her heavy breathing or the blush pinkening her round cheeks.

If I watch her lick her lips while my hand is on my dick, I'll explode.

She wanted to watch him? She wanted to see what she did to him? Fine. *Let her watch.*

Between furious strokes, Draven panted, "See how

hard I am for you? Huh? Is this what you wanted, wearing those tight little shorts?"

He kept his eyes closed, knowing she thought she was successfully spying as he touched himself.

She would see it as him talking to himself. But he spoke to her. "Flashing that perfect ass at me. Did you know I could see the outline of your pussy through those shorts? Fuck, baby, I'm jerking it, thinking about ripping those off you and devouring that wet little pussy until you pass out."

Sexual madness—a frenzied haze—ruled every part of his body. Each feverish tug of his cock sent him closer to spiraling toward orgasm. He could hear her breathing. Was she trying not to touch herself while she watched? What would make her dip a hand between her legs?

Keep your eyes closed, and you can pretend this never happened, you bastard.

Moaning, he stroked himself harder, his heartbeat erratic. "They think you're such a good girl, don't they, Thea? But you couldn't help yourself from watching me. You just had to come in here and watch me jerk off."

Biting his lip, he grunted and squeezed at the sensitive tip of his dick. "Do you like the way I touch myself, wishing it was your hand on me?" His stomach muscles twitched. Hollowed. "Are you going to watch me come, sweetheart? Thea—" His balls tightened. Heart skipped.

"Fuck, Thea," he bellowed as streams of his release shot out from the thick, dusky pink mushroom tip of his cock. Again and again, he grunted and moaned from each jet. "Thea."

He strived to catch his breath. Finally unable to control himself any longer, he glanced over to the door, which was pulled closed again.

Had she seen the finale?

Had she read her name on his lips when he came?

"Babe, are you taking me to Mal and Wren's wedding, or do you still need time to calm down? When are you going to move back in? I miss you," Alec texted her.

The message lighting up her screen burned into her eyes.

"We need to talk. Maybe coffee tomorrow morning?" Alec texted.

When her phone buzzed again, she reluctantly checked it but shot up straight on the couch when she read, *"Hello! I am writing on behalf of Director Pamela Hutchins about needing a makeup artist assistant for Thursday and Friday. Would you be available? She loved what you did to the members of Medusa's Tears on Halloween."*

An excited, shocked scream bubbled out of Thea's vocal cords as she hopped onto the couch, standing tall on the cushions, and jumped up and down in elation.

She got a job! It was a two-day job, but it was a resume

builder. It was a big step in the right direction. Finding out she got a finance job would have never felt like this.

Her happy dance was interrupted by Draven skidding in his socks on the hardwood floor in front of the couch. His frightened, frantic eyes scanned her for injuries.

He pointed to his ears and mimed someone screaming. She nodded, grinning as she jumped up and down on the couch some more.

Realizing she was not hurt or in danger, Draven pressed a palm over his chest and shot her a curious brow. She handed him her phone, showing the message. He read it, looked up at her, calmly joined her in standing on the opposite side of the couch, and began jumping up and down along with her.

Laughing and jumping, they performed joint, goofy, happy dances. When he stopped and began typing something onto her phone, she froze.

Horror flooded her at the thought of Draven: A) sending a response to the job for her or B) seeing Alec's texts. She slapped at his hands, trying to take back her phone, but he held it out of reach.

Using her vantage point of standing on the couch, she half-tackled him, wrapping her legs around his back and securing herself to him as she fought to take back her phone. His body vibrated under hers, laughing and clearly finding her fear amusing.

When she got the device back, she saw that he had opened her notes app and typed, *"We should go out and celebrate tonight."*

Fear dissipated, her stomach full of nothing but butterflies. She smiled at him and typed back, *"You'll buy me dinner?"*

She handed her phone back, and he typed, *"I was thinking shots so that I could finally meet 'Drunk Thea.' But, yeah, let's do dinner. My treat."*

"Somewhere with lobster, please," she replied.

He flung his head back and chuckled. *"Not a cheap date, are you?"* he typed.

Her smile fell. She bit her lip. Because she wanted to ask: *Would it really be a date?*

And she wanted his answer to be: *Yes, Thea. A real date.*

Chapter Nineteen

I want to kiss him, she thought as he opened her car door for her and offered his arm—like a tattooed gentleman—to walk her to the fancy restaurant's entrance. *I want to devour his lips and lick his face and tattoo my name on his chin.*

Thea had never felt so possessive and giddy and visceral and ardently about anyone before in her life. She had loved Alec, but the spark had dimmed somewhere along the line of breaking up and getting back together over the years.

There was something about a man proving he could live without her that rubbed her the wrong way. Maybe it was obnoxious and silly—and definitely stemmed from a childhood of sometimes being ignored—but she wanted her partner to feel like time away from her was the equivalent of a chainsaw to the chest. Fatal.

She wanted a partner who jumped on her if they spent several days apart, like one of those reunions of a soldier returning home to his golden retriever. Pure joy and excitement.

Her mind rushed back to the way she watched Draven touch himself and how she swore his lips mouthed her name. Late that night, she had laid awake, grinding her pussy against the heel of her hand as she replayed Draven's chest heaving with breaths and his thighs trembling from his release.

New flames danced over Thea's pores, keeping a blush warming her cheeks anytime she looked him in the eyes. Thankfully, the restaurant was chilly; hopefully, that would help deter her body and brain from thinking dirty thoughts.

Draven's big, warm palm on her lower back, guiding her through the waiting room, did *not* help deter the dirty thoughts.

As Draven greeted the hostess and told her about the reservation, Thea watched his polite, neutral face. It didn't glow; he didn't smirk; his eyes didn't sparkle with flirtatious promises. *He doesn't look at other people the way he looks at me.* That was a good sign, right? But why was he holding back?

A single golden candle lit their intimate area when they sat at their table. Thea grabbed the drink menu and pointed to what she wanted. When a waitress came, Draven ordered for both of them. And when the waitress leaned *way* further down than she needed to, Draven did not even *glance* at the woman's overflowing cleavage.

Draven pulled his phone out from across the table

and motioned for Thea to do the same. She pulled it out of her purse, and a few seconds later, it vibrated in her hand.

Draven texted her, "*When was the last time you came to a place like this? Maybe with Wall Street guy?*"

She rolled her eyes and bit back a smile. "*Alec did not work on Wall Street. We live in L.A., not NY, dummy.*"

She hit send and began typing again. "*I don't go to restaurants very often. Servers don't know sign language, and I don't always like the expression I get from people when I point at what I want on the menu. They act like I'm being rude for not trying to say it out loud.*"

He frowned from across the table. "*That happens a lot?*"

"*One time, I signed to a waitress that I was deaf, and she brought me a menu in braille.*" Thea added the face-palming emoji.

Draven pursed his lips, seeming not at all pleased by that. "*I hate that anyone has ever made you feel unaccepted.*"

Her heart warmed—stuck in an oven, which Draven mastered the temperature controls.

"*Is it upsetting to you when I order for us?*" Draven texted, "*I don't want to ever make it seem like you can't do something yourself.*"

Heart toasting to a crisp now. "*Draven, it's hard to imagine you upsetting me.*"

He dramatically put a hand over his chest and gaped. "*This is coming from the same woman who turned my ther-*

mostat down to fifty-eight degrees just to get me to put on a shirt?" he texted.

She giggled and messaged back, *"I've become much more comfortable with your shirtless-ness."*

Draven read her text and looked back at her with narrowed eyes and a smolder that twisted her lungs. His heated expression turned her organs to stretchable taffy. A single cocky, arched eyebrow rose at her statement. *"Oh, reeaaalllyyy?"* he texted.

"Really."

"Because," he replied, *"I've been thinking about establishing our apartment as a topless apartment. Legally. Like some French beaches."*

She snorted at his joke, and his answering grin shot giddy hormones through her.

After the first glass of wine, Draven ordered their meals for them. When she pointed at the manicotti, he frowned and pointed at the lobster. She texted, *"I am allergic to shellfish. I just wanted to see if you'd still agree to pay for it."* He chuckled.

The dinner was going great. Then, ten minutes into waiting for their food, Draven made some off-handed joke about Alec, and Thea texted, *"I've been thinking about meeting him for coffee. Maybe this week."*

Draven's eyebrows furrowed; his lips pressed into a thin line as he read her message. *"Fucking why?"* he sent back.

Bristling, she wrote, *"Because we were together for years and he deserves closure."*

"HE deserves closure?"

Frowning back, she typed, *"Yes."*

"You already have your closure?" Draven texted.

Pausing for just a moment, Thea nodded. She had fallen out of love with Alec before the cheating scandal, but her family and friends loved him. She would have stayed with him had he been faithful to her. *I would have settled.* All to make other people happy.

"Then, why the hell do you need to meet up with him? He cheated. He doesn't deserve closure."

"Draven..."

"You are not meeting up with him, Thea."

Her spine straightened at the command. It reminded her too much of when her parents made active decisions in her life and told her to follow them mindlessly.

"You can't tell me what to do, Draven."

They must have looked like quite a pair, texting furiously back and forth at the five-star restaurant.

"If you try to meet him somewhere, I will hide all of your shoes," Draven messaged with a straight face. *"Are you going to meet him without any shoes?"*

"You're really that immature and stubborn?" she questioned.

"I was already thinking about hiding all your underwear, Thea. Your shoes would be an easy feat."

His humor did nothing to cut through this new tension. After living under the roof of over-protective and controlling parents, she despised being told what to do. There was being underestimated, and then there was being treated like a subordinate. *It's demeaning.* "*You wouldn't,*" she texted.

"*Don't test me,*" he shot back. "*Do not see that prick. You'll let him apologize and forgive him and go back to him, and he doesn't deserve you.*"

Her mouth opened, and she sucked in a lungful of air at his words. Her thumbs jabbed at her phone as she typed. "*That's the type of person you think I am? Such a people pleaser, so weak-willed, that I could be cheated on—with a close friend—and still go back to that person?*"

Draven glowered at the message.

That was how he saw her? After everything, he thought she could be "talked into" falling back in Alec's arms?

What hurt the most was that she worried he was right. If she had never moved in with Draven, if she had accepted her family's calls about how perfect Alec was for her, how they were a match, if she had taken another boring finance job and continued down the path of making everyone else happy, Thea might have gone back to Alec.

She might have never hoped for anything more.

Draven doesn't see me the way I thought he did.

"*Thea, I didn't mean it like that,*" he messaged.

She typed, "*I'm not hungry anymore.*"

"*The food will be out any minute. We already ordered.*"

She texted, "*I don't want to sit at this table with you a minute longer.*"

She watched as something shattered in Draven's expression. Something broke behind those light green eyes.

She shook her head.

The thing about being "quiet" was that shallow people saw that as her entire personality. Was she a wallflower? No. But people thought they could walk over her like disrespected dandelions in a field.

I don't want Draven to see me as a spineless wallflower, bending to however the wind blows. She wanted to be the wind.

She wanted him to see her like a force of nature. Volcano, tornado, hurricane, earthquake...

She wanted to feel like a natural disaster to his past and a brand new start to his future.

But he doesn't know me like I thought he did.

Draven drove her home in silence. Silence that was too goddamn loud.

His fingers tightened around the wheel; his knuckles turned white from the grip.

He blew out a breath of frustration as he drove back to the apartment. She had worn black lace and red lipstick, and Draven was fairly certain she aimed to seduce him before his dumbness struck. Her black dress shifted up her thighs as she crossed her legs and stared out the passenger window.

"I didn't mean it like that, Thea," he said aloud, knowing she couldn't hear and didn't *care* to hear him.

Thea's disappointment emanated from her smooth skin like an airborne poison, killing him. Taking years off his life.

It was for the best that she didn't like him. After all, she was off-limits. In the eyes of her and his friends, he was not "*good enough*" for her. He was a stamp on her passport, a single stop in the big adventure of her life. Regrettable or forgettable.

Even as Draven thought that, he pulled his car to the side of the road. Thea gasped and glanced at him as he parked the vehicle.

The second the car stopped moving, Draven unbuckled his seatbelt and turned to Thea. She gaped at him and glanced around the dark, empty street as he leaned into her space.

His fingers pinched her chin, directing her gaze onto him. Meeting her eyes, he cupped her cheeks and moved forward until the scent of grapefruit tickled his nose. She inhaled sharply as he eliminated the distance between them.

Her eyelids fell to half-mast.

Her lips separated, pursing for him.

Baby, I'll only kiss you when you like me again.

With nothing but an inch or two separating their faces, Draven said, "I didn't mean that you were someone who would go back to a cheater. I didn't mean anything about you."

He admitted, "I said that because of my own fear. I am terrified of you going back to him. Back to a life that doesn't excite you and to a man who doesn't deserve you. Back to a life where we're strangers, and you hate me and think I'm nothing but a manwhore."

He continued, "I was talking out of my ass. I think you are strong, amazing, and resilient. And you scare me with your love of horror movies. And I think if I go back to living in an empty apartment or with anyone else, I might go insane. I want you there. I don't want you meeting up with him because I'm jealous and stupid. I was being stupid. I won't hide all your shoes, I promise. Just stop looking at me like I ruined everything. Can you do that, baby? Please?"

She blinked, her expression slack, while her eyes sparkled in the dim light of the car's blue dashboard. Her tongue emerged to lick her lips as she stared back at him.

Reluctantly, he let go of her face and sat back in his seat.

Just before transitioning the car back into drive and pulling onto the road, Draven reached into his pocket to grab his phone.

He texted her, "*I'm sorry.*"

For the rest of the drive, instead of peering out her passenger window, positioned as far away from him as possible in the tight car, she looked straight onto the road ahead of them.

Chapter Twenty

When Thea emerged from her bedroom, sleepy-eyed and ready for decaf coffee and sugar-filled cereal, she stumbled and clutched at her heart when she saw a stranger in their kitchen.

A stranger wearing nothing but an oversized T-shirt that fell to her mid-thigh. A *man's* T-shirt.

A gorgeous young stranger. Maybe twenty or twenty-one years old?

Draven. Man-slut. Maxwell.

Thea's rage did nothing to cauterize the bleeding cracks in her heart as she realized Draven—having surpassed the seven-day sex ban—had hooked up with someone last night after their fight at the restaurant.

Why do I feel so damn angry? We've never even kissed. Yet, the organ in her chest acted like it had been violently stabbed and dipped in a lemon juice and bleach cocktail. Did learning about Alec's cheating even feel this bad?

Thea pressed her lips into a thin line as she bit her tongue and suppressed the need to scream.

The half-clad blonde danced in front of the coffee machine while she waited for it to finish brewing. The stranger swung her hips side to side, reached into the fridge, and pulled out a carton of almond milk as Thea watched silently.

That is my milk, Thea growled to herself.

Ruled by immature instinct and jealousy and whatever the heck was toxically pumping through her veins, Thea snatched the milk carton from the woman.

She gasped at seeing Thea. Then, she smiled and began talking, probably introducing herself as Draven's latest lay.

Thea pointed to the milk carton and flattened a hand over her chest. "*My milk.*"

The blonde laughed and lifted her hands in the air as surrender.

If Thea signed that Draven was hers too, would the stranger back down so easily?

The blonde said something else.

"*I'm deaf,*" Thea signed.

The blonde slapped her forehead as if she had been told Thea was deaf but forgotten.

Draven mentioned me to his one-night stand?

Finally, Draven—the legend, the myth, the dead man —shuffled through the kitchen, yawning. He rubbed his eyes and nodded to Thea and the blonde.

Just as the blonde finished pouring herself a cup of coffee, Draven stole the mug from her. He lifted it to his lips and blew, making eye contact with Thea as his lips pursed over the cup.

Thea glared and mimed taking an invisible dagger out of her back and placing it onto the counter.

He frowned, putting the mug down. Glancing between her and the blonde, Draven blinked, and understanding washed over his expression. He shook his head at Thea. After pointing to the blonde, Draven mimed a pregnancy belly.

Thea's jaw dropped.

Had he gotten this woman pregnant?

Seeing her reaction, Draven rapidly shook his head *no* again.

In a desperate rush to explain, Draven grabbed the blonde, pulling and positioning her so they stood side by side. He then shoved the blonde down by her head, so she was much, much shorter than him. Meanwhile, the blonde slapped at him to let her stand back at her normal height.

Shit, shit, shitake mushrooms. Hadn't he told Thea his sister was crashing at the apartment last night? Oh, right. His previous two interactions with Thea were: A) their fight yesterday and B) her secretly watching as he jerked off to orgasm in his room. So, no, he had not told her.

And she clearly thought Summer was some hookup. *Gross.*

"Jesus, Summer, can't you put on some pants?" Draven asked his little sister.

She shrugged. "I'm your sister. Don't look at my legs."

"*I'm* not looking at them. You're painting the wrong picture to my roommate right now." When he glanced back to Thea, he mouthed, "Sister. Sister." He groaned. "Damn it, where is a notepad and pen?"

Thea grabbed the Post-its they kept in the kitchen and wrote in marker, "*Your hookups are not allowed to use my milk. And she is way too young for you. Pig. –Your respectful tenant.*"

Back to passive-aggressive notes? *Noooooo.*

Draven grabbed the pad of Post-its from her and wrote back, "*She is my younger sister. I haven't hooked up with anyone since you moved in. –Your celibate and incredibly sexy landlord with blue balls, the color of a first-place ribbon.*"

Thea narrowed her gray blues on him, suspicious.

He underlined "*I haven't*" on his note.

"You guys don't act like roommates," Summer remarked, intrigued by watching them. "Seems like a jealous lover's spat to me." She sipped the coffee and cringed, spitting it back into the cup. "What the heck is this?"

"Decaf coffee."

"Ex-fucking-cuse me?" Summer replied, never sounding quite like people imagined of a prodigy cellist.

Draven responded in a huffy, impatient tone, "Thea

likes coffee in the morning, but caffeine makes her ears ring."

Thea still glared at him.

He shot her a "*What gives?*" expression.

Her scowl replied, "*You know.*"

Summer whistled. "Wow, is it just me, or is she hot when she glares at you like that?"

"Do not call my roommate hot, Summer." If his little sister hit on Thea...

"What did you do to make her glare like that?" she asked.

"Something stupid."

"Obviously. It's *you.*"

"Thanks, sis."

Summer smiled and leaned against the fridge. "No prob, bro."

"I said something last night that she took the wrong way."

Summer hummed. "Seems more realistic that you said something wrong you didn't mean to say. Not 'she took it the wrong way.'"

"That too," Draven grunted. "I was jealous, and I implied she would go back to her cheating ex."

Summer stole the pen and a blank Post-it from Draven. He tried to retrieve it, but his little sister kicked him in the thigh, and he lurched over. The masculine instinct to protect his balls gifted Summer enough time to write a note to Thea.

Thea read it and quirked an eyebrow. Then, she looked directly into Draven's eyes and stopped glaring.

"Damn, Summer, how did you do that? Want to move in?" Draven joked before reading the note she wrote.

"*My brother says he was a dumb, jealous asshole and is sorry about hurting your feelings last night. He didn't mean it.*"

"Dammit!" Draven grabbed a fistful of his hair. "Offer revoked," he told Summer. "What the hell? You just told her I was jealous."

Summer flipped her blond hair over her shoulder and commented, "*Duh-doy*. You just told me you were jealous."

"Yeah, but she's not supposed to know that." Sweat broke out on the back of Draven's neck. "She can't know I'm into her."

Thea moved around Summer to retrieve a bowl and her cereal box. Summer checked her out as she did; her gaze roamed up and down Thea's body. "Why can't she know you're into her?"

"Because Wren said she is off-limits."

"Why?" Summer asked.

"Because she is the best friend of his fiancé, and he thinks a rift between us will hurt his marriage, and he will have to kick me out of the band."

"Why?"

"Summer," Draven groaned.

"What?" Forgetting it was decaf, Summer lowered her mouth to the coffee cup once more to take another sip but spat it back out. "If she is the best friend, I assume you are both in the wedding parties?"

"Yes."

"You'll hook up at the wedding, then."

"*What?*" Draven exclaimed.

"Oh, come on, people always hook up at weddings. I'm sure the vows, champagne, cake, and dancing will get you two so horny for each other that you hook up in a hotel room down the street or something."

"What part of 'Wren will kick me out of the band' do you not understand?"

"You're Draven Maxwell. Half of Medusa's Tears fans are just women who go to see you shirtless. He can't kick you out."

"Judas Maximo said he has a replacement drummer all lined up."

Summer's green eyes widened, and her mouth formed a solemn "*O.*" If Judas Maximo wanted Draven gone, he would be gone. Wren just had to give the green light.

"You shouldn't pay for my school anymore," Summer said softly.

"What?"

"If you lose the band, you won't be able to pay for Mimi's nursing home or me and Geo's college. You shouldn't have to pay for it to begin with. You are too generous with your money, Draven."

Draven did not respond, but his tense shoulders and adamant expression said it all. He *wanted* to take care of his family—the way his parents had not taken care of him.

But he needed a new income stream fast. Medusa's Tears would go on tour soon, but Judas made it clear Draven would not see a penny before then. He needed to verify everything was fully funded for the time he would be abroad, performing.

I guess I need to call my agent about that semi-nude photoshoot. He needed the money.

The kitchen was quiet as Thea sat on a barstool at the kitchen island and poured herself a bowl of cereal. Draven watched her as she lifted the spoon to her lips.

"I take it back," Summer said. "You guys won't hook up at the wedding. You'll hook up before then."

Chapter Twenty-One

"Good luck on your first day. Don't make anyone else look like a sexy tiger, or I'll get jealous," Draven had texted her.

Thea stared at that text, stroking her phone's screen, as she waited for the production assistant to welcome her onto the set and introduce her to the makeup artist she was assisting for the film. *I still can't believe I'm really here,* she thought.

Her phone buzzed, and she smiled at it, assuming it was another inspirational text from Draven. Nope.

"We're meeting for dinner or coffee or something. I'm not taking no for an answer," Alec texted her.

Deep sigh. *"Alec, I know you want closure, but I'm not ready,"* she messaged. *I'm too busy trying to follow my dream and not fall any harder for a drumming bad boy who seems to have a heart of gold.*

"Your parents invited me to Thanksgiving dinner,

Thea. They expect us back together in the next few weeks," he texted.

Her lungs expelled all of their unused oxygen. Her family invited her cheating ex to Thanksgiving dinner.

She bit the tip of her tongue as anger simmered down her limbs. *More people who think they know what is best for me.*

"They are worried about you, babe," Alec sent. *"So am I. Where are you staying? Did you find a new job? Please come back home."*

What would he think if he knew she was staying with and lusting after the drummer from *Medusa's Tears*? Or that she was on a movie set *right now*, waiting to pursue her dream career?

Switching to the different messaging chain, she texted Draven, *"Thanks, I'm nervous."*

Several seconds later, the drummer replied, *"Maybe you should do some yoga? You know. For the Zen. The peace. In your shorts. I hear yoga in shorts is super peaceful."*

"You are such a flirt," she sent, biting back a smile.

He messaged, *"Two voyeurs, sitting in a tree. W-A-T-C-H-I-N-G."*

She gasped at his words. Did that mean he had seen her watch him masturbate in his room? He had his eyes closed the whole time; he didn't acknowledge her at all. Had he seen her? When? Before or after his perfectly toned and sculpted body shuddered, and he came all over his stomach and hand?

Great, now her body heated from the illicit memory.

Someone tapped her shoulder, and her head swung up from her phone.

"Hi! I'm here to escort you to Chanelle. The makeup artist," the young woman signed.

"You are deaf?" Thea signed back.

"Yup, there are a couple of us on set. I'll introduce you during the lunch break."

And just like that, Thea's heart soared.

"Ready?"

"Beyond ready."

The day flew by—a whirlwind. Thea did the makeup of some of the extras on the set; the true artist did the stars of the movie. When the actors were dismissed to go back to filming, the makeup artist, Chanelle, wrote a note to Thea saying, *"You did great! I've never seen a first-time assistant so calm when applying fake blood and eyeliner."*

Thea kept the note in her dress pocket for the rest of the day, grinning to herself.

The entire day, she floated on air, anxiety, and pride. Before she could stop it, a traitor thought drifted through her mind, *"I can't wait to tell Draven about my day."*

But when she got home, the apartment was empty. When she realized he was out, she swore the space felt colder than usual, but a glance at the thermostat revealed the chill was in her head.

She hugged herself as she walked to the kitchen for a snack. A hot pink cupcake with a fake little pearl on the top sat on the counter.

A Post-it note sat beside it, reading, *"I will be out late for practice tonight. Hope your day was amazing. Don't eat this cupcake. It's mine. Unless you break rules when people write things on doors like 'Don't come in.' –Your rule-abiding roommate with a big ole cock, but I don't need to tell you that (Enjoy this well-earned treat)."*

Oh God, he really had caught her watching him. *He must think of me as a horny stalker-groupie now.* She groaned at herself as a deep, hot blush claimed her cheeks, even in the privacy of the empty apartment.

I am eating that damn cupcake.

And I will touch myself to the memory of him doing the same.

"They want me to come in *today*?" Draven asked his manager over the phone. Just the day before, Draven had told him to say yes to the semi-nude underwear modeling shoot, so Draven could grab a big payday. He blew out a breath. "They're not wasting any time, are they?"

Draven laid back on his couch in the silent apartment. Thea had gone to her work early in the morning, and his alarm clock had treacherously not woken him up in time to see her leave.

Marty, his manager, replied, "They're probably worried if they give you too much time to think about it, you'll drop out."

"I'm not dropping out," Draven grumbled, sinking further into the couch cushions and wishing they would swallow him whole. *If you keep me from this photoshoot, I'll join the dust bunnies, crumbs, and lost, forgotten remotes in your folds, old couch.*

"When I originally pitched it to you, you said it was the most demeaning thing you had ever heard, and you would sooner die than pose for it," his manager reminded him.

"You caught me. I died. I'm a ghost now," Draven said. "*OoOooOoOHhhH*," he mimicked a ghost's wail. "I am doing the shoot."

"Well, I know Raquel will be excited. She has been begging me to beg you to do this for months."

"Raquel just wants to see me in my tighty-whities."

"As does the world," Marty said smoothly. "That's why the paycheck is over two million, Drave. That'll buy Mimi the best care for a while."

I am stripping and selling images of my body for the health of my grandmother. Perfect. Thanksgiving dinner would be fun this year. Odds were that Geo and Summer would team up with making puns all night, such as "Pass me the buns—Draven, not the buns you showed on that magazine" and "Can I have the breast of the turkey—Draven! Put your pec away!" Brats. They learned it from him.

"When and where?" Draven asked Marty.

"She said she can set everything up at your apartment. You won't even have to make a trip. The whole crew would get there around five o'clock. Set up. It could all be done by seven thirty."

"Couldn't do any earlier?" Draven asked, dreading the idea of Thea arriving home from work only to see him standing in nothing but tight briefs. "Or maybe reschedule to a different day?" *One when I know Thea won't be home.*

Marty snorted. "No, Draven, they hired *two* air brushers to paint your abs with special tanning oil today after you told me yesterday to do everything I could to book it as soon as possible."

"I don't want to model so close to dinner time. I get hungry."

"They will be there at five o'clock, Draven."

Shit.

If Thea thought Draven was arrogant and shallow before, seeing him photographed in his underwear for money was sure to lose all of her respect. *And I can't handle that.*

He sent her a quick text before pressing his face into the couch cushions and groaning.

"Can you try not to come back to the apartment before 8PM?"

Thea stared at the message from Draven and ground her teeth. Why didn't he want her home? Did he have someone over?

"You can't just tell me when I can and can't be in our apartment," she texted back angrily. *"It's a shared space."*

He, of course, did not respond.

More hours passed before the very last scene was shot, and Thea was dismissed to leave. She had made it to the end of her first makeup job, and her roommate had banished her from the apartment. A quick glance at her phone showed that it was six o'clock. She was supposed to stay out for another two hours? *I don't think so.*

Thea's muscles ached from standing all day, but she cherished the pain. It was surreal to be on a set, in a studio complex full of backgrounds from famous films and TV shows. Sure, the movie business was very much "Hurry up and wait," but she had soaked in every interaction and experience with unmatched gratitude.

Would working on a set every day make the movie magic fade? Or would every day feel like this?

I need to find another job, she thought as she unlocked the door to their apartment and shuffled inside.

She kicked off her shoes, shook her jacket off, and looked up to see seven strangers in their apartment.

Someone had moved the couch out of the way.

A large white sheet created a backdrop and covered up the TV and drum set in their living room.

And Draven stood. Naked.

Chapter Twenty-Two

No, not naked, she realized.

He wore the smallest pair of briefs she had ever seen. Thin, *tight* briefs. She did not need to wonder if a sock was tucked in them because she knew from experience the significant size of his, *ahem*, appendage.

His chest *glistened* with oil. His full, toned thighs were on display. The yummy, masculine happy trail dusted a straight line between narrow hips, like an arrow directing Thea's eyesight to the briefs and that bulge again.

If this were any other situation, Thea might have dropped her panties and jumped on him—who wouldn't at a tantalizing sight like that? But the seven strangers, including two holding ring lights and one woman snapping photo after photo of him, gave her pause.

Was he doing some kind of photoshoot in their apartment?

Or was this the start of some insane orgy?

Two women giggled and twisted locks of their hair around their fingers as they watched him from the barstools in the kitchen. That's what he did to smart women—transformed them into giggly schoolgirls.

Draven made everything feel like high school. Feelings turned on high volume. Every look was worthy of a diary entry. Getting his attention felt holy. Cosmic.

The women giggled louder.

Draven's hand drifted lower, running over his abdomen and sinking to the waistband of those briefs. Every person in the apartment seemed to gasp. More flashes went off for photos. He teased the camera.

Would he really... Thea held her breath in anticipation. Would he take them off?

The second Draven saw Thea, he dropped the sensual pose and straightened. Sex spell broken.

Limbs loose at their sides, they stared at each other for a moment.

He *blushed*. His face turning red, Draven yelled at the people and motioned for them to clean everything up and leave. The photographer woman scowled and said something back.

Meanwhile, Thea stood, frozen, by the front door.

Draven grew more and more upset the longer the photo crew delayed packing up the equipment.

With furrowed eyebrows, stern lips, and ticks of his jaw, he watched Thea from across the room, stealing glances at her as he rushed them out of the apartment.

When Draven and Thea stood alone in their apartment once more, his hands were clenched into fists at his sides. Not anger. Embarrassment? The inner turmoil darkening his face pulled Thea forward, closer to him as he stood, still as a statue.

The more distance she eliminated between them, the clearer the glimmering emotion in his green eyes became to her.

Shame.

The sex god—who had a six-pack, thighs like a warrior, a sinful face, and thousands of women begging to have sex with him at each of his concerts—stood before Thea, unable to meet her eyes as she shifted closer to him, and emitted shockwaves of shame.

There was no way cocky, self-assured, and flirty Draven was insecure about his body.

So, why could he not look at her?

He stared at his feet until she reached up and touched his chin. At the slight graze of her fingertips, his face abruptly turned, and they locked gazes.

This close, Draven's lime and mint scent filled her lungs, making her think of clean bedsheets and all the dirty things they could do in them. He leaned down a bit, so she didn't have to crane her neck back. *He is so tall*. How could a man make her feel small and delicate, yet strong and larger than life at the same time?

She quirked an eyebrow and shot him an expression of, "*What's wrong?*"

Apparently, her silent questioning was too prodding because he looked away again.

She poked a finger into his naked, shiny chest.

He had no reaction other than he seemed to sink inside himself, hiding even further behind an invisible shell. He had never emotionally hidden from her before.

She pulled her phone out and typed a message, *"What's wrong? Why are you so upset?"*

When he read it, he flexed his jaw and wrote back, *"I told you not to come home until eight."*

"What? Were you embarrassed for me to see you doing some underwear modeling?"

More jaw clenching.

"Draven, I'm sorry I interrupted. I had a long day, and I just wanted to shower and...I'm sorry. I should have stayed out like you asked."

He took her phone and typed back, *"I didn't want you to see me like this."*

"You always walk around shirtless. How is this any different?"

He huffed and crossed his arms, blocking the view of his stunning chest.

She swallowed and wrote honestly, *"We both know I've seen more of you than this. You joked about it. So, what's wrong?"*

He said something; his lips moved. She held out her phone for him to type. Taking it, he turned and sank onto the couch as he texted.

"It's demeaning, okay? I didn't want you to see me like that." He handed her phone back, his face cast downward to look at his feet.

How did he think she saw him? Standing in front of his sitting form, she wrote, *"You're embarrassed because I saw you with oil on your abs?"*

He ran a hand over his abdomen and wiped the grease onto his thigh, gazing down at himself in disgust.

I don't like this. I don't like seeing him so sad. Stepping forward, she stood between his legs and touched his cheek as he sat there, glaring at himself. *"Tell me,"* she signed.

He gripped her phone in tense, straining fingers before typing, *"It used to be fun, you know? But now, not wearing a shirt while I drum is in my contract. I make sixty-five percent more if I wear tight leather pants and get my abs airbrushed. The last few times on tour, some reviewers said I was nothing more than man candy that could hold a mediocre beat. Wren and Tomi got an award for their lyric writing, and I got called candy. Something people consume and feel guilty about afterward."*

Draven paused and hung his head for a moment. *"I wanted to do all this because of the music. At one point, I would have sold my soul to do music full-time. And now... Now, I sell my body. Because nobody seems to want my soul."*

Lightheaded, Thea swayed when she read the last few sentences. Her heart broke into such jagged pieces that it was sure to cause internal bleeding. *Nobody seems to want my soul.* She wanted to slap him. She wanted to cradle him. She wanted to show him that he was so much more than a body, a sex symbol, a piece of meat. He was Draven.

"I didn't want you to see me selling myself for money,

Thea. I can't handle you thinking of me that way. Just shallow and…"

She cupped both his cheeks in her hands and leaned down to keep intense eye contact between her standing position and his sitting one. Their breathing intermingled, puffs of air that screamed of anticipated intimacy and warmth. Sharing oxygen with him felt better than breathing in her own.

After a moment of mentally shouting at him that he was perfect, she took her phone back and wrote, *"You want to know how I see you, Draven? You are the man who bought me a pink cupcake with a pearl on it and pushed me to follow my dream. You saw me with a black eye and acted like you would burn the world down to protect me. You learned sign language to greet my friends and make them feel welcome in your home. I see a man who is kind, generous, accepting… A man who is dedicated to his art and makes me laugh."*

She squeezed one of his broad shoulders. *"I see a man who knows exactly how I feel—aligned to a stereotype and doomed never to be seen as more. A man begging for acceptance and connection."*

She put her phone down on his thigh, so she could grip his face in both hands again. On her screen, a message glowed, *"I see you, Draven."*

In a sudden turn of events, his hands slid down her back, down, down, and then up, under the skirt of her knee-length dress. He gripped the backs of her thighs and yanked her forward until she tumbled onto his lap.

She was splayed before him. Straddling him.

Chapter Twenty-Three

Thea gasped at how the backs of her bare thighs sat upon the tops of his muscular ones. With her legs spread, her panties rubbed against her sensitive sex, the material teasing her as much as his closeness.

Draven sat naked under her, other than that small pair of briefs. The thin fabrics did nothing to calm the electricity bouncing between them. His clean, manly scent melted her brain. Lust simmered within her as she rocked her hips, finding a comfortable position to sit herself on the tops of his thighs.

Skin against skin, the timeless but unique and new sensation reminded her of poetry. Others may have a different interpretation of Draven, but she read between the lines of him.

His heart was a sunset of unexpected bubblegum pink, purple, and gold. His body was midnight—a time when decisions were hazy, and thoughts turned sinful. His soul was morning dew, detoxifying and protecting the delicate surfaces of anyone he cared for, making them shine.

Straddling him, Thea circled her arms around the back of his neck, their faces so close. She shivered over him as his fingers trailed the sides of her thighs, moving under her dress. She swore her pores and goosebumps rose to create some type of braille to entertain him, to tempt him into touching her forever.

He said something, moving his lips. She could not tear her gaze from his mouth.

His warm thumbs continued swiping up and down the sides of her thighs as she settled on top of him.

At the touch and the sensual position, her breasts ached; the tips tightened and peaked for him. As her legs happily enjoyed Draven's rough yet smooth fingertips, the rest of her body lit up with jealous competition. Her lips yelled, "*Touch me!*" Her breasts whimpered, "*Me next.*"

There was not enough time in the world for Draven to appease every part of her—not with every fiber of her wanting him this badly.

Sitting there, they breathed heavily, staring at one another as if they had finally reached the top of a mountain they had climbed for a while. Oxygen was thinner at this altitude, but the *view*... Would he kiss her? Could she kiss him?

He just got done saying he hated how everyone saw him as a piece of meat, yet, she was ready to grind herself on his hard, toned thigh.

Eyebrows furrowed, Draven leaned in closer and licked

his lips. She hoped her answering whimper was not too loud.

He moved his hand up her sides, up her waist. His palms traveled over the sides of her breasts and continued moving up, not pausing even when she silently begged him with her eyes to cup her there. Finally, he held her face in his hands.

With a mesmerized and hungry expression, Draven dragged his thumb over Thea's lip. Such a soft, slow caress, the action occurred in slow motion. He released a ragged breath, and a tortured, pining look claimed his face.

He pressed his finger firmly into the dip of the middle of her lower lip. Then, he retracted his hand to tap his own lip, as if unknowingly signing, *"May I kiss you?"*

Stunned, she blinked but remained in a trance too deep to respond with anything other than a hitched breath in the back of her throat.

He did it again, painstakingly slowly. He tenderly touched her lip then touched his. Those hypnotic eyes asked a silent question, *"May I kiss you?"*

Then, he rubbed his palm flat against his chest in a circle. *"Please,"* he signed. He bit his sensual lip and rubbed another circle with his hand. *"Please."*

He is signing to kiss me. How could she possibly say no? Tilting her head up and down, she jerkily nodded. She would have blinded him with her green hue if she were a traffic light. *Kiss me, please.*

His jaw ticked, and his eyes narrowed onto her lips. One of his wide palms sank around the back of her neck and cupped her there, dominant fingers sliding into her hair.

Kiss me, she silently whispered.

He brushed his forehead to hers, taking his goddamn time as he cradled the back of her head and flattened his other hand over her spine, gently guiding her forward. His patience reminded her of the film crew mindset: *hurry up and wait.*

Kiss me.

He hesitated, pursing his lips.

Her hands shot out, grabbed his neck, and tugged him to her.

Contact.

Softly, smoothly, their lips joined and pressed and mingled. Exploring and conquering. Like a scene in a silent movie where the couple kisses and where the screen fades to a single word like "*Smooch.*" Except their screen should have said, "*Magical. Spellbinding. Bewitching.*" Draven's mystical lips would have been hung at the Salem witch trials in the 1600s. Burned at the stake for their enchanting sorcery.

His kiss felt like Halloween, which—to a fan of horror—made Thea climb further into his lap. He was the feeling of dressing up in a costume and being whoever you wanted. He was the hypnotic golden flicker of candles in pumpkins carved with crooked smiles. He was forbidden candies melting in her mouth well after midnight.

He sucked on her bottom lip before dragging his teeth over it.

Yes.

Because suddenly, the magic of the gentle kiss became dark. Thrilling. Salacious. They sold their souls to each other, knowing the buyer could be trusted. His fingers curved around the side of her throat. His palm rested on her collarbone as his hand acted as a leash, keeping her there. Held hostage by the kiss.

His rough lips surpassed intoxicating to become searing. Demanding. Primal. Claiming.

The curve of his mouth transformed her into a thousand-pound anchor, and she sank into him instantly. Lost at sea. No amount of wax could have clogged her ears and prevented her from becoming a victim to this male siren.

Or maybe he was some kind of incubus, feeding off of her soul with each movement of their lips.

Because she couldn't stop fusing their lips together. She couldn't stop sipping on his mouth like it was a fine wine, aged to perfection just for her and her alone.

Want him. Need him.

Her thighs quivered over him. Her pussy grew slick as it hovered an inch away from the bulge of his briefs.

There will never be anyone else I will want this badly.

Her hips began to rock.

Draven's heart beat wildly out of his chest. Kissing Thea was either body-awakening or bad for his health. The kiss began as warm and relaxing as a cup of coffee—now, the heat of it burned his tongue, and the caffeine-like feeling it inspired infiltrated his bloodstream. Her breathy little intakes and whimpers in the back of her throat drove him to the brink of insanity.

Wren will kick you out of the band, he reminded himself.

She sucked on the tip of his tongue, and his groan vibrated his chest against hers. *Want to rip that dress from her and suck and lick and make her scream.*

Shit, he was losing control. He had not had sex since a few days before she moved into the apartment, over a week ago. He had been too busy thrusting into his fist at the thought of Thea's mischievous smiles and twinkling eyes.

She is kissing me, he thought and felt his chest inflate; pride and happiness acted like helium. *She is kissing me.*

He wanted to consume her, so even when she inevitably walked away, he would still have a piece of her.

Cursing, he grabbed her hips and squeezed, stilling her movements just as she began undulating and grinding dangerously close to his growing erection.

Wren will kick you out of the band.

Screw. Wren.

Wrenching his lips from hers, he grunted at seeing her dilated pupils and puffy, well-kissed mouth. "Baby, this is beginning to escalate," he warned aloud, hoping she could somehow understand him.

She purred and rubbed her cheek against his, maneuvering their lips to lock again. Seeking and teasing and possessing.

Her taste is perfection.

Pulling away again, Draven closed his eyes and groaned. His cock pulsed violently under her. All he had to do was lift her skirt, and he could grind her soft pussy over his shaft, pleasuring them both. Even now, she rubbed her chest against his, her needy nipples poking through the fabric of her dress.

"You have no idea what you're doing to me right now, do you?" he asked, his voice embarrassingly hoarse. *Thank God she can't hear me.*

She moaned and wiggled on his lap, rubbing her breasts firmly against his chest.

"Fuck, baby, rubbing up against me..." He kissed down her neck, unable to keep his mouth off her magnetic skin. "You need it that bad?"

One of her palms fell to grope his chest. She rocked her hips again, seeking out something stiff to grind against her. Her little clit probably swelled for his touch. She leaned back just enough to sign with her free hand, *"Please."*

Resistance. Shattered. Maybe she heard it break because Thea moaned and churned her hips in a silent plea.

Draven, ever the thoughtful gentleman, shifted forward on the couch, jostling the woman in his lap as he repositioned so her legs wrapped around his waist, and she laid her pussy over his stiff erection.

His hands fooled with the skirt of her dress, bunching it up her legs as he slid his palms under and cupped her ass through her panties. He had to hold onto her for balance after all—to ensure she did not fall off him. *Just being mindful.* A loud moan vibrated deep in his chest as his fingers bit into the swell of her delicious backside.

She surged her hips forward, rocking against him and creating an unreal, mind-blanking friction.

He cursed under his breath again as he kissed the side of her neck, her earlobe, and her chin. "You have to tell me what you want, Thea."

She breathily moaned and wriggled over him again, seeking the perfect alignment.

"Fuck, what do you want from me, huh?"

Another sexy twist of her hips.

"You want this stiff cock?"

"*Mmmmm.*"

"You want me to fuck you, baby?"

Not knowing what he said, she rubbed her flat palm over her chest in a circle. "*Please,*" she signed again, lost in lust.

"Baby, you never need to say please again," Draven rasped. "You tell me what you want, and I'll give it to you. Always."

Chapter Twenty-Four

Draven's hand drifted down her spine, fingers tracing the zipper at the back of her dress. Would he take it off her? *If he doesn't do it soon, the fabric might burst into flames against my skin.*

Flushed, she breathed heavily as his fingers closed around the zipper and gave a little tug. Not far enough for the dress to slip from her shoulders.

She squeezed at his pectoral muscles, egging him on. *Tug.* The zipper slid down further.

The moment her dress slipped down her arms to reveal her lack of a bra—*thank you, B cups*—Draven froze. His gaze fastened onto her bare breasts and puckered, pink nipples, as if he were a man frozen in ice who saw and felt the sun for the first time in years.

His chest shuddered from a broken inhale. Draven slowly cupped her waist and pressed his face into the crook of where her neck met her shoulder. He breathed her in, a pained expression on his face as if he grappled with his self-control not to maul her and ravish her right on the couch.

Seeming to summon droplets of control, he pulled back and stared darkly and possessively at her breasts and the tight tips reaching out for him, whining for his mouth. His tongue dabbed out to wet his lips again.

Flicking his molten gaze back to hers, he pressed his thumb to his plush bottom lip then hovered the digit a hairbreadth above her tender nipple.

His eyes shimmered with a question. He made the motion again, signing in his own way, *"Can I kiss them?"* the same way he asked to kiss her lips. He circled his palm over his chest, *"Please."*

Having a man like Draven ask if he could please suck her nipples was quite possibly the hottest experience of her life.

"Please," he signed again.

Shivering, she nodded.

Draven hissed and ran his palms up and down her waist. His hands curved around her sides, slipped under her dress, and palmed her ass. He bunched up her panties as he held her firmly against him. His head leaned down, mouth hovering above her taut nipple, as he tightly gripped her ass and kneaded the flesh there.

Lust and heat rippled down her spine, blossoming low in her stomach.

His hands guided her lower body, grinding her over the bulge at his crotch just as he dipped forward and sucked her entire breast into his mouth.

She squawked, and he grinned at her. The sentiment clear: *I want to swallow you up.* Devour her whole. Gulping, she watched as he burrowed his face in her chest and vibrated the skin there as he groaned.

His tongue flattened and dragged over a tight nipple. The rough, smooth, wet sensation was more than she had ever felt.

He expertly swirled and circled his tongue, pebbling the tips of her breasts as they tingled. Every stroke of that merciless tongue sent her nerve endings on a fritz.

There must have been actual electrical wires connecting her nipples and clit because each time he sucked or grazed his teeth over her, she felt the same tight, all-consuming feeling between her legs.

Massaging her ass, he tilted her, changing the angle as he rotated her hips. *Rapture.* Her choked moan told him he moved right against her throbbing clit.

Tugging and laving and suckling at her sensitive nipples, Draven studied her the entire time with hooded eyelids. When she ground against him harder, he smirked around her breast—the sight of which had her pussy contracting and begging to be filled by the wicked, talented man.

Heart thundering, she clutched him, fingers digging into his toned back. God, could he feel how wet she was for him? Her panties were soaked. Dampening his briefs.

She kept bearing down on him, rocking and wiggling and twisting as her clit scraped over his rigid bulge. His mouth grew more insistent on her breasts, leaving scalding kisses all over her delicate skin.

Tearing his brazen lips from the tender peaks, Draven lifted her off his lap and had her stand up between his legs in front of the couch. Dazed, she whined in alarm, fearing he put a stop to this. Instead, he jerked her dress down her legs as if it offended him.

Before she had the chance to step out of it, he lifted her by the hips, leaving the fabric on the floor, and turned to position her until she sat with her back against the arm of the couch, her legs folded and spread.

His nostrils flared. His expression ignited into one of mindless need as he saw the damp spot on the center of her thin panties. Her clit pulsated with each galloping heartbeat. Panting, she bucked her hips toward him as he sat back on the couch between her legs.

He pushed his thumb to his lower lip, then he drew that same thumb down between her breasts, down her hallowing stomach, down, down, to lightly swipe over her swollen bud of nerves.

Her head fell back before she remembered he tried to ask her something.

At the loss of her attention, he began anew. The thick atmosphere of the living room was charged with sexual tension. She held her breath in anticipation as he touched his bottom lip, lightly grazed the top of her slit over her panties, and circled his palm over his chest.

"*Please*," he signed.

The man was asking if he could "please" kiss her between the legs.

Nodding rapidly, so emphatically it might have been embarrassing, she widened her pose, spreading her legs as much as she could. Hell, she threw her left leg over the back of the couch to provide him with all the access he could ever need.

She gestured for him to please begin, her expression communicating, "*Bon appétit.*"

His savage grin reminded her of a sexy villain finally getting everything he ever wanted.

Draven fought the magnetic pull of her pussy as long as he could, cherishing the sight of her splayed before him. Crawling up so he could balance on his elbows and align his face with her panties, he raked his nose up and down her slit.

She smells like pleasure. Softly, he laid a single kiss on her clit. The edges of his lips curled at her shriek.

"You want me to eat this pretty pussy, Thea?" he asked, laying another barely-there kiss over where she ached.

Whimpering, she threaded her fingers through his long, dark hair and guided him to use more force.

A guttural rumble of approval shook his chest. "What if I tell you that once I lick it, it's mine?"

More pushing at the back of his head.

Kiss. Press. Suck. Lift. He teased her. His cock wept for her, but he took his time. Ignoring the brazen throbbing between his legs, he dragged his tongue over the center seam of her, hardly able to taste her through the thin fabric.

Okay, maybe patience was overrated.

He grabbed at the top of the panties and *ripped* them into two shreds of material, baring her glistening pussy to his face. *Merciful God.* His cock lurched under the briefs, pointing and pleading to explore her.

Her fingers yanked at his hair, and he glanced up at her angry expression. She glanced at the shredded fabric and scowled at him.

"I'll buy you another pair," he promised. "Better quality that won't rip."

She pursed her lips at him.

"You caught me. I lied. I'm only buying you edible underwear from now on. Maybe they have matching pairs for couples." His cock twitched at the idea of her licking candy off it.

Her glare remained, but it weakened as he moved his hands up to lay on her inner thighs. Her breath caught as his thumbs separated her lower lips, spreading her and leaving her utterly vulnerable. Wet heaven.

"Fuck, baby, can I live here?" he muttered to himself as he bit his lip and examined the soaked pink flesh. "Aw, look at that little clit, all swollen and slick for me."

His gentle fingers eased the hood back to reveal the little hypersensitive bud. "Did I just find my new favorite toy?" he purred.

He flattened his tongue and swept it over the bundle of nerves. Sick, twisted satisfaction filled his lungs as Thea's glare *melted* off her beautiful, flushed face. Her mouth dropped open; the sound escaping it made a surprised "*puh*" sound.

"This is called a French kiss," he told her, leaning in to perform a wet suction technique as he tongued her. *Suck, lick, swipe, swirl.* She trembled violently at his erotic talent. "Mmm, my girl likes the French."

Bucking, she closed her eyes, but the lids fluttered back open as he blew on her clit, demanding her attention.

"Eyes on me, sweetheart." He gestured for her to keep watching him. Settling back in for more of his new favorite treat, he delved his right hand under her while his left kept her spread.

Long, thick fingers pet her entrance and swirled the sweet wetness around. *Gotta spread the love.* His cock panged and pined, jealous, as he delved the tip of his index finger inside her.

He cursed, his own hips jerking forward on instinct as he felt her tight heat squeezing his finger. He could imagine it—that pussy wrapping around him, a vice-like grip.

Not tonight, he reminded himself. Tonight was about her.

There was also a greater chance that if he didn't have penetrative sex with Thea, Wren might not throw him out of the band. After all, he said not to have sex with her. Loophole? What was a little tongue play and fingering between two good friends? No way Wren could get upset over that.

Draven winced when he thought of Wren's reaction. *I am going to hell.* Thea's pussy clamped around his finger, pulling him back into the moment. He dismissed his previous thought. *I hear it is warm there.*

"Now, let's see if I can...there it is." Curling his finger just right, he caressed her hidden ribbed flesh. *Hello, Thea's G-spot. Nice to formally meet you.*

She threw her head back and weakly wailed as he licked and suckled her clit while fingering her. The sounds of her wetness grew louder under his manipulations. *How soaked can I get this girl?* He wanted to know. He wanted to know her body better than anyone else in the world.

He sped up his mouth and fingers, pushing her toward orgasm because he had to see it. He had to. He had to watch ecstasy break across her face, watch her cheeks and breasts turn pink, and hear the sounds she made.

"Give it to me," he demanded as he fingered her with a precision and speed that had her body quivering so bad, it vibrated the damn couch. "I want it," he whispered between leisurely laves and desperate sucks on her swollen clit. "Give it to me. Be a good girl, and come on my tongue."

She gave him everything.

She came with a broken, husky scream. Her eyes rolled back as her body tightened and spasmed with release. He lapped her up like a cat with cream.

Don't fuck her; don't fuck her, he chanted in his head as

she arched her back and thrust those pretty hips against his hand, riding out her orgasm.

His dick ached so painfully now that he knew he needed to either jerk off or cut that damn appendage from his body. When she calmed, laying back on the couch with her legs stretched, her panting slowed to semi-fast breathing.

Easing the fingers from her, he watched her entrance shine and practically beg for more.

Leave right now, or you won't be able to resist her.

Jolting away, he rushed to the bathroom and slammed the door.

"*Have you ever hooked up with someone, and then he ran away?*" Thea texted her friend Fifi after Thea had gone to her bedroom for the night.

She did not know whether her blushing cheeks were from the most powerful orgasm of her life or the humiliation of being abandoned immediately afterward.

Out on the couch, Draven had blown her mind. Wait, more than that. He had annihilated—straight up nuclear mushroom cloud-ed—her previous notions of lust. Was that normal? Alec had never instilled in her such animalistic urges.

She had *screamed*.

Palming her face, she waited for Fifi's reply.

"*OMG, you had sex with Draven, didn't you?*" Fifi texted. "*He ran away afterward?!?!??*"

Thea scowled. "*I didn't say it was Draven! I am just asking if things like that happen.*"

Fifi messaged, "*What the hell was he running away from? The chance of a real relationship? LOL!*"

Thea bit her lip. Could he have run because he did not want a relationship with her? Did he see what they did as just a casual hookup? If so, why did he only pleasure her? Why run away to take a shower?

She had even tried to follow him in, maybe join him under the streams of water, but he locked the door.

Why did men become more confusing once women liked them?

I also need to find a new makeup artist gig to make some money for next month's rent payment.

It was a sleepless night.

The next morning, she chewed on her cereal, sitting on one of the barstools at the kitchen island. Swinging her legs back and forth underneath her, she stared over to the hallway, where Draven would emerge soon.

She would see him for the first time since the "incident." The incident being: him having eaten the hell out of her pussy.

She shivered on the barstool and crossed her legs just thinking about it. Her body remained awake all night, whispering for her to join him in his bedroom. She awoke in the morning with a hand between her legs and some naughty memories from wet dreams.

Her phone buzzed, and she read a new, unwanted message from Alec. "*I'm serious, Thea. We need to talk.*"

Really not the man I'm looking to talk to this morning.

After finishing her cereal, she impatiently paced around the kitchen. She grabbed the caffeinated coffee beans and brewed a fresh pot for him. She tapped her fingers against the granite countertops. She opened and closed cabinets, not looking for anything specific.

Finally, Draven emerged for breakfast. Dark, spiky hair. Pouty lips. Morning stubble dusted his chin. He yawned, raising his arms out to stretch. Her gaze locked onto the straining of his muscular biceps and the prominent vein there she wanted to lick.

No. No licking until she understood what they were to each other now.

Did he plan to ignore last night? Erase it from his memory?

She stood there, waiting for him to do or say something to suggest how they were supposed to interact with each other now. Did he regret it? Did he worry she was another groupie obsessed with him now?

He trudged over to the coffee maker, grabbed a mug, and paused when he noticed the pitcher of his coffee beans already being brewed. Turning to her, he caught her gaze and signed, "*Thank you.*"

"*You're welcome,*" she signed back. Every time he used sign language, she grew slick between her legs. Was there anything sexier than a man putting effort into communication?

Again, she tried to read him, but his calm and collected exterior had advanced to university-level poetry that never made sense to her—an enigma of advanced metaphors lost on her. He poured a large amount of cereal into his bowl as she wondered to herself, "*What does that MEAN?*"

"*Hungry?*" she wrote on a Post-it note and passed it to him.

He glanced up at her after reading it and nodded.

Again, his reaction told her nothing. Were they truly going to pretend it didn't happen? That she didn't come all over his face and fingers while he brazenly smirked?

"*Did you eat dinner last night?*" she wrote to him.

His lips pursed, and he twirled a pen in his fingers before responding, "*I ate on the couch. Remember?*"

Okay, so they were acknowledging it now? Her phone buzzed, but she ignored it. She wrote to him, "*I remember it quite well, especially the part when you ran away.*"

He blew out a sharp breath and wrote, "*People don't want us together, Thea.*"

"*What are you talking about? Who?*" Other than Mallory's warnings, Thea had no idea what he talked about.

"*It doesn't matter. I'm not your type, and I'm not a rebound.*"

Thea scoffed. "*I don't have a type.*" Her phone vibrated once more. Who was contacting her so insistently this morning?

"*You go for straight-laced, tie-wearing hedge fund types.*"

She gaped at his note. "*Excuse me?*" Her phone buzzed again.

Draven frowned and nodded for her to answer it. He jerked a thumb toward the bathroom and began his journey over to it. Was that his official new hiding place for when things got too real between them?

Left alone, Thea read the new messages on her phone. All from Alec.

"*Your parents gave me your new address and asked me to check in on you. They said they're worried about you. I'm on my way.*"

"*Just parked. Will find your door soon.*"

"*I'm here, Thea. Let me in.*"

"*Thea, I'm here. Check your phone, beautiful.*"

Here? Alec? Was here? Right now? She stopped breathing. Quietly sprinting to the front door, she looked through the peephole and saw a blurry man standing there who resembled Alec.

Oh no.

Living with Draven and pursuing her dream career felt like a brand-new life. Was this when reality crashed the party?

Taking a deep breath, she unlocked the door and opened it.

Alec's short, blond hair was professionally slicked to the side, with no strand out of place. He wore a light blue button-down shirt, a dark blue tie, and black slacks. His shoes and gold watch cost an ungodly amount of money.

She used to see him as an all-powerful man. Deaf and

dominating and inspiring and full of promise. Then, years passed of off and on, of suspicious behavior. And, of course, there was the cheating Thea had just recently learned about.

Alec's eyes scanned her, examining her lilac lace dress and pearl necklace. He always did like her "look." "*You wouldn't answer my texts*," he signed. No *hello* or *how are you* or *I'm sorry*. "*I had to see you.*"

Ignoring her accelerating heart, she signed calmly, "*Why?*"

"*Why?*" Alec gawked. "*Because you are throwing away your whole life over one mistake.*"

Throwing away her life? Throwing away a man was not throwing away her life. "*I'm not*," she replied.

"*It just happened once, baby. It won't happen again, I promise.*"

"*I don't trust you*," she signed. "*And even if I did, I don't want to go back to the way things were.*"

He scoffed and looked around the apartment. "*You think any of this is real? Your mom told me about your trouble finding a new finance job. And the whole makeup thing? Come on, Thea. That's not real life. You are living a temporary vacation. I don't even know how you are paying half for a place like this.*"

She bit her lip. She paid less than a third, actually. It helped that she was roommates with a drummer who no one else wanted to live with.

"*Come back home. We will figure this out. I'll go to therapy.*"

"Alec, I like my life right now. It's mine. I am not going back to you," she signed, adamant.

"You are acting crazy," he signed.

"Crazy?"

"You made your point, okay? I messed up. Now come back home."

She crossed her arms and shook her head.

Instead of appearing frustratingly amused, Alec began to glare. Refuse to give a powerful man what he wants, and he tends to scowl. *"Thea, your parents expect us both to attend Thanksgiving dinner—together."*

"They shouldn't have invited you. It's completely inappropriate for them to meddle with my life like this," she signed. *"Alec, we were over a long time ago. I just needed the push."*

He frowned. *"What are you talking about? We are perfect together."*

"Everyone thinks *we are perfect together. But the last year or so, I mean, when was the last time we were really happy? Do you remember?"*

He signed slowly, as if she were a child first learning, *"Babe, we match."*

"Just because we speak the same language? Because we have similar upbringings and families? Alec, do you love me, or do you love how other people see us together? Are we settling for each other, for a certain life, because we are too afraid— because we have been taught *not to ask for more?"*

He began to sign back a heated response, but something behind Thea caught his attention. She glanced over her shoulder to see Draven, shirtless, re-entering the living room. Abs and bedhead on full display.

Draven caught sight of the two of them and froze.

Thea tried to get Alec's attention back, but her ex's lips thinned into an angry line. A vein in Alec's forehead pulsed and became prominent as his cheeks reddened.

"*This is who you're living with?*" Alec signed, "*The manwhore of that rock group?*"

Thea gasped at the hateful, horrible words. "*He is not a manwhore.*"

"*Don't tell me you fell for his act.*" Alec shook his head, disappointment and anger warring for front and center time on his face. "*Do we need to get you checked for STDs?*"

Air sawed through her lungs. "*How dare you?*"

"*I made a mistake, and you ran off to screw the most available man in L.A.?*"

She signed, "*Get out.*"

"*You know what, I'm not interested in getting you back anymore. I'm looking for a wife, not a slut.*"

A slut. Thea's heart clamored in her chest. A slut? A ringing sound speared through her ears.

Before she had time to react, Draven appeared beside her. A soft gust of wind blew pieces of her hair at how fast he moved to her.

She blinked.

And Draven's fist collided with Alec's jaw.

Chapter Twenty-Six

"You *punched* a man?" Wren repeated in a shocked, exasperated tone. A little dramatic, if you asked Draven.

"Yes," Draven said again, holding a frozen bag of peas around his throbbing hand.

The band had been scheduled for their typical "practice hang out" to draft and revise songs for the new album at Draven's apartment. Of course, his bandmates noticed his injury and cursed. It was horrible timing. Drumming required hands; the act of punching someone injured hands.

Ever since Alec ran out clutching his jaw, Thea flitted around the apartment in a blur of chaos.

She found bags of frozen vegetables and made Draven "try out" each one on his hand and choose the best fit. She searched the medicine cabinet for aspirin, tossing the condoms to the back of the shelving unit while she glared at the little packages, and Draven chuckled to himself.

As the big brother in a family with busy parents, it had been a *while* since anyone cared for him like she did. Thea pointed for him to sit on the couch and hold the bag of frozen peas to his hand while she made him hot chicken noodle soup, heating a can of it she found in a cabinet.

Even though he could have held a spoon, he let her feed him the soup, reveling in the way her lips formed the perfect, sexy "O" when she blew on the steaming liquid for him. Amused, comforted, and touched, Draven sipped the broth.

He knew the hot soup would do nothing to heal his hand, but he also knew he could deny her nothing when she looked at him with those big gray-blue eyes.

Keeping his right hand under the bag of peas, he tapped on his phone to use voice-to-message to text her, "*You make a sexy nurse.*"

The sight of Thea's blush had made his heart lurch forward and his dick tingle—the stuff of poetry.

She texted him back, "*How did you know he called me that word?*" She did not repeat it.

Slut.

Draven blushed, his stubble unable to mask the pink blooming over his cheeks.

She poked at his side when he hesitated to answer, shooting him those pretty pleading blues.

Huffing out a sigh, Draven clicked on the voice-to-text and replied, "How do you know I knew what he called you? Your ex has a very punch-able face."

She rolled her eyes and poked him again.

He took his time in replying. His phone screen circled as it waited for his dictation of a new message. "I may or may not have learned that word after I may or may not have watched videos on how to talk dirty in sign language."

Both of them blushed.

An hour and a half later, his bandmates came over for their practice and brainstorming session, saw his injured hand, and cursed.

"Dude, are you going to be able to drum?"

"We go on tour in less than two months!"

"What the hell happened? You get into a drunk bar fight?"

"God, Draven, you've got to grow up, man."

"A drummer hurting his hand *punching* someone? How much more immature can you be?"

Everything they said was a new, invisible, painful nail hammered into Draven's body. Hammered into the sensitive parts—like everywhere a tattoo artist warned, *"Okay, but it's going to really hurt."* Wrist. Foot. Back shoulder blade.

Their complete lack of support—or interest in *why* Draven punched someone—hurt him worse than his hand did.

There used to be a time when all of the members of Medusa's Tears were dumb, young rock stars who stood by each other no matter what crazy thing one of them did. Tomi once accidentally got married in Vegas, and Draven had the self-control to mention it only once a year. *Once.* Okay, maybe four times a year.

Ever since his friends got married and had kids, they looked at Draven like he was an irresponsible token from their past. *I'm getting pretty damn tired of it.*

Convincing his bandmates that he wasn't the same twenty-two-year-old they witnessed have a threesome in the green room after a concert was not easily done.

Worst of all, the idea of having to explain and *prove* to his closest friends that he was a grown man and not the archetype they saw him as—well, it sucked.

Was it unrealistic to crave utter acceptance from someone? To want someone to have his back no matter what? It was not Draven's job to tell his friends he spent his money on Mimi's care or Summer and Geo's college to win back their respect. *Having to constantly prove yourself is exhausting.*

"How did it happen?" Tomi asked, prying for the dramatic details of the punch.

"It doesn't matter," Draven said, disappointment welling inside him and brimming in his chest.

"Let me guess, jealous boyfriend?"

If anything, *Draven* seemed like the jealous boyfriend in the scenario. Someone said something horrible about his woman—his, uh, roommate—and he flipped.

"Are you going to be able to play in the next week or so?" Wren's serious tone took the carefree joking out of Tomi and Yin's prying.

"It was just a punch; my hand isn't made of glass. I'm

sure I'll be fine before the tour, if that is what you are worried about," Draven replied.

"Do we need a backup drummer on call when we're in Europe, or will you be able to control yourself?" Wren asked.

"Like I'm normally some violent guy? You're the one who killed every spider he saw on our tour busses." Draven clucked his tongue. "And mentioning the possibility of kicking me out of the band again. Awesome."

"Honestly, Draven, you've been kind of unhinged lately. Can you blame me?"

"Unhinged?" he echoed.

Wren continued, "You've missed more practices in the last year than you ever have before." Draven had been visiting Mimi after concerning news from her caregivers. "You asked our record label for money." For Mimi's care and his siblings' college. "You have nothing but mindless hookups with groupies."

Draven rolled his eyes at that.

"And now, you punch some random guy and won't tell us who it is?"

Draven shrugged stiffly. "You don't need to know. You shouldn't *have* to know."

Tomi cracked open another beer as he leaned back on the couch. "If you told us why, maybe we wouldn't be so upset with you."

Draven snorted.

"What?"

"You guys love to be upset with me nowadays," Draven commented.

"You *hit* someone, Draven," Wren stressed from his seat in the armchair. The "leader's" seat. "What if it becomes a lawsuit or something? You never think about how your actions impact all of us—"

A balled-up piece of paper whacked Wren in the cheek, startling all the men.

Dumbstruck, the rock stars glanced at where the soft weapon came from. Thea stood just behind the couch, her chest heaving up and down like she just barely held back from screaming. Her intense scowl chilled Draven down to his bone marrow, and she wasn't even directing it at him. She glared at his bandmates.

Wren signed something to her, which Draven assumed was something along the lines of, *"What the hell? What was that for?"*

She rapidly signed back at him. Thea's quick hands moving in the air mesmerized Draven and the other men who did not know sign language.

"What's she saying?" Draven asked Wren, who was fluent.

Wren ignored him as he stared, slack-jawed, at what Thea signed.

"What is she saying?" Draven repeated; Tomi and Yin asked the same.

"She says that she was using the voice-to-text app to eavesdrop on us. She says we're all assholes for calling Draven immature and that we should apologize," Wren translated. He shook his head at that and signed something back.

Whatever Wren signed seemed to piss her off even more. Thea's eyes narrowed into slits, and her tiny, cute nostrils flared as she furiously signed back.

Draven sat on the edge of his seat, feeling like he could tip over at any moment in front of this fireball of a woman. "What's she saying now?" he asked, hoping his tone didn't sound as desperate and begging to the others as it sounded to his own ears. Was she standing up for him? Was someone finally standing up for him?

"She says, 'Draven is amazing and doesn't deserve to be talked to that way.' Now she is *demanding* we apologize." Wren scoffed and signed back to her, narrating his words to the men, "*Thea, he punched someone.*"

She rolled her eyes and signed some more.

Wren translated, "She says her ex came by and got mad at her for living here. That he—he *what*?" Wren growled. She signed it again. Wren glared at her hands as he said, "Her ex called her a 'slut,' and Draven punched him."

Wren took a deep breath and continued, "She says she is glad Draven punched him. She is proud of him." *Proud of me?* "She... She has never had someone stand up for her before, and he did. Without hesitation, he did."

Finishing with the translating, Wren blinked and glanced at Draven for several seconds. He jerked his head up and down in a nod of solidarity. Tomi leaned forward and clapped a hand over Draven's shoulder.

"Oh, so now you are all proud of me?" Draven asked.

Hurt bled from his voice even though he attempted to cauterize it. Still, his heart thudded behind his ribcage at Thea's words.

She signed again.

Wren translated, "She says she will make sure his hand heals before the tour. She won't let him use it if that is what it takes. She says we don't deserve him. And she... She says if any of us dare to make him sad about the punch or anything, the next time she does our makeup, she will draw a dick on our faces in black eyeliner and let us go out and perform like that."

Tomi cackled while Yin scoffed and turned to Draven. "Dude, be honest, you told her to say that."

"I didn't," Draven whispered, dumbfounded. *She threatened to draw a dick on them for me.* For some reason, that felt like a love proclamation. A woman who wore pearls every day was willing to do something so childish for *him*.

I...love her.

No, no. Obviously not. Emotions ran high. It was a powerfully charged moment. She was beautiful and sexy and caring, and her pussy tasted like heaven, but love? So soon?

We hardly know each other.

Distraught and confused, Draven stared at Thea as she glared at his bandmates and pointed her judge-y little finger at them like she was a kindergarten teacher scolding a group of kids. They were famous rock stars, but she scowled at them and demanded an apology for Draven.

His upper body swayed to the side for a moment, his brain going lightheaded.

Dear God, had he just *swooned?*

"I need everyone to leave right now," Draven said evenly, not sparing a glance at his friends because all he saw was Thea. All he focused on was Thea.

"Excuse me?" Tomi asked. "We haven't even done any songwriting."

"Out," Draven said, maintaining heavy eye contact with Thea. "Right now."

They needed to be alone. Right. Now.

"Dude—"

"Get out of my apartment," he told them, standing from the couch and walking around it to get to Thea. She inched closer to him, only looking back at the other guys to silently chide them.

I want her so bad.

Draven cupped her throat lightly, a little leash of affection as he peered down at her smooth, round face and gut-wrenching eyes. "You used the voice-to-text app to eavesdrop, huh?" he teased.

A small smile curled at her mouth even though she didn't understand his words. *Because she hears me like no one else.*

"A regular James Bond, huh, baby?" Draven smirked. "That's sexy as hell."

One of the men made an alarmed coughing noise, and Draven shouted, "Get out."

Once the door slammed closed and they were left

alone, Draven grinned at her, his face aching from the stretch of such a dominating smile. *When was the last time anything felt like this?*

"You said you wouldn't let me use my hand until it fully heals," he said, stroking a thumb over the center of her throat. "Will you help me shower, Thea?"

<h1 style="text-align:center">Chapter Twenty-Seven</h1>

"Help me shower?" Draven wrote on a Post-it note and handed it to her before striding to the bathroom. He did not need to glance over his shoulder to see if she followed. He knew she would. Sexy, cocky man.

Her uncertainty from earlier in the morning began to clear.

Though Draven had not kissed her in front of his friends, he cupped her throat in front of them, which made her think maybe he didn't see her as only a hookup. If he wanted his friends to know, then what happened between them was most likely serious, right?

He punched Alec for me, she reminded herself. He cared about her.

She had been unable to get their kiss—or his head between her legs—out of her mind.

Just the memory of his expert fingers playing with her clit and G-spot, his erotic, talented tongue dancing over her, teasing and coaxing...it made her nipples tighten to tingling peaks.

I want him more than I've ever wanted anything. Was that a dangerous thought? Maybe. But for the first time, she chose not to question it.

He asked her to help him shower. Sign her up.

She followed him to the bathroom, body thrumming. Draven had already turned on the water, waiting for the streams to heat. She closed the door behind her and smiled at the pleased sparkle in Draven's eyes when he saw that she wanted to play his game. Or maybe it was not a game at all.

He reached down to grip the hem of his shirt, but she shooed his hands away.

"Stripping you is my job," her stern expression informed him. *"One I take very seriously."*

A smile consumed his smirk as he lifted his arms and allowed her control.

She lifted the shirt, revealing line after line of muscle, of tanned, taut skin. *This man is a fantasy.* She covertly pinched herself. Not a dream. So maybe it would not end in a nightmare.

He leaned forward, helping her pull the pesky article of clothing from him. *There,* she sighed. Shirtless Draven. His natural habitat. The way he belonged.

The only barrier left was his pants.

She swallowed thickly as her gaze roamed his dark sweatpants. All she needed to do was loosen the knot in the center and tug, and the material would fall down his toned legs. Easy.

Thea hesitated and bit her lip, glancing up at him from under her lashes as she silently asked for permission.

He rolled his eyes at her, clearly saying something along the lines of, "*You watched me jerk off. Nothing you haven't seen before.*"

Right. Yes. She held her breath as she pulled the laces loose and glided the waistband down his body.

Plop. His thickening erection bounced up to his stomach as she lowered and let the sweatpants fall to the tiled floor. Large, hard, and glistening at the dusky pink tip. A vein stretched the length of him, and she wanted to trace it with her tongue.

Mine, she thought as she gazed upon him. She had never been a particularly selfish or possessive person. Growing up, she shared her lunch and snacks with any kid who asked—but Thea thought, *I want him all to myself.* He was the treasured fruit cup she dared not share.

She stared at his mouthwatering cock as it grew before her eyes. Harder and harder. Thicker and thicker. It twitched like it felt the caress of her gaze.

Impatient, Draven spun Thea around and unzipped the back of her lilac dress. He unzipped it with his injured hand.

She scolded him, pointing to his right hand, but he ignored her and tugged the dress down her shoulders. It slipped to the floor, leaving her in nothing but green panties.

He seemed to like it when she didn't wear a bra. In fact, the way he looked at her, the amount of raw desire in his expression, suggested one of these days, she might wake up to a *thank you* note addressed to her breasts.

She recalled a time when she once thought of her body as nothing special; Draven and his over-emotive, vulnerable, genuine reactions to her annihilated any self-doubts or insecurities.

When someone completely accepts you as you are, you realize everyone before him who didn't was either dumb or never worthy—or both.

They stood basically naked in front of each other, breathing heavily as steam painted the glass of the shower door. Draven's engorged erection was hard to ignore. Thea licked her lips, gaze fastened on it. *Want to touch him. Want him inside me.*

He made the first move—and it was tender.

He held out his left hand for her to take. She nearly didn't see how it shook ever so slightly as he waited for her. She draped her hand over his, and his fingers wrapped around it, securing them.

Holding her hand, he walked her to the shower.

Heart racing and sweat beading at the back of her neck, Thea stepped after him into the shower. He slid the glass door shut behind her. Letting go of her hand, Draven walked backward until the spray of the shower head drizzled over his hair and face, droplets traipsing down the curves and angles of his body.

He slicked himself in the water as she drowned in a downpour of invisible lust.

When he dripped like a wet siren, he opened his piercing eyes and waved for her to step closer. Into the hazy, damp fog of desire.

He lifted his injured hand, faked a pout as if it hurt him, then gestured to the bar of soap.

I get to wash him, she realized, biting back a goofy grin.

Stealing the bar of soap, Thea lathered her hands with it. His pupils dilated inside his light green irises as he watched. Was he imagining the feel of her hands on him already?

Her sudsy palms connected with the tops of his shoulders as she washed down his strong arms. Then, his hard pectorals.

His muscular abdomen rippled when she ran her soapy hands over it. Unable to stop herself from looking down, she noticed his hard erection jerk against his lower stomach.

Draven bit his lip and gazed up desperately at the ceiling as she skimmed her fingers over his sides, his hips, never quite touching his cock. Her wrist grazed the tip when she washed his stomach, and he jolted and stiffened.

She grinned evilly and turned him around, so he faced the streaming water. She hissed at his bare ass—firm, curved, and bitable.

She ran her hands over his sculpted back faster this time. Her palms dragged up and down his spine and the backs of his thighs.

Just as she lowered her hands to tease over his ass, before she had time to give it a little squeeze, Draven spun around, caged her against the side of the shower, and clasped the back of her neck. She gasped at the cold tile on her back but moaned at the new position.

His wet, dark hair dripped over his chiseled face as he slammed his lips to hers. The searing kiss fused their mouths, welding them together until no crowbar could rip them apart. Ferocious. Animalistic.

He snapped his teeth at her, demanding she give him all she could, which she did. If Draven nipped, she nibbled. If Draven licked, she devoured.

She was fairly certain that her heartbeat would follow any rhythm his drummer-hands demanded.

His erection scalded her stomach, where it ground against her as they kissed. Maybe it was the shower's hot water or that every intake of breath was pure steam, but Thea melted.

His mouth seared her soul. It whispered, *"I've never felt like this. How are you doing this to me?"* It promised, *"No one else will ever come close."*

She retracted her fingernails from his back and grabbed the soap from the dish beside them. After lathering her hands again, she waterfalled her fingers down his cock, lightly grazing the tip and shaft as she pet the skin there.

His entire chest shuddered and heaved as he sucked at her lips.

His large, hot palms cupped her breasts and kneaded

the needy flesh, plucking and tugging and playing with her puckering nipples. He wrenched her panties down her legs.

Moaning, she rubbed her hand over his cock more firmly, soaping up the stiff erection and the tops of his quivering thighs. Breaking away from the ravishing kiss, she saw the dusky purple-pink color of the tip of his cock as she teased him with her fingers. Precum glazed her thumb as she stroked over the hypersensitive slit.

Jolting, Draven turned and grabbed at the detachable shower head, bringing it down.

One moment, Thea had all the power with his dick in her hands. The next, Draven's mouth sucked at her nipple; his right hand lowered the spraying shower head over her mound, aligning it to stream powerfully over her pulsing clitoris. At the same time, he used his left hand to plunge a finger inside her throbbing pussy. He hooked that finger, performing some masterful sexual artistry.

He kept her like that as she screamed at the onslaught of tantalizing sensations. Coming and coming again.

She had never been much for Jacuzzi jets. She had never had a detachable shower head. Yet, suddenly, with it spritzing against her swollen bud, her eyes rolled back, and she realized the hype for such things.

She swore his smug smirk counted, *"That's one... Mmm, that's two. And there's a good girl. That's three,"* as she came on his sinful fingers. She had never had someone be so dedicated to her pleasure and only her. He just...kept working on her. Not stopping after she came.

Only when she fought to stand on wobbling legs did he move the shower head back. He went to move it to its rightful place, but she grabbed at his wrist, fighting to take the metal circle spouting warm water. Confused, he quirked an eyebrow but let her have it.

She laid one hand over his hip and used her other to position the streaming shower head over his sizable arousal. The water shot out and stroked over his jutting cock, causing it to twitch and lean toward the jet.

She did not need to be fluent in lip reading to understand the words that shot out of his mouth as she watched for his reaction.

His jaw went slack, his eyes widened, and he fell toward the wall, one elbow resting against the shower wall at the side of her head as he rasped, "Oh, *fuck*."

Chapter Twenty-Eight

Lust for this woman is heaven and hell. Draven burned for her. Thank God he was in the shower because he sweat after being rubbed squeaky clean by her pretty hands.

Her teeth sank into her plush bottom lip as she watched him through hooded eyes. Holding the shower head over his shaft, she shifted it up and down until the powerful streaks of water felt like wicked tongues.

He cursed again, fists clenching as he leaned over her, and she worked him into a frenzy. His hips rocked into the cascading current. His cock throbbed so hard, he thought he might die if she kept up her teasing. RIP, Draven. Prey to lethal lust.

She dropped the shower head low and sprayed it over the hypersensitive underside of his shaft, where the mushroom tip leaked.

"*Thea,*" he gasped. His stomach hollowed; his balls

tightened. Groaning, he clenched his jaw to fight off the need to come.

I want more of her teasing. This cannot end yet.

He clutched at her hips, at her tits, her perfect, round backside, as she kept up the sexy assault of unrelenting, provocative water on his pulsating arousal.

When he could not stand it anymore, she stopped and pulled away.

Shooting her a tortured expression, he moaned, "Why?"

She pointed for him to put the shower head back up on the metal holder where it belonged.

"Why?" he whined again.

The sexy woman smirked and repeated her motion for him to put the shower head back.

Hard and aching, he begrudgingly followed directions.

Smiling softly at him, she touched her lips, pressed those same fingers to his shaft, then signed, *"Please?"*

Gaping and panting and wondering if this was all some kind of concussion or coma dream, he nodded. *She wants me in her mouth.* No man had ever felt luckier.

She had said *please*.

As she lowered to her knees, his thighs trembled. He knew he would come within minutes of her beautiful lips on his cock, but he summoned all of his resolve. *Keep it together, Draven.*

He'd had blowjobs before. He had been *bored* during blowjobs before. But right now, he was the opposite of disassociated. He was one hundred and twenty percent present in the moment. He could have answered questions like, *"How many freckles are dusted across her nose and cheeks?"* Or *"Are the silver blue specks in her eyes more gray or pearlescent?"*

Her grapefruit scent wrapped around him in the mist.

Her soft hands slid up the sides of his clenching thighs.

Her alluring mouth opened as she leaned forward.

"Fuck, baby, are you really going to suck me?" he asked in a hoarse voice. "Make my dreams come true?"

She grazed her lips over the base of his shaft, acclimating herself to the length of him. The lightest caress. She teased him, driving him to the brink of madness.

"Is it possible to die from needing another person this much?" he asked.

His heart beat so fast, it felt near explosion. Was this what caused strokes at a young age? What if his body couldn't handle her? It already struggled to keep up with how she made him feel.

Other women threw themselves at Draven after shows or groped him as he walked by on the street or at a club. Like they were entitled to him. Other women used him for a good time.

Meanwhile, Thea had asked permission to suck him and said *please*.

Lightheaded again, Draven leaned back toward the wall as she settled onto her knees and kissed his throbbing erection. She gently suckled the tip, leading it into her warm, wet mouth, licking and kissing and, *oh, fuck*—

Draven's head fell back as he moaned. His hips bucked

forward as she sucked him down her throat. "Thea," he rasped.

A deep rumbling growl of approval poured out of him as her mouth closed around him in a powerful suck. "That's it, baby."

Tentatively, then gaining a quicker pace, she bobbed her head over him, taking him in and out. "Uh, y-yeah, that's it," he muttered, a bit mindless already. Sultry, warm water droplets raced down their bodies as the shower filled with steam.

"Goddamn, you're a fantasy, Thea. It's never felt like this," he admitted as the sharp pressure between his legs built and built. His nerve endings shrieked as Thea twirled her tongue over his cockhead and sucked him deeper. "You're taking me so good, baby. Fuck, I'm so goddamn lucky. Can we live in this shower?"

Through slitted eyes, he watched her lips dance over him. When she moved a hand up to cup his balls, his entire body jerked. Emitting a hoarse cry, he planted his palms against the slick wall behind her.

"Little vixen, you want it that bad? Goddamn, you're like a succubus trying to suck bits of my soul. And I'm so damn pent up for you. Only for you." His hips rocked of their own volition, driving his cock into her pliant, bewitching mouth. "Trying to hold back," he strained.

She narrowed her eyes and sucked on him harder. Faster. Swirls and twists of tongue. A tightening of her fingers around the base of his shaft. This succubus demanded he come for her.

As his legs began to shake, her lips stretched into a salacious *smirk* around his cock.

"Oh, shit," he cursed.

His muscles bunched.

His back bowed.

"Oh, fuck, baby, you're taking it from me. Little succubus, my soul—it's all for you."

His mouth opened; his breath caught as warm droplets from the shower dripped over his face. Praises and curses bubbled up from his inner essence—some deep part of him he had no control over. Thighs widening and trembling, Draven leaned his weight toward the wall.

Tingles darted from his shoulders to the base of his spine. *Rapture.*

At the first violent spurt of release, Thea buried his cock deeper between her lips.

Draven's mouth hung open as she swallowed him down her throat. This kind of pleasure was like nothing he experienced before. She did not stop. She milked him for more. Her eyes demanded he fill her up with everything he had to give. Like she wanted all of him.

Someone finally wanted all of him.

He lifted her gently by her hair to pop Thea's still-sucking mouth off his dick. She had taken every drop of him.

She leaned forward to kiss the tip, causing it to jerk and spasm.

Great, now he hardened immediately after coming his brains out. Who the hell was this woman?

She released him but only to pinch her fingers and tap them together. "*More*," she signed.

More. She wanted more of him.

He knew he was in way over his head.

But drowning in Thea sounded like the best way to go.

He helped her to stand once more. His palms folded onto her lower back as he pulled her close and nuzzled her.

She dug her nails into his back, clutching onto him as much as he did her. Both of them felt how vulnerable and important the moment was. Like the water washed away every distraction, every past mistake or heartbreak. How could someone who inspired such dirty thoughts leave him feeling so *clean*?

She leaned back and looked at him with an inquisitive and nervous expression.

"What is it, baby?" he asked, petting her spine, two fingers tracing it up and down.

She reached between them and drew a question mark with her finger onto the fogged-over glass door. She motioned between them and pointed to the question mark.

Maybe it was the post-orgasm haze, but Draven did what first came to mind.

Following pure instinct, he drew a heart onto the mist-coated glass shower door.

A heart.

"That's what we are, Thea," he whispered into her damp hair and held her tighter.

Their friends believed they were not a good match.

They came from two different worlds.

"You're mine, and I'm yours," he promised, kissing the side of her head as he clasped her to his chest.

They hung onto each other until the water ran ice cold.

Chapter Twenty-Nine

Thea yawned and stretched on the vast, massive mattress, breathing in the smell of lime, mint, and the crisp softness of clean sheets. The wide-shouldered man lying in deep slumber beside her emitted the body heat of a large bear, soothing her into a cocoon of warmth.

She smiled to herself. *He is like a big lion.* He was caring, doting, prone to licking and biting, and obsessed with his glorious mane of hair—and protective and loyal to anyone in his chosen tribe.

After the many orgasms in the shower, Draven had toweled her off, eaten her out once more as she attempted to balance on the sink counter, and carried her to his bed. There, they cuddled and wrote notes to each other all night, eventually passing out from exhaustion.

Thea grabbed at the sheet of paper they used last night to communicate back and forth, so she could read and reminisce.

"So, why the pearl necklace?" He had written.

She had played with the pen before responding, *"My parents sent me to spend a lot of weekends with my grandparents growing up. My grandmother had lost most of her hearing, so they always used subtitles on the TV and wrote notes to each other. My grandfather's family used to work in the production of silent movies, and he would run these old tapes in his dusty attic. We would sit side by side and watch and eat popcorn."*

"He made outdated silent movies my favorite. The dramatic acting. The outfits." She smiled softly. Her grandfather instilled in her a love for old, "classic" things. *"Grandpa knew I was having trouble fitting in at school, and he would point to the women on screen who always wore pearls and elaborate, classy dresses. He told me, 'Nobody can disrespect someone in pearls.' And I believed him."*

She knew it sounded silly, but when she looked at Draven, she saw how seriously he absorbed her written words. *"So, there I was, a fourth grader wearing a strand of pearls every day after that."*

From there, the old movies and the over emotive Lucille Ball shaped her retro style of dressing. Once Thea saw vintage 1950s cocktail dresses, and how they poof-ed out at the skirt, she fell in love.

Draven smiled and wrote, *"No one made fun of you for it?"*

She rolled her eyes. *"Of course, they did. A nine-year-old in pearls? Duh. But I never told Grandpa. He was so happy seeing me wear them, and that was enough."*

"*That's how I feel about my grandmother, Mimi,*" Draven wrote back. "*I would do anything for her. She was my strand of pearls.*"

"*Is she still around?*"

"*Yeah. I visit her a lot. She got diagnosed with dementia several years ago, so she lives in a nursing home. It's been rough. Maybe we can visit her together sometime? I got her a foosball table. She loves to defeat new people. The woman is competitive as hell.*"

Thea smiled. "*When you guys play, you let her win, don't you?*"

Draven scoffed dramatically and wrote, "*Mimi is a foosball legend. She vanquishes all.*"

Thea underlined her note, "*You let her win, don't you?*"

Revealing nothing, Draven grinned at her with so much affection in his eyes that she knew he would do anything for his grandmother's happiness, including purposefully losing at foosball.

Thea shook herself from the flashback of their notes over the span of the previous night.

Now, in the soft morning light, Thea's gaze raked over the magnificent male beside her on the bed. Last night, she had learned so much more about him, falling even harder for him than before.

He loved cooking and soap operas and action comedies, where the normal average person who was least likely to become an action hero was tasked to save the world. He cheered for underdogs. He fought imposter syndrome. He made money to survive but played music to live. He used humor as a defense mechanism because he worried others did not want or care to hear his true thoughts and feelings.

Draven had written, "*There comes a time when being underestimated or being viewed as a stereotype starts to sink in and poison you. It's a lot of back and forth of 'I want to prove to them I'm not what they think' and 'Why waste energy trying to prove who I am to people who will never change?'*"

As a deaf child raised in a hearing family with other hearing children, Thea had never felt two sentences better represented her than what he wrote.

She had held his hand in her left one as she wrote back, "*I understand that completely. Growing up, I always felt like people expected me to be the shy, wallflower deaf kid. My parents put me in public schools for most of my childhood, thinking that was the way for me to learn lip-reading, which is so ridiculous. Only about thirty-five percent of English can be read on the lips, and it's extremely difficult.*"

She added, "*In the public hearing school, everyone expected me to be slow in classes, teachers told me I would have trouble keeping up. So, I worked harder than anyone else. I studied until my eyes stung each night. I had the highest grade point average at my school. One teacher accused me of cheating. I sent that teacher my college transcripts after graduating with my Bachelor's. All A's. 4.0 GPA.*"

Draven had bitten his lip and written, "*Damn, that's hot.*"

They had fooled around some more on his bed, but

when she mounted him and stroked his cock against the junction between her thighs, aligning him with her entrance, he shook his head and said something.

He wouldn't write it down, but she strained to understand the shapes of his mouth. It looked like, "*When you are ready.*"

She was ready for sex with him now, but he distracted her with his fingers and mouth until they fell asleep.

Thea smiled to herself again as she watched him sleep. His hair was bunched in sexy bedhead spikes around his pillow. *I like this man. A lot.*

She grabbed at her phone and texted her friend group chat. "*Draven and I got together last night,*" she sent, holding her phone to her chest as excitement bubbled behind her ribcage.

In mere minutes, her phone buzzed with new messages.

Elisa: "*OMG, tell us everything! Scale of 1 to 10, how good? Scale of 1 to 10, how big?*"

Fifi: "*Good for you, Thea! After Alec, you needed a rebound. Proud of you for dipping your toe into hookup culture, lol.*"

Thea's smile dipped into a soft frown as she read their reactions.

Elisa: "*A one-night stand with your roommate/landlord is a bit messy, but we applaud your wild child status. After everything that went down with Asshole Alec—yes, that is his new legal name—you deserved to let your hair down and have some frivolous fun!*"

Frivolous fun? Thea glanced back over to Draven, a pang rattling in her chest. He had drawn a heart in the shower. They had stayed up writing notes back and forth. This was more than a hookup. As a finance major, she knew when she was fully invested.

Thea clarified in text, *"No, we're actually together. Like a relationship."*

Fifi sent back almost immediately, *"You and Draven?!?!? Is this a different man named Draven? Not 'Medusa's Tears' Draven?"*

"How many other Dravens are there in California?" Elisa wrote. *"Thea, what do you mean you guys are in a relationship? You mean just a rebound, exclusive, friends-with-benefits relationship?"*

"I like him," Thea sent back, her fingertips furiously typing. *"It is not a rebound."*

"Babe," Fifi messaged. *"You and Alec were together for years. You just broke up less than a month ago."*

"We were over before that," Thea replied. *"Draven is not a rebound to me."*

"Thea, he doesn't speak sign language," Elisa texted.

"He is learning it."

"For how long?" Fifi asked.

Fifi's words triggered a box of emotion Thea had long ago locked away.

Years of group projects where her peers were not interested in providing Thea "playbacks" and "explanations" of what the others talked about, so they submitted things without her. Years where her hearing friends invited her to movies but not the ones with subtitles on the screen. Years where her co-workers said they did not have the time to "recap" meetings or phone calls for her, so they would handle those tasks themselves. People acted like it was too much effort to include her.

What happened when Draven realized it was too much effort to keep learning sign language to talk to her?

What if he drops me too?

When Draven awoke, his bed smelled like grapefruit. His heart felt like a stomach after a buffet—painfully full with no regret. He reached over to pull Thea into his arms but found the bed empty. Glancing around in alarm, he frowned at her absence.

Then, he saw the note.

"Your breakfast is on the kitchen table."

Grinning but also disappointed that he couldn't make her breakfast this morning since she beat him to it, he strode down the hallway and to the kitchen.

He staggered at the banquet.

On the long, dark wood table, Thea laid back, legs spread, wearing nothing but the skimpiest of lacy, light pink lingerie. She had left pieces of their favorite cereal over her chest and abdomen, and she munched on some of them after getting hungry from waiting for him to wake.

Staring at his sexy-as-hell roommate—who had a big

heart, goofy sense of humor, and love of the same sugar-ridden cereal—Draven noticed she wore one other item in addition to the erection-invoking lingerie. Her pearl necklace; the one that made her feel less like an outsider. Her shield. Her security blanket.

Nude and covered in cereal, she smiled at him, spread her legs wider, and continued munching on some of the pieces.

He thought to himself, *"I might love this enigma of a woman."*

Chapter Thirty

Thea's feet balanced on Draven's lap as she stretched out on the couch. With her laptop on her lap, she applied to more film set makeup jobs and emailed any makeup artists she could find.

Draven peacefully watched TV and stroked a finger up and down her shin and calf. She curled her toes into his thigh. The two of them could not keep their hands off each other. Though Draven still pressed pause whenever they got close to sex, he never left her unsatisfied.

The amount of orgasms... He had appreciated—an understatement—how she spread herself across the dining table like a feast. *Hungry man.* Alec had never made Thea feel wicked and sinful. She had never wanted to do things like that for him.

Draven inspires more in me. Yet another reason why he was not a "rebound." Her friends would come around eventually.

Abruptly, Draven jerked on the couch, body jolting in alarm. Concerned, Thea sat up, moving her feet from his lap as he looked over at the door. He made a gesture to tell her someone knocked at the door.

She slowly stood and followed him over.

When he opened the door, the air shot out of her lungs because her parents barged right inside.

Her mother's lime green dress was louder than any sound could be, seeming to trigger an alarm in Thea's head. Ears ringing, she watched as her parents strode into the living room, passing Thea and Draven as they examined the space. Investigative officers without a warrant.

Mouth agape, Thea signed, *"Mom, Dad, what are you doing here?"*

Her father glared at Draven's naked chest, then he scowled at Thea as if she were living in a strip club.

Thea motioned to Draven to go and put on a shirt. He hesitated but jerked his head in a nod and walked to his room to find one.

"What are you doing here?" Thea signed to them again.

They had never become fluent in sign language but knew enough to interact with their daughter. *"Alec told us about his jaw,"* her mom signed. *"Did that man hit him? What is going on?"*

"Draven defended me. Alec had no right to be here and say the things he did."

"Thea, what are you doing?" her father signed. *"This isn't your life. Doing makeup to pay the bills? Living with...*

that?" Her father made a gesture about how Draven had so many tattoos.

"Draven is great. And I don't want to work in finance anymore. I want to do makeup. It makes me happy."

Her father mimed writing something down, informing Thea that he was already tired of signing. Right. She grabbed a notepad and pen and wrote her statement.

He read it and pushed his glasses up his nose, squinting—not because he had trouble reading, but because he did not like what she wrote.

Her father took the pen and pad. *"Thea, you and Alec are meant to be together. He is your perfect match. He can take care of you."*

"I don't need a man to take care of me."

"You clearly do," her father wrote. *"I assume makeup jobs don't pay the full bill for this apartment, let alone half. Alec has a good job; he'll provide for you. He understands you."*

"Just because we're both deaf and he makes good money does not mean we should be together," Thea shot back, her handwriting sloppy from the speed and force at which she wrote it. *"I didn't like my life, Daddy. I'm trying to rebuild."*

"You're my daughter, and I love you, so I know when you need tough love. You're taking a step back in life. Do you think this fantasy of doing makeup and living with some drummer is real life?"

He pointed to where Draven had disappeared. *"Honey, what happens when he goes on tour? Will he still be paying for most of the rent, then? Do you think you can just jump into the movie business—one of the most competitive fields in existence? Alec is your normal. Finance is how you succeed in life. It's safe."*

"I'm not going back to a man who cheated on me," Thea signed.

Her mother crossed her arms and huffed.

Her father signed, *"The man made a mistake. He's your best option, honey. You may never find another match like him."*

"I don't want him. I like my life right now."

Her mother signed, *"This—"* She gestured to the apartment. *"—is a temporary arrangement. We gave you several weeks to calm down. Now, it's time to be a responsible adult and go back to a normal life. Forgive Alec."*

"This is my life now. Accept it," Thea signed.

Draven reentered the room wearing a black shirt with skulls on it.

Adrenaline coursed through Draven's veins as if this were a paintball game, not simply Thea's parents in his apartment. His gaze zigzagged between his woman and the people who gave her life. The intense glaring was not a good sign.

When he walked back into the living room, they stopped signing and looked at him. "Um, can I offer anyone a beverage?" he asked, clearing his throat. "I have water, soda—"

"What do you want with our daughter?" Thea's father asked Draven.

Draven's eyebrows rose, and he fumbled out the genius, well-articulated response, "What do you mean?"

"You're letting her stay here for cheap. Why?"

"It's hard for a drummer in a rock band to keep a roommate. Thea's perfect for me," he said. *She is perfect for me*. But not because she couldn't hear his drumming. Because she was *Thea*.

Her mother clacked closer to him in her heels. "Thea was months away from getting engaged. She didn't need you swooping in to offer her a place to stay. This apartment gives her an excuse to not go back to her normal life."

Engaged? Normal life? "What would you call the last few weeks she has been living here?" Draven asked.

"A vacation," her mother replied stonily. "She was always the studious, straight-A student. We knew a day might come when she had to break the mold and rebel somehow. But this stops now. You're going to stop renting this apartment to her."

Thea slapped a hand against her notepad, glaring at everyone in the room. Draven read her expressions well enough by now to know she was pissed that no one was signing or writing or communicating in any way that she could follow along.

"I'm not making Thea move out," Draven said evenly, shocking himself, considering no part of him felt "even." His equilibrium was uncentered, out of orbit.

The idea of Thea moving out and never talking to him

again was a nightmare. No, worse than a nightmare. It was a chainsaw to the chest.

"You letting her stay here is giving her unrealistic expectations for her future," her father said. "You understand that, don't you? What happens when you eventually move? Where does she go? She had a home, a future career, a future fiancé all lined up."

"She didn't want any of it. And she has a home and future career here too." Also, maybe a future fiancé. *Hi, hello, new boyfriend here.*

"It's clear we are not going to get what we came here for, Margaret," Thea's father stated.

"This is ridiculous." Her mother narrowed her eyes at Draven, practically spitting at him. "She's a brokenhearted woman feeling confused and lost. Months from now, she'll wake up and realize what a step back she has taken, and she'll regret it. You think our daughter deserves to throw her future away to live here with you?"

Draven's chest cracked at her words. Could they tell? Was blood seeping into his shirt? *They don't think I'm good enough for their daughter.* Wasn't that what his bandmates thought too? "Thea is a grown woman who can make her own decisions."

And right now, she chose Draven. She chose to live with him and be with him. *And one day, she might change her mind.* She might wake up and realize this had all been an ill-timed vacation from real life to help heal a heartbreak.

He swallowed and shoved the painful, weary thoughts aside.

Thea's mother and father turned back to their daughter, whose red face and flared nostrils projected her anger at being left out of the conversation with Draven.

Her mother signed something, and Thea's wrathful glare fell away. Instead, she was left with pursed lips, furrowed brows, big, hurt eyes, and a vulnerability in her face that cracked a few more of Draven's ribs.

What the hell did they say to her to make her look so sad? She looked like they slapped her.

Thea closed the door after her parents exited the apartment. She kept her palms against the piece of wood, staring at it, until Draven slinked up from behind and wrapped his arms around her, cooing and kissing the side of her neck and her hair for comfort.

"What did they say to you, baby?" he purred.

She turned toward him, and his heart broke at her barely suppressed tears. She pressed her lips together, but the edges curved down sharply.

"*What?*" he signed.

After a moment of recharging in his arms, Thea wrote on her notepad, "*They said they don't want to see me until I choose to stop playing pretend. My own family uninvited me to Thanksgiving dinner.*"

A growl shook Draven's chest, but the need to comfort her overruled the anger at seeing her hurt.

He wrote back, "*Then you'll come to mine.*"

Chapter Thirty-One

Meeting his family. Big step. She should have been nervous, right? Instead, all she felt was warmth.

Draven bought her a small whiteboard so she didn't have to flip through a notepad to converse during the evening. His parents were out of the country doing "science-y" things, as Draven put it. Draven would meet his siblings at his grandmother Mimi's nursing home to spend dinner with her.

Draven baked a pumpkin pie from scratch in their apartment kitchen as Thea watched with big, uncontrollable hearts in her eyes.

She grew dizzy watching the muscles in his arms bulge, the chords tense and release, as he carved into the pumpkin and removed the pulp. He noticed how turned on she was—evident from her swollen, bitten bottom lip and hardened nipples poking through the front of her dress.

Smirking, he wrote on a Post-it: "*I bought an entire can of whipped cream for when we get home tonight.*"

To lick off her? *Yes, please.*

Still, Draven was not pursuing full-on sex with her. They "satisfied" each other all over the apartment, but when she tried to hand him a condom, he shook his head. They had discussed being sexually clean. They had discussed her being on birth control.

After asking him about why he paused whenever she pushed for more, he told her, "*I want you to know this is more to me than sex. I've never had sex with someone I've loved. I'd like to wait until then.*"

Did that mean he did not love her yet? Or was he waiting for her to say it first?

Love was a big word; it should have had more consonants and vowels. People threw four-letter words around without meaning them all the time. "Love" should be changed to something that won more points during a Scrabble game, like "Queistiousnyheinburg." Fewer people would say it without meaning it if it were more difficult to pronounce.

I'm falling into Queistiousnyheinburg with you, Draven. Especially when he baked in front of her and wrote notes about how his grandmother taught him cooking tricks and how they used to have baking challenges together.

"*What should I know about your family?*"

Draven pursed his lips as he wrote back, "*I come from a long line of geniuses. Mimi was a doctor. My parents are scientists. Summer is a prestigious cellist prodigy, and Geo is going to med school to save the world from disease. I am the lowly drummer among them."*

Thea frowned, but Draven shrugged. She wrote, *"They must be proud of you for how successful your band is."*

He shrugged again, but his shoulders seemed stiffer. *"I'm not out there curing diseases."*

"Summer plays music."

"She plays in front of diplomats and politicians."

"Draven, if I see you trying to blow up balloons for your pity party, I will pop each one," Thea replied sternly. *"Your art is just as important as what they do."*

The side of his mouth curved up but dropped back to create a flat line. *"My family is great, but sometimes it feels obvious that I'm the black sheep. The disappointment."*

Did he have any idea how similar they were? Because in moments like this, it felt like Draven peered into her past and her soul.

No matter what her friends said, he was not a rebound. This was not a "vacation from life" like her parents thought.

Why can't everyone else see it?

As he drove them to dinner, he turned on heavy rock music with a loud bass and drum, so Thea felt the vibrations in her seat and on the dash speakers. They head-banged to the rhythm until he pulled up to a massive mansion-looking nursing home. Thea gaped at its size and splendor as Draven laughed off her dramatic reaction.

Holding the door open for Thea, Draven clutched his pumpkin pie tighter. His stomach transformed into Boy Scout-level knots—the impossible kind that earned someone a new badge.

He had never introduced a woman to Mimi or his siblings. He had no idea what type of questions he should prepare for. All he knew was that Thea would meet them, and maybe she would want to come to future Thanksgivings.

Maybe she will want to stay with me.

Ever since her parents visited them, he caught her staring off into space around their apartment, deep in thought. Was she thinking about what parts of her new life were "real" or not? Was he real to her? Or temporary?

After all, women used him as an escape. *How much longer until she wakes up and realizes she doesn't want me?*

Upon checking in with the front desk, Draven reached for Thea's hand and walked her toward Mimi's room. Their fingers interlocked, squeezing mutual little *"I'm here. Don't worry"* pulses in their own unique Morse code. Draven only let go to knock on the door.

His sister Summer ripped open the door, yelled "Drave," and hugged him.

"Shit, Summer, the pie," he warned, trying to hold onto it as she tackled him into a welcoming embrace. Her long blond hair floated everywhere, coming close to his dessert.

"Oops, sorry." Summer laughed and hugged Thea as well. "And don't think I forgot about you, you sexy little —"

"Summer," Draven warned again.

"Sorry, sorry." She snorted, grinning—not sorry at all. "I see you two are together now. Did I call it or what?"

"How is Mimi doing?" Draven asked.

Summer's smile faded, and tension stabbed at his back. "She's doing okay. She was a little confused when I got here, but she knows it's Thanksgiving now. She has been asking for her 'Baking Buddy.'"

Draven swallowed, his mouth dry. *Dementia sucks.* Mimi often forgot Draven's name over the last few years, but she always remembered him as her Baking Buddy.

"Oh look, I learned some sign language," Summer said. She then signed something at Thea.

Thea blinked several times in a row.

"What did you say to her?"

Summer giggled and sashayed away, further into his grandmother's unit.

Thea wrote on her whiteboard. "*I think your sister just flirted with me.*"

Draven shook his head and snorted. Taking her whiteboard, he wrote, "*Summer is gay and thinks you're hot. It will most likely happen again.*"

Thea nodded and held out her hand for him to take again.

Here we go.

Twenty minutes later, Thea played Mimi in foosball while Geo, Summer, and Draven cheered them on, losing their minds and drunk on the excess sugar in sparkling grape juice.

"She's the perfect opponent," Mimi shouted over them. "She doesn't hear my trash talk. No distractions. It's all about pure talent."

Thea had better hand-eye coordination than his grandmother, but in the end, she let Mimi win. Thea smiled at Draven as the ball shot through her un-defended goal, making it clear that she let Mimi win for *him.*

I think I love her.

Later, Thea spotted Mimi's bags of almonds and jumped up and down, writing on her whiteboard, "*Do you like spiced nuts?*" She then gathered all the needed spices and ingredients, turned on the stove, and began candying almonds in cinnamon and brown sugar.

Mimi had turned to Draven and asked, "Can she live with me?"

"Get your own roommate, Mimi. She's mine," he shot back through a wide smile.

As Thea served the hot, sugary nuts to his grandmother and siblings, she mimed for Mimi to blow on hers before eating them.

When she spotted that Mimi's glass of water was empty, she filled it before Draven could grab it himself.

I think I love her.

When they asked Thea questions, she used her voice-to-text app to understand. She wrote back replies that had Mimi and Summer cackling with laughter while Geo nodded, ever the too-serious one.

"What do you do for a living, Thea?"

"I've been picking up jobs as a movie makeup artist assistant. I also wipe Draven's tears when he watches a horror movie. Both pay basically nothing."

"I like her, boy," Mimi said, avoiding making it obvious that she could not remember Draven's name.

Considering Thea still had her voice-to-text app open, she knew what Mimi said and blushed.

"She's pretty much perfect, huh?" Draven replied to his grandmother, watching Thea stare at the phone app as it typed out his words.

Thea's blush darkened.

I think I love her.

When Mimi and Geo got distracted by a story Summer told, Draven sneaked a kiss onto Thea's forehead. She blinked, smiled, and *yanked* his head down so she could kiss his forehead too. And his nose.

Do I love her? Would that be crazy? Too fast?

When the nursing home brought up their plates on the Thanksgiving trays they ordered, they sat around Mimi's long dining table.

Sweat dampened the back of Draven's neck as he prepared for the annual go-around-the-table question.

Summer started, "What are you thankful for, Mimi?"

"I am thankful for my family and the way you all visit me even though I'm in this place," Mimi said. "I am thankful for this man right here—" Mimi tapped the table in Draven's direction. "—and the way he pays out of the roof to keep me here. Did you know they had lobster last week for dinner?"

Mimi laughed throatily, coughing a bit toward the end. "I feel like a queen," she said. "And I am also thankful for my unbeatable foosball skills."

They went around the table, leaving Thea and Draven to answer last.

Thea wrote, *"I am thankful for my life and all I have. I am thankful for the chance to be here with all of you."*

Draven winced at the fact that she was only here because her own family uninvited her to Thanksgiving dinner because they disapproved of her recent life choices. What if Draven really wasn't good enough for her? When would she realize it?

Everyone stared at him, expecting his answer next. *Here we go.* He had rehearsed this. He could do it. Shaking like a high schooler expected to converse in a foreign language, Draven nervously ran a hand through his hair.

He signed so Thea could understand it.

He signed, *"I am thankful for my amazing girlfriend. I am thankful for the time we spend making each other laugh and feel appreciated. I am thankful for her ex messing up and leading her to me. I am thankful for the way she makes my apartment feel like home. I am thankful for the way she makes me feel seen and heard more than anyone else."*

Thea stared at his hands from her seat beside him. Wide-eyed. Lost in thought. Unresponsive. Comatose.

Seconds felt like minutes as they ticked by, and Draven waited for a new topic of conversation to bloom.

Thea erased her whiteboard to jot down a new message.

She wrote, "*I am thankful for my amazing boyfriend Draven, who is a musical genius and the sweetest man I've ever met. I am thankful that my past life fell apart, so I could create a new one I love more. I am thankful he will be a part of it. And later, I am sure I will be thankful for his homemade pumpkin pie.*"

Thea placed her whiteboard down, took his hand from off the tabletop, and kissed the back of his palm, as if *he* were a Southern Belle treasure and *she* was a Regency gentleman.

He thought, *Oh God, I love her.*

Chapter Thirty-Two

Thea could not keep her hands to herself. If this were a prison, she would have been written up for breaking the "no touching rule" at least thirty-seven times tonight.

She touched his hand, his back, his chest. When no one looked, she let her palm run down the plump curve of his backside through his black jeans, and he winked at her.

Her hands changed their molecular makeup, altering electrons until Draven's body became a magnet to them. Invisible strings yanked her to him at all times.

Watching Draven dote on his eighty-two-year-old grandmother all night, watching him sign complete sentences, one after another, to express how grateful he was for Thea in his life... Was a person's heart supposed to feel like this? Like a marshmallow dropped into a campfire. Hissing and popping and melting to liquid goo.

He was a summer night bonfire, filling her lungs with a smoky haze. Too hot to sit close to. Too beautiful and entrancing to look away from. She wondered if one quick touch would be enough to burn. Would the pain be worth the aftercare?

How could one man be a scorching flame and a soothing salve all at once?

After returning to their apartment, Thea left him for only as long as it took her to change into comfortable pajamas. Reemerging from her room in fuzzy, light blue shorts and an oversized white T-shirt, she beamed at him as he ran a hand over his mouth and staggered back, acting like the sight of her in such simple pajamas had the same effect as a five-thousand-dollar ballgown.

Was it unusual to look at a partner and think, *"I would like to keep him forever, please?"* Was that how soulmates felt?

Draven walked to her, striding forward until the toes of his feet touched hers. He handed her a note. *"I want you in my bed again tonight, Thea."*

She tapped her chin, pretending to think about it. Then, she shot him a goofy I-have-the-biggest-crush-on-this-man grin as she rapidly nodded. Yes. His bed. Sleep. Chatting. Sex. *Whatever you want, because odds are, I want it too*, she thought.

He scooped her up like she weighed nothing as she yelped in alarm before happily settling into his arms and nuzzling her face into his warm chest. *Can I nest here?* All she needed was some water, maybe some vitamins.

Honestly, the word "home" was a synonym for Draven

Maxwell's arms. *How do I contact the people who handle Thesauruses?*

He gently set her down on his soft mattress and gestured for her to stay. He signed, *"I'm going to go get,"* then mimicked shaking and spraying a can of whipped cream.

Giggling, she laid back on the bed and flailed her arms and legs out, making a bedsheet version of a snow angel, leaving evidence that she was once here.

Waiting for her boyfriend—that term felt so small compared to the man she referenced—Thea peered around his room. Her gaze caught on all those crumpled balls of paper on the floor.

She recalled once, after waking in his bed with a hangover, that when she tried to see what the papers were, he dove for them. He had been desperate to keep her eyes off them.

Were they bills? Was he in debt?

She fiddled with her thumbs, fighting the temptation to uncrumple and read a few and solve the pending mystery. She had never seen Draven mad before, but she had also never invaded his privacy before. *Other than watching him masturbate that one time*—but he seemed happy to allow her a front-row seat.

What harm would it do if he walked in and saw her looking at one of those balls of paper?

Jumping from the mattress, abandoning all self-control, Thea grabbed the closest paper ball and straightened it, recognizing Draven's handwriting.

"Need insecticide
for these butterflies.
Infiltration in my chest.
Call an exterminator;
we'll need the best."

Poetry? *No.* Song lyrics. Draven was writing songs? Why had he crumpled them up? She scanned further down the page. Even through the heavy crossed-out words, she read, *"Thea, like a tree—ahh, sappy for you. Wow, I'm an idiot."*

He was writing songs about *her?*

She sprinted to the next balled-up piece of paper, greedy for more of his inner thoughts and feelings.

"You're a horror movie,
where I can't look away.
I'd follow you to the basement,
be any dumb character you want me to play.
Would summon the ghosts
to hold your hand through the haunting.
Would walk into the chainsaw
To eliminate space between us.
My woman loves horror movies.
Honey, the scariest scene is yet to come.
If you leave, I will never..."

He had stopped writing it.

She snatched up another ball of paper. She knew he would find her reading. He would walk into the room any moment and catch her, but she could not stop herself.

"I'd reopen every wound

to let you crawl through.
Every scar sliced anew
just to see you under my skin,
to show you how deep of an imprint.
Burned your initials into my bones,
so even the archaeologists will know.
Tattooed your name onto my lips;
they'll never know another lonely kiss."

Emotion simmered beneath her skin. The pores opened to purge the overwhelming rise of giddiness and hope and affection and pain and love and fear. Fear over the potential heartbreak.

"He is more than a rebound," she had told herself. What a joke.

He is everything. How he became everything in so short a time, she could not recall. There was no one moment. There were simply *many.* Many small and big. Words. Gestures. Actions. Facial expressions.

His bright green eyes reminded her of the sly Cheshire cat from *Alice in Wonderland.* This whole time, she fell down the rabbit hole, never realizing how deep it was until she landed here, in Draven's bedroom, holding his poetic thoughts about her. Pieces of his soul, touched by hers, memorialized on paper.

When he walked back into his bedroom, holding a can of whipped cream, and saw her holding the crumpled pieces of paper, he froze.

No anger rolled across his face, only shock. Nervousness. Fear.

She placed the papers carefully onto his bedside dresser.

Stepping toward him, she took the can from his hands and tossed it behind her onto the bed. She grabbed his shirt by the collar, yanked him to her, and kissed him like this was the end of a romantic movie.

But she didn't watch romantic movies. She watched high-stakes action and horror. Her lips attacked his. Space between them was enemy number one. Bodies pressed together; they fell onto the bed as one. The mattress bounced them into the air, but soon, they sank so deep that they discovered the center of the earth. His lips never left hers.

Invisible bullets shot through her chest, only to find that her heart was no longer there. He had it now. And she knew he would die to protect it.

His mouth possessed hers as he turned her to her back, lifting himself above her on two strong, delicious forearms. Her spine arched against the bed; her vertebrae bent just to get her closer to him. He cupped her face in his hands and kissed every inch of it. Cheeks, forehead, lips, nose, chin.

He pulled back to say something to her. She memorized the motion of his lips. She knew that familiar order of mouth movements.

Either he was asking for *"olive juice"* or saying, *"I love you."*

He loves me too.

An atomic bomb of *feeling* went off behind her ribcage. Lust and love combined in a combustion sure to wipe out civilization if she ever let it. Fighting the over-whelming desire to maul him, she pressed a palm to his heart, then to her own, and she nodded.

She signed, "*I love you.*"

A dark, brazen expression blazed across his features as he saw what she signed. An intense, wicked, and blistering gleam shone in those green eyes.

He knew exactly what she signed.

She had a feeling his "waiting to have sex" inkling burned into ashes.

Because his cock surged between them, and his hand slid down to cup her throat. His thighs glided between her legs, splaying them open as his bulge pressed firmly to her aching core. She panted and moaned, her throat vibrating under his gentle, dominating fingers.

He whispered something against her jaw.

She imagined it was something along the lines of: "I fucking love you, and now I'm going to love fucking you."

Chapter Thirty-Three

Draven had gone without sex since Thea moved in with him, sure, but nothing explained how pent-up he felt over her.

His cock did not simply "ache." It wept. The bulbous tip slicked with precum just at the thought of thrusting inside her. Inside the woman he loved.

Was this what fishermen lost at sea for a decade felt like? Maybe that was what love was—finally finding that one lighthouse to bring a person to shore. To remind them what stable, firm ground felt like instead of constant waves. *For years, I've just been bobbing up and down in darkness.* A buoy constantly moving in an effort to forget how stuck he was.

She has changed everything.

His blood sizzled at how she stared at him with such a ravenous, hungry expression.

Cock swelling behind his mesh joggers, Draven had never wanted another person more. He never would again.

"What have you done to me, Thea?" he asked, brows furrowed and sounding tortured.

She shot him a prideful, wicked expression that he swore said, "*I hexed you, of course.*"

She leaned forward off the bed, causing him to sit back on his ankles to give her room. Thea wrangled off her T-shirt and threw it to the side, baring her supple, mouthwatering breasts. The pink little nipples saluted him as if to say, "*Hello, soldier. At attention, please!*"

She proudly stuck her chin up and preened like she knew exactly what the sight of her pert breasts did to him. She knew how badly he wanted her.

That was so damn sexy.

"Little witch," he grunted, shooting his hips forward so his dick rubbed between her legs, bunching up those fuzzy sleep shorts. "Think you can tease me with your perfect fucking body?"

She smiled smugly at him, clearly projecting silent agreement to his words.

"Oh, really? You think you're in control here, baby?"

Her grin grew as she ran a pink fingernail down her collarbone, down her chest, to twirl around her right nipple.

Draven cursed. Yup, she was in utter control of him. But she wasn't supposed to know that. He dove forward and sucked the hardened tip of her breast into his mouth.

"These are mine now, you hear me?" he muttered to himself through a mouthful of her flesh. He licked and sucked and nibbled, all while rocking his erection between her legs.

She thrashed her head side to side on the pillow, tangling her dark hair as she moaned.

He released her nipple with a soft *pop*. "This body is mine. If you ever move out, I will demand visiting rights. You own every damn inch of me. Give me something in return, Thea."

Promise you feel the same way I do. Promise I'm good enough for you even if no one else sees it.

He kneaded her tits as his mouth performed skillful tricks over the tight peaks. She yelped when he grazed her with his teeth. One of his hands fell between her legs to press through her thin, fuzzy shorts and rub over her.

"You think you can hide your pretty pussy from me?" He yanked her legs up straight and wrenched her sleep shorts and panties off her in a single, savage move.

She gasped and bit her lip as he tossed the material behind him. Her pupils dilated, black eating up the icy blue.

Then, she stared straight into his eyes, unblinking, as she opened her legs wide, letting them fall apart and reveal her glistening pink core. The woman spread herself for him. Vulnerable. Wet. Enthralling. Perfection.

"Damn, you get it already, don't you, baby?" He lowered himself on the bed until his face hovered above her quivering abdomen. "That I'll dominate this body..." He nipped at the top of her sex, causing her to whimper and her hips to buck. "But you'll master me," he whispered.

And he feasted. Rubbing his nose and stubble over her, he dragged his tongue from the rim of her entrance to the swollen bead at the top of her sex. He snaked over her clit, teasing it, stroking it, and playing with the hood.

When he suckled, she sucked in a loud breath, chest shuddering at the sensation. Her desperate fingers tangled in his hair, gripping him against her.

With a strong suck, he tugged at her hypersensitive clit, and her hips shot up, off the mattress. "That's it," he purred as she grew wetter for him still.

He lapped her up; his new favorite treat was her pleasure. Who needed energy drinks when he had Thea's orgasms to revitalize him?

"They think I'm not good enough, but this wet pussy likes me just fine, doesn't it?"

A whine caught at the back of her throat as he continued the merciless tongue lashings and sucking lips.

"No one gives it to you this good, do they?" he asked between punishing kisses and practiced licks.

His tongue batted her swollen nub. He pressed a long finger to her slick entrance and prodded in and out, teasing her. "If I have to make your pussy addicted to me just to keep you forever, I will."

Beginning to finger her, he set back in to tongue-fuck the life out of her.

Her eyes rolled back in her pretty head as he kissed, licked, sucked, pressed, and devoured, all while driving his thick finger in and out of her fluttering core. *She is close.* Her inner muscles convulsed around his invasion. Once. Twice.

"Fuck yes, baby, squeeze my fingers. So damn tight."

His cock throbbed harder with each heartbeat, to the point that he slipped his free hand beneath him to clasp the shaft in his hand and squeeze the tip, commanding it to calm the hell down while he enjoyed his favorite meal.

"Can't get enough of you." His low growl rumbled onto her, vibrating the tender flesh until she shrieked with release.

Coming around his fingers, she thrashed on the bed. When he stilled his fingers, she undulated her hips to fuck herself on the digit. In and out. His little vixen rode out her orgasm, insisting and ensuring her pleasure.

So. Damn. Hot. He groaned into her pussy, clutching his dick in a tighter grip to control himself. His cock lurched forward, begging to release on her soft skin.

Coming down from the erotic torrent of pleasure, she tried to catch her breath. She thought she was done. She thought that he was finished. *That's cute, baby.*

His arms curled around her thighs, clamping down to hold her open to him.

He *consumed* her. "More," he rasped, demanding it. His tongue darted back and forth, performing expertly crafted flicks at the hood of her clit. "I want another. Give me another."

Her fingernails dug into his scalp. Her thighs shook so hard, they reminded him of little earthquakes. She gaped up at the ceiling, moaning and panting as he worked her.

"Another," he demanded, slapping her thigh lightly and clasping it in a large, dominating palm.

Back arching off the bed, she came again. Her eyes glazed over from endorphins. Masculine pride filled his chest at the sight of her flushed cheeks and reddened nipples, swollen from his masterful manipulations.

Her breasts quivered as she rushed to even her breathing after the two back-to-back orgasms.

Just getting started.

Draven's cock leaked precum from his excitement of watching his woman come twice. The engorged appendage chanted to him, "*Want her. Need her. Inside. Thrust. Ravish.*"

His balls were heavy for her and had been for weeks, aching and full of Thea-induced seed. He had never put much importance on sex—but now? He wanted her heart and body at the same time. He had been prepared to wait for it.

But she says she loves me too.

That knowledge broke the dams of waiting. The bridge of resistance went tumbling down.

He was about to have sex with the woman he loved, which meant all of this felt new. His cock was so full and throbbing for her; he swore he was back to being a randy virgin on the verge of coming. Like she took away his entire past, his sexual history wiped clean. *There is only her.*

Thea bucked her hips and whined. She reached for his

jutting erection and motioned for him to get inside her already. They had already gotten tested and shown each other negative results. Thea had told him she was on birth control. And with his woman openly glaring at him to hurry up and fuck her, they were all set to continue.

He hesitated.

What did she like? What did she expect?

He knew she had heard the rumors about him. The sexual tales of his exploits. Did she expect him to nibble at her neck, pull her hair, or leash her throat in a loose grip?

He was a dominating man who loved dirty talk, but this was the woman he loved. Was he supposed to still do those things? What if he disappointed her somehow?

She frowned at his sudden, concerned expression. Reaching forward, she cupped his face and silently asked, *"What's wrong?"*

He exhaled deeply. "What if I really am not good enough for you, baby?"

Not understanding him, she petted his cheeks, trying to comfort him.

He grabbed his phone and opened a new voice-to-text app he downloaded for her.

Handing her his phone, she quirked an eyebrow.

"I don't know how to make love, Thea."

As she read his words appearing on the screen, her eyes widened, and her expression softened.

"What if I do it wrong? What if I accidentally say something you don't like? I mean, you wouldn't hear it, but what if I wanted you to hear it? I'm messing up with words again."

Her eyebrows rose as she read the voice-to-text app.

Blushing, he said, "I dirty-talk, and I don't know if you'll like it. But I also wanted to try this app to see if you might."

He leaned forward, balancing his weight on his toned forearms. "I learned some dirty talk in sign language, but I thought you'd appreciate my hands being free."

Draven's hand, which had rested on her inner thigh, skimmed back up to trace the seam of her pussy. His finger dipped into her wetness, pushing inside her and curling to find her G-spot. She whimpered and spread her legs wider for him as he stroked her. The weariness eased in his chest.

"You like this, baby?" he asked.

Reading his words on the phone screen, Thea nodded.

"You want my cock to replace this finger? To stretch that pretty little pussy and hit you nice and deep?"

Rapid nodding from Thea. Another soft, breathy moan.

He moved forward, aligning the bulbous tip to her slick entrance. *Need* her. The head of his cock prodded her, inching inside but easing back out.

"Will you tell me again, Thea?"

Her hooded eyelids fluttered as his words appeared on the phone screen she held.

"Tell me what I want to hear, and I'll give you this cock all night long."

Thea shivered beneath him, put his phone down, and signed, "*I love you.*"

You can do this. Make love. Be soft.

His intense gaze bored into hers, projecting his every emotion and thought. His hips pushed forward as he plunged his shaft inside her gripping pussy.

Perfect. Tight, wet heaven.

Fuck.

How was a man supposed to hold back and *not* unravel for a woman who felt like utter bliss?

When she bucked, her pussy clamped around his rigid cock. A strangled noise wrangled its way out of Draven's throat. "Now, now, baby," he said. "Trying to make love here. Would appreciate some patience."

Another quirked eyebrow from her.

He reached forward and stretched their arms out over the pillow, weaving their fingers together. There. Romantic.

Sweat sheened his chest as he grappled with self-control. Slow thrusts. In. Out. *In. Out.* Slow was torture. His body hummed to slam against hers. His cock wept to rail her perfect pussy until she came around it—hard.

No fucking. Just making love. Was it obvious he had no idea what he was doing? Obvious by the way he gritted his teeth and the tendons in his neck strained? All he wanted to do was ravenously ram himself inside her until her eyes rolled back in her pretty head and she'd realize she would never want another man.

Words like *"mine,"* *"claim,"* and *"thrust"* consumed his thoughts.

No, go slow.

With furrowed, impatient eyebrows, Thea jerked her hips up and sank herself fully onto him, pinning herself on his cock. He filled her to the hilt. Her inner muscles closed around him and seemed to tug.

"Fuck," he barked, face tight with agony as his balls tingled and cock twitched inside her. *Do not immediately come in her.* "Are you trying to annihilate my self-control?" he asked her.

Her expression said, *"Yes."*

He swallowed. "You want it rough, baby?"

Her hands slid down the ropes of his muscled back until her fingernails dug into his ass cheeks and shoved him forward.

He coughed out a gasp-laugh hybrid. Maybe she didn't want to make love? Maybe anything they did was making love because they loved each other.

"You want to be fucked, Thea?" he asked.

Those wicked, pale blue eyes sang a siren song. The kind that led a man to his death—happily.

To the rhythm of her soft, mewling moans, he thrust. Her grapefruit scent imprinted in his lungs until every breath he took contained a trace of her.

He maneuvered her legs in a way that tipped her hips and allowed him to sink even deeper. His hips punched forward, and she whined gibberish that he translated as, *"More. Please, more."*

Her small breasts jounced as he thrust until the two of them ran out of breath, out of oxygen, and survived only on each other.

Her pussy pulsated around him, the beat of his new favorite song. One he could play again and again and never tire of.

"You know the best part about hooking up with a drummer?" Draven grunted into her ear as he shoved those hips forward and rocked them to grind his dick against the most sensitive parts of her. "*Rhythm*."

Chapter Thirty-Four

I get it now, she thought to herself as his hips kept moving. The reason women looked at Draven like he was a sex god —he was.

Even when she came around his dick, shrieking out her pleasure, he kept thrusting. She fumbled as she flung a hand over the sheets until she had his phone again and opened the voice-to-text app.

"*Fuck.*" His words appeared on the screen as his lips moved. "I can feel your pussy coming for me. So damn tight. Milking me. Greedy girl, you need it that bad?"

She blinked up at him, his gaze raking over her eyes, lips, neck, and breasts as he continued pistoning between her legs, pumping himself inside her. *God, he's just so good.*

"Too damn beautiful. Can't fucking look at you, or I'll come," he said, clenching his eyes shut. "Can't come yet."

She moaned as his words appeared on the screen; her inner muscles squeezed around him.

"Damn it," he cursed. Pulling his shaft out of her, she gasped out her discontentment, but he turned her and positioned her to face the bed. She held onto his phone and watched the app as he said, "Be a good girl and hold the headboard for me."

She did as she was told, laying up on her knees and holding the bed's headboard. She sat his phone on the pillow, so she could see what he said as he slowly guided his cock back inside her.

"From this position, I can..." He tilted her hips, and she fought to balance her weight on her knees as he slammed his dick forward and stroked that special mind-bending spot inside her.

"There it is," he grunted. "There's the spot that makes you purr for me. You like it when my cock rubs you there, baby?"

She moaned as their flesh slapped against each other. His expert hand sank low to play with her clit as he churned his hips, stirring himself in her.

"How am I going to ever stop touching you, Thea?" His words lit up on the screen. "When you feel this perfect..." His body surged forward, keeping up that steady, fast rhythm like nothing she had ever known.

His dirty, dominating words on the phone screen sank into her mind like some sexy form of brainwashing.

He strummed her swollen little bud of nerves, and she moaned gibberish as her fingernails bit into the bedsheets.

"That's my girl."

Harder thrust. Right against that deep spot inside her

that made her whimper and her entire body tremble. He hammered that spot again and again. Heat and building tension ricocheted through her.

"I want you to come for me again. Can you do that for me, baby? Be a good girl, and come around this hard cock. Show me you feel this too."

She gasped for breath as his hips jackhammered against her ass. The smooth globes of her backside quivered against him.

"Your pussy just keeps getting tighter and tighter. *Fuck*."

She cried out and wantonly met his every thrust, rocking herself against him.

"Making me...lose control."

Heat coiled tight in her abdomen. Her core jittered with pulsations. *Soaring*, soaring up into the clouds. Readying to free fall.

His hips steadily lost their rhythm; his full balls slapped against her rear as he thrust.

"Wearing those pearls all the time and making me think you wanted it soft and slow. But my girlfriend likes it hard. Rough. Dirty. Fuck, you're so perfect."

He sank a palm around her front to lightly hold her throat as he thrust inside her from behind and fingered her clit. "I like that I'm the only one who knows what a dirty girl you are, Thea. They think I'm going to corrupt you, but you're going to corrupt me, aren't you, baby? Fuck, nothing has ever felt this good. Time for you to come again."

Her head shot back, and her body went completely still just before she screamed.

Her vision splintered. Her pussy clutched him in such a tight grip that his hips stuttered, and his cock began to release inside her. Through their orgasms, his hips kept moving.

Finally, he pulled her back down to lay beside him. Their chests rose and fell, fighting to catch their breath.

She glanced at his veined shaft, which already jerked and began to harden again.

But all he did was hold her close.

Her body was exhausted, but her mind remained utterly awake. Thinking about their situation. About the timing.

His band would go on tour soon. Her parents did not accept her living with him. Her friends warned her to stay away from him.

They were like forbidden lovers. Romeo and Juliet.

She cuddled with him, burying her face into his chest, and assured herself, *We will have a different ending.*

"But you're not getting invested in him or anything, are you?" Elisa signed to Thea as Wren and Mallory set up the board game on their large dining table for game night.

Mal always hosted game nights for their friend group. Since Mal now lived with her fiancé and his young daughter, Thea sat on the couch beside Draven in Wren's massive apartment. She grinned at all the black furniture trying to make the place masculine and "rocker" whilst hosting traces of pink glitter from his daughter Armie's crafts.

When Elisa, Fifi, Mallory, and Wren realized Thea brought Draven over for game night, they all had similar uncomfortable expressions. Mouths drawn into thin lines. A few apparent frowns.

It was enough to crack Thea's heart.

Draven sat beside Thea, patiently waiting for the board game to begin as Elisa and Fifi signed to her.

"I told you he is my boyfriend. Of course, I am invested," Thea signed back.

She swore Draven's leg jumped when she signed "boyfriend." How much did he understand of what they were signing? Soon, he would know what her friends thought about him. He was picking up sign language faster than she expected.

"Signing in front of him like this is rude."

"Thea, what happens when he leaves for the band's tour in a month? He'll be gone for over half a year. Has he invited you to go with him?"

No. No, he had not. But they were newly together. She did not want to push him. Still, the idea of touring the world with him made her giddy.

Fifi added, *"And if he doesn't invite you along, would you guys do long distance? Groupies toss their thongs at him at every show. How can you feel confident in something like this? It's not like you."*

"*We are worried you are not being realistic,*" Elisa signed.

They sounded like her parents. Why didn't they understand that being "realistic" was a synonym for settling? "*Can't you just be happy that I'm happy?*"

Elisa and Fifi shared a knowing, concerned look.

Thea signed, "*Look, he will ask me to go on tour with him, okay? I know he will.*" But did she?

Mallory strode back into the living room and gestured for everyone to go sit at the table.

This week's board game was revealed. Scrabble.

Delightful, Thea huffed to herself. More words from a group of people she did not appreciate hearing from at the moment.

Could they not see Draven holding her hand as they walked to the table? Did they not perceive the little smiles they exchanged whenever their gazes met?

Wren sat across from Draven at the table and glared at his drummer. Wren was too busy directing all of his negative attention at Draven to notice Thea scowling back at him.

"*Anyone want drinks before we start?*" Mallory signed.

"*Beer, please,*" Draven signed back.

Wren's glare deepened as he scoffed at Draven's answer.

The tingles of rising fury prickled through Thea as she witnessed Draven sink further into his chair and sign, "*Never mind.*"

What the hell did Wren care what Draven drank at

game night? He had once seen Mallory and Thea tip back three shots of bubblegum vodka in a row while playing a distressing game of Monopoly.

Raising her chin defiantly, Thea signed, *"Two beers, please. We'll both have one."*

When Mallory returned with drinks, Draven squeezed Thea's thigh under the table as she set a beer in front of them.

Draven's hypnotic green eyes whispered, *"Thank you."*

Thea squeezed his thigh, telepathically telling him, *"I've got you. Wren is an ass."*

Lost in their own silent language, they nodded at each other and grinned before glancing back at the others.

See? *He loves me*, she thought. *He will ask me to go on tour with him.*

But Mal, Fifi, and Elisa looked at Thea with scrunched expressions of pity and dread, like they already foresaw her broken heart.

Chapter Thirty-Five

Draven was used to the looks of judgment, but they had never inspired as much inner turmoil as they did tonight. Because these were Thea's friends, and they didn't like him. They did not *know* him, and they did not like him. No—it was not about disliking him, it was about disliking him *for Thea*.

They don't think I'm good enough for her. Just like her parents.

He wished he lived in fifteenth-century Scotland where he could do some physical trials and "win" her, so no one could say Draven was not worthy. *Tell me what to do to earn her, and I will*. Shoot some arrows? Give him a bow. Lift a boulder? *Just point to it, baby*.

As Mallory dished out the Scrabble pieces, Draven slowly lifted the beer bottle to his lips and took a swig.

From across the table, Wren stared him down with icy

eyes and shook his head. *Hello, familiar expression of disgust.*

"What's your problem with me, man?" Draven asked.

Wren shrugged but kept his disapproving gaze on the beer.

Draven let out a defeated sigh and shoved his beer bottle to the side, away from him, to symbolize he would not drink any more.

Suddenly, Thea's fingers wrapped around his beer bottle and lifted it off the table. Wren and Draven looked over to watch Thea tip the bottle back and *chug* it.

Draven's jaw dropped. The brazen workings of her swallowing throat and lips mesmerized him as she gulped down the contents of the bottle. As she drank, she focused her narrowed, angry eyes on Wren. Draven could *hear* her inner thought, *Anything to say now, asshole?*

There it was again—that bright, sparkling love taking up room in his chest. They stood up for each other, always. She was his... God, she was his best friend.

Draven vibrated in his seat, withholding laughter and unadulterated lust as Thea swallowed the last swig of beer in the bottle. She politely placed the bottle back onto the table, putting a coaster under it to catch the condensation.

Draven performed a slow clap before proudly signing, "*That's my girlfriend.*"

"For how long?" Wren asked.

Good mood dwindling, Draven shot back, "What is that supposed to mean?"

"We go on tour in less than a month," Wren reminded

him. "Are you taking her with us?"

Draven sat up straighter in the chair. "And if I do?"

"So, you will ask her to go on tour with us?"

"Just say what you want to say, Wren," Draven told him.

"If you take her on tour, you make her press pause on everything here. No more makeup jobs. Or opportunities. Over six months of just following you around to shows," Wren said.

Wren hit Draven with hard facts as he continued, "Are you willing to hold her back from what she wants in life? Willing to ask her to drop her whole career? Loving someone is about looking out for their best interests. If you take her with us, then you don't love her. Because love isn't selfish. If you take her away from working toward her dream career, how are you any better than her asshole ex?"

So, this is what it feels like to spiral, Draven thought to himself. He could not banish Wren's words from his mind. Even while making grilled cheese sandwiches on the stove, he felt overwhelmed.

Not knowing what to do made it hurt to breathe. The tour was weeks away. He needed to start packing—waiting till the last minute never worked for him; he always forgot something.

"Are you willing to hold her back from what she wants

in life?"

Were they supposed to do long distance? He would—for her. But what if, in that distance, she realized he was not what she wanted? Thea needed just as much validation and attention as he did. They were equally needy, their love languages in perfect sync.

"If you take her away from working toward her dream career, how are you any better than her asshole ex?"

Dammit. It wasn't fair. Wren could take Mallory all over the world because she was his daughter's nanny. But if Draven wanted to explore areas of the continents with his woman, it was selfish?

He wanted to hold Thea's hand and walk on pink sand. Or eat Belgium waffles in Belgium. Or take her to ritzy, high afternoon tea in some London castle, so she could wear her favorite dress and strand of pearls and feel like royalty.

Maybe he could find some international movie sets for her to have some makeup gigs while his band went on tour. That would fix everything, right?

"If you take her with us, you don't love her." What did Wren know? He had screwed things up with Mallory, too, before groveling to win her back.

As days melted into weeks, Draven's kisses lengthened. He took his time. Savored. Thea's lips slanted over his, and all he could do was whisper to her mouth, *"What do I do, Thea? I want to be good enough for you. I want to make the right decision."* Desperately, he kissed her, praying his lips did not taste like a bitter goodbye.

He wanted her to go on tour with him, but he wanted to do right by her. Asking her to drop everything to go with him was not fair. Pressing pause on her dream, that was what her parents wanted. Or her asshole ex.

"*Are you okay?*" Thea signed to him after he accidentally burned their grilled cheese sandwiches.

Draven signed back, "*I'm fine,*" because he did not yet know how to sign, "*It feels like there is a clock ticking, counting down the seconds until you blink and see that I'm not the man you are meant to be with. I don't wear ties. I'm selfish. And I'm about to be gone for half a year. And you'll realize you never loved me; I was just a 'good time.'*"

No one wants us together. If she went with him, she would regret him. He knew it, deep down.

What had his ex once said? Oh, yeah. "*You fuck a drummer. You don't date one.*"

How long until Thea realized that too?

Draven was slipping away from her, and Thea could not figure out why or how to stop it. His grins were dim and even —not crooked and bright and teasing. Not *normal* Draven grins. But whenever she asked what was wrong, he shrugged and kissed her until she forgot what they were talking about.

He cooked her meals, cuddled her on the couch, kissed and pleasured her in his bed, but she could see the dark premonition shining in his chartreuse-green eyes. They continued playing house, but each passing day was another invisible stab to her stomach.

Why hasn't he asked me to go on tour with him? Did he see her as a burden? Too much effort to take her along? Did he worry about the time he would spend translating everything to her?

All of those doubts swarmed her chest as she recalled why so many hearing people had walked out of her life before. *Too much effort for them.* As much as she was over Alec, *that* had never worried her. Draven was not a member of the deaf community. He did not get it.

Work was not any better. She had secured a five-day makeup assistant job on another film set, but she seemed to make a mistake every hour—or at least, get in trouble every hour.

"I told her I needed to be on set at nine. Not my fault she made me late."

"She is deaf; she needs you to write that kind of thing down."

How was she supposed to be blamed for an actor taking too long in makeup when the famed celebrity arrived forty-five minutes late for Thea to work on him?

"I told her I am allergic to parabens! She did this on purpose."

"Why would she do it on purpose? Did you write down that you were allergic?"

How was Thea supposed to know one of the female

leads was allergic to a particular type of makeup if no one told her?

On the fourth day, the Director took her to the side and gave her a note that read, *"Look, I get that you're disabled, and I'm all for diversity. But I hire people because of their talent, and I don't know that it's worth it to keep someone on set if they require…more than the others. Do you know what I mean?"*

Too much effort.

"I think if we had more deaf actors, you would be a better fit," he added to the note. *"But this film doesn't, and a few cast members have complained."*

Burden.

Thea walked to her apartment in a daze. She had been fired. Again. But this time from her dream job. Because they didn't think she was good enough.

Tears streamed down her face as she opened the door and trudged inside. Draven stirred chili on the stove and stopped when he noticed her fling herself dramatically onto the couch.

Rushing over, he saw her tears and froze. A dark, menacing stoniness overtook his face. *"What's wrong? Who made you cry?"* he signed.

He is still learning sign language. Maybe Draven didn't see her as too much effort. Yet. She signed, *"I got fired."*

He frowned at the words. He did not know the sign for "fired" yet. He grabbed a notepad and pen and handed them to her.

Too much effort.

"*I got fired from the set today. Even when I got fired from my old finance firm, it didn't feel like this.*" Her face hot and wet with tears, she wrote, "*What if this was all a mistake, Draven? I know finance. It fits me. I work by myself, and no one has to bend to me. I'm not a burden with numbers. What if I'm not supposed to be doing movie makeup? What if this was all a big mistake?*"

He shook his head back and forth at her note. He signed, "*Thea, no, you're so talented.*"

He memorized how to tell me I am talented. Her heart broke deeper in her chest, fragments of it traveling in her veins and clogging up her arteries.

Invite me with you, Draven. Say I'm not too much effort. Say I'm worth it.

"*What if I'm asking for too much?*" she wrote.

"*Fuck that,*" he wrote. "*You deserve anything you want. Anything, Thea.*"

A tear dripped down her cheeks and over her lips. "*My parents won't respond to my text messages. They think I'm living a lie.*"

When Draven saw her words, he held her so closely, her ear on his chest, she swore she felt each beat of his heart. The tempo was much faster than she expected, like the heartbeat of someone running.

She signed, "*I just want to feel good enough.*" She wanted to feel good enough for a career and for him. Why had he not asked her to go on tour yet?

But his eyes were closed as he held her.

Chapter Thirty-Six

The tour was three weeks away.

And everything held on by a delicate, thinning thread.

Because Thea realized Draven was not going to ask her to go on tour with him.

She saw his packed suitcases in his bedroom. The three cases mocked her. Silent symbols that her boyfriend would roll the suitcases around the world but wouldn't haul her around with him.

I would be too much baggage.

The two of them danced around the subject. They disassociated and stared at the walls. It was a quiet battle of who would be the first to break and confront the issue.

Thea finally snapped as they ate their morning cereal. She slapped the kitchen countertop and signed to him, "*Why?*"

He stared solemnly at her hands, a blank expression telling her nothing.

"*I know you understand me. Why?*" she signed. "*Why haven't you invited me on tour? We haven't talked about it.*"

Calm and way too collected, like he had already seen this scene play out on the big screen, Draven reached for the pen and notepad. He wrote, "*Thea, your parents aren't talking to you. You're fighting with your friends. It's all my fault.*"

Her eyebrows shot up into her hairline. "*What do you mean?*" she signed.

"*They all see it. Why don't you?*" he wrote, tossing the pen down. He signed, "*I'm not good enough for you. The sooner you realize that, the easier it will be for both of us.*"

"*What are you talking about? I love you, Draven.*"

"*No, you don't, baby,*" he wrote. "*You have loved your vacation from normal life. You have loved feeling free, and I want you to be free. I want you to do anything you want. But we both know I was just temporary.*"

Lungs wringing behind her ribs, she stood from her barstool and signed, "*No. You were never temporary to me. Draven, don't talk like that.*"

"*I love you, Thea. But everyone can see it. You were never meant to be mine. This life is making you sad. You've cried over it.*"

"*Not over you! I just had that bad day. I wasn't crying over you.*"

"*If this were easier, I would never let you go. But I can't fucking stand it to see you sad. It makes me want to rip my damn skin off. This isn't working, Thea. Too many things stand in our way.*"

Too much effort. That was what she understood him to say. Too many things stood in their way, and being with her was too much effort.

Thea's ability to breathe dissipated into the ether.

He wanted to give up on her because of her disapproving family and their friends? Screw that. What about Romeo and Juliet?

Thea wanted him to fight for her. To die for her if she asked—and yes, she realized that was dramatic, but that was who she was. She was a ride-or-die kind of woman. Either she felt loved utterly and completely, from head to toe, or she didn't. There was no "*I love you, but...*" Either someone saw her, heard her, "got" her, or they never would.

Was it too much to ask for someone who loved her to willingly put in the effort?

Screw him.

Thea wrote in messy swipes of the pen, "*For the first time in my life, I decided to stop worrying about making other people happy. I stopped actively trying to be what they wanted me to be. I don't care what anyone else thinks about us. I just want you.*"

She pressed her lips into a thin line as she wrote, "*I have spent my life bending to make it easier for people to relate to me. Stretching myself so thin to prove myself in everything I did. And you're not willing to face a few sour people to be with me?*"

She threw the notepad in front of him on the countertop and signed, *"Screw you, Draven. You're right. You're not good enough for me."*

Heart mangled, lungs strangled, and eyes prickling with tears, Thea turned and strode out of their apartment in her pajamas.

She walked away.

She did not stop walking away until she got to Mallory's place. She did not stop until Mal saw her brutal, broken expression and wrapped Thea in her arms.

Finally held still, Thea crumpled. Her knees gave out from under her.

Because a human body can only get so far without a heart.

"What the FUCK did you do?" Wren's text message lit up Draven's phone. He ignored it.

Four minutes passed.

"Thea is over here SOBBING on Mal's shoulder. She can't even sign because she keeps hugging herself like she's got appendicitis or some shit."

Draven closed his eyes and pressed his face down into the pillows of his bed, smothering himself. The sheets still smelled like her.

Thea's words speared through his gut. *"You're not willing to face a few sour people to be with me?"* *He* felt like he had appendicitis. She might as well have kicked him in the liver, kidneys, appendix, and stomach.

He knew it had been coming. "It" being her leaving. She was always going to realize he wasn't the one for her.

After all, Draven was only good for one thing. *A good time.* Hell, his friends knew it.

Half an hour later, a loud *BOOM* came from outside his bedroom. Robbers? They could take anything they wanted. After all, Draven's most valuable possession was no longer in the apartment.

Then, his bedroom door swung open, banging against the wall as Wren barged inside the room.

Blinking through swollen eyelids, Draven saw Wren and murmured into his pillow, "Did you break my door down?"

"No, you idiot, I still have a spare key."

Face down on the pillow, Draven shrugged.

"What the hell are you doing?"

Another shrug.

"Thea is crying her eyes out at my place, and you're lying in bed—"

Wren yanked at his shoulder, forcing Draven to turn over on the bed and look at his bandmate. Wren cut himself off and blinked a few times, registering Draven's pink face, damp cheeks, and red eyes. Draven's mussed dark hair spiked out at different angles like he had pulled on it every which way.

"Aw, hell," Wren said. His husky voice dripped thick disbelief. "You actually love her?"

"They say if you love something, let it go. So I did, Wren. I did. And it feels like I'm dying." Draven clutched at his heart, fingernails digging into his pectoral muscles like his new instinct was to rip out the organ that caused him so much pain. "Am I dying?"

Wren cursed and grabbed Draven's hand to prevent him from clawing at himself anymore.

"I was just trying to do the right thing. You told me not to be selfish, so I wasn't. I did it, Wren. And now I—I feel like I can't breathe."

"Shit." Wren squeezed Draven's shoulder. "I've never seen you like this, man. I'm not sure what to do. You're scaring the hell out of me."

"Why do you hate me, Wren? I don't get it."

Wren's brows furrowed. "I don't hate you, Drave. I don't."

"You're mean to me, Wren. Your little snide comments about how irresponsible I am and shit. It hurts my feelings," Draven admitted, too tender and vulnerable to care how he worded it. "You don't think I'm good enough for Thea."

Taken aback, Wren hesitated to reply. "I... A lot changed when I suddenly had Armie to take care of, Drave. I couldn't go out and party, or drink, or do any of that. It's tough being around someone who is still so—"

"There you go." Draven pointed at him. "You were about to say something else mean."

"Stop using the word 'mean.' I feel like we're on an elementary school playground."

"Another dig at how immature I am compared to you." Draven tried to turn back around to press his face into the pillows again, but Wren did not let him.

"Dammit," Draven cursed. "You don't even know anything about my life anymore. You don't *ask*. I get that Armie keeps you busy, but judging me with snide comments all the time, when you don't even know what's going on in my life, is messed up."

Wren snorted. "Draven, I know what's going on in your life."

"No. You don't. Remember Mimi? Well, she started getting dementia right after we graduated. Did you know that? How about how the second we signed with Maximo, I started paying for the best doctors, the best care, and got her into an expensive as hell nursing home, all while paying my own school loans? The entirety of my first paycheck went to that. But no, you thought I spent it all on beer or something."

Draven added, "Then, Summer decided to go to school for music, much to my parents' dismay, and they wouldn't help her out either. So, to save my future cellist baby sister from student loans, I paid for her NYU classes. Her summer programs. Her apartment. Then, Geo went to college last year, and you know what? Even though he chose a smart science-related major, I'm paying for his school too. Because that speck of respect I saw in my parents' eyes when they found out I was paying for Summer's was the first respect I'd seen from them since I became a drummer."

Wren gaped at his friend. "Why didn't you tell us any of that? We could help you—"

"Because having to prove who you are to *your closest friends* feels a lot like rock bottom. I shouldn't have to explain myself to you. You should believe in me. Thea always believed in me." At the mention of Thea, Draven tried to face plant in his pillows again.

"Stop that," Wren scolded. "God, the two of you are so dramatic."

"She doesn't want me anymore. She'll stay in L.A. and keep pursuing makeup and live out her dream. That's what needed to happen, right?"

"Drave..."

"I've just been feeling so fucking alone. You guys don't care about me being in the band anymore. Mimi can't remember my name. And then, Thea came here, and she saw me. She *got* me. I want to give her everything she's ever wanted in life. I've never loved anyone like this," Draven said, feeling like a raw sack of emotions.

Draven continued, "I want to spoil her and feed her and take care of her. I want her to win some makeup award at a Hollywood event—does that exist? I want to stand and clap and cry as she walks up to accept it. I want her to feel the spotlight warming her and making her feel like every choice she ever made in life was worth it. I want to be worth it."

"Draven," Wren mumbled. "I'm sorry I told you to break things off. I didn't realize."

"Does she hate me now too? Why does everyone hate me?"

With a tortured, guilty expression, Wren stressed, "Nobody hates you, Drave. No one who knows you could ever hate you." He let out a deep sigh. "You really love her?"

Draven's expression twisted into: *"Are you dumb enough to ask me that, motherfucker?"*

Wren snorted again and patted his friend's shoulder. "Then, do everything you can to keep her, man. Win her back."

"Even if I'm not good enough?"

Wren smirked. "Can you think of anyone good enough for Thea?"

Draven's lips curled downward. "No one is good enough for Thea," he answered adamantly.

Wren nodded and smiled. "Then, yeah. You're more than enough for her."

Chapter Thirty-Seven

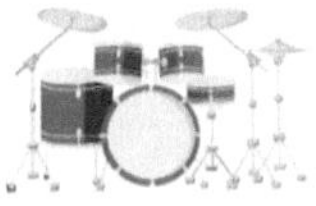

Lesson learned, Thea thought to herself as she stood in front of their apartment the next day after the breakup. *Always trust your friends, even when you think they are wrong.* Mallory had warned her that Draven would break her heart.

Now, Thea was moving out, having to find a new apartment, and most likely having to go back to a stable nine-to-five finance job to pay for rent.

All last night, Draven had called her. She finally texted him back, "*I don't do phone calls, dummy.*"

So, he texted her thirty-five apologies. One had caught her eye the most. "*I didn't want to invite you on tour because I didn't want to be the reason you press pause on your dream. You're in L.A., the land of movie set jobs. On tour for six months, you could lose your momentum. I never want to hold you back, Thea. Ever.*"

Leaving with him would have been her decision. And

hello? Touring the world with him was a once-in-a-lifetime opportunity. She could have practiced and learned her craft during that time. It wasn't just "pressing pause." *Life happens in every moment.* More time with Draven would never feel like pressing pause.

It didn't matter *why* he pushed her away. It happened and could happen again.

She needed to start over. She needed space—a lie. She hated space.

Her life had been filled with too much space. Space in her childhood home where her parents and siblings struggled to connect with her. Space in her school classrooms where hearing students avoided her, scared of passing notes and being yelled at.

She wanted a grade-A clinger. A *"I never want you to leave my arms"* teddy bear of a man. That was what she *thought* Draven was.

Taking a deep breath, she opened the apartment door and stepped inside.

Pink Post-it notes. Everywhere. On the table. Couch. TV. Fridge. Microwave. Walls. Everywhere.

She gasped as she found one on the floor beside her shoe. She picked it up and read, *"Before you move out and leave me heartbroken and destitute, read each of these. I triple-dog dare you, baby. So, you have to do it. It's the law. – The Man Who Loves You."*

Swallowing, mouth suddenly dry, she followed the trail of notes, reading them and feeling the tension in her chest sinking.

"*I promise to watch horror movies with you even when you scarily chuckle as people get murdered. Every moment holding you in my arms on the couch makes the nightmares worth it. -A Scaredy Cat With Big Muscles.*"

"*I love the way you do everything way too loudly. You laugh and chew like a menace. You bang cabinet doors shut cause you can't tell you're doing it. Life is too quiet without your noise, baby. I miss you. -A Very Lonely Man In Love With You.*"

"*I want you to teach me how to dance. The way you flail your arms and shriek with laughter. Nothing has ever been so stunning to me. So beautiful. Your lawnmower move changed my perspective on life. -A Drummer In Need Of A Dance Partner.*"

"*How are you going to move out if I hide all your underwear? Joking. Don't hold this one against me. -Your Inappropriate Landlord Looking For An Excuse To Hide Your Panties.*"

Thea breathily laughed, striving to swallow down the sound. Swallow down the rising emotions.

"*Kissing you feels like wrapping a fuzzy blanket around my soul. I don't know if that's a weird thing to write, but it's true. -The Man Who Does Not Write Song Lyrics For A Reason.*"

She grabbed another note. And another.

"*If you stay, you can have all the almond milk you want. I will buy an almond tree and milk the nuts myself. -Someone Who Doesn't Know How Almond Milk Is Made But Will Do Anything For You.*"

"*I'm sorry you ever felt the need to bend yourself to others' expectations. The only bending you will ever do with me is of the sexual yoga position variety. -A Man Who Would Literally Die Just To See You In Those Yoga Shorts Again And Also Die Before Ever Asking You To Change Yourself.*"

"*I promise never to use up all the hot water before you shower. -A Man Cursed To Cold Showers For The Woman He Loves.*"

"*If I have to bribe your friends to like me, I will. Do they like fresh pumpkin pie? -A Baker Driven To Bribery.*"

"*I promise to let you practice your makeup on me. Whatever You Want. Always. I'm Yours. -Your Helplessly-In-Love Roommate.*"

"*I loved hearing how close you were with your grandfather. I'm sorry I can't meet him. I will buy you a hundred pearl necklaces in his absence just because they bring you comfort. -A Man Willing To Make An Enemy Of Every Oyster He Meets.*"

"*I'm an idiot who thought I was doing the right thing by letting you go. Forgive me? -The Clown Who Listened To Wren.*"

Dazedly stumbling, she made it to her bedroom door, which was also covered in pink notes.

"*I am more than willing to face a few sour people to be with you, Thea. I'm fairly certain I would have a fistfight against a chainsaw for you. -Someone Who Will Always Put In The Effort.*"

"*You are perfect to me. More than enough. I know I'll*

never be worthy of you, but since no one else ever will be either, I will dedicate my life to being all that you need. – Draven (I couldn't think of something fun for this one. I take loving you very seriously)."

Opening the door, she found Draven sitting on the floor, his legs crisscrossed under him as he wrote on more squares of pink paper.

His head shot up, his lips parted, and he dropped his marker. He signed, *"No! I'm not done yet. You were supposed to come later. I still have more to write—"*

She fell to her knees in front of him and tackled him to the ground.

Slack-jawed, he caught her, maneuvering their bodies so none of her limbs hit the floor. Protecting her. Always.

Warm tears streaked her face, but she did not care. They were tears of love—salty, overflowing love. More written notes littered the floor all around them. This man loved her so much, he wrote a year's worth of love notes.

She cupped his face, bit her lip, and blinked at him through watery eyes. *My dreams are full of bright green irises. Of crooked smiles. Of dirty jokes.* Of Draven.

She had never wanted that Prince Charming and Princess fairytale. Draven and Thea were knights, ready to fight for each other at every turn. They fumbled around in thick armor, which was invisible to the world, but they saw it and the hidden scars beneath. Their wounds matched like couple tattoos.

She kissed his chin. His cheek. His nose.

He held her close and teared up before her eyes. Both

of them were blubbering, weepy messes as they kissed each other's faces but not the lips. Not yet.

When their mouths finally met, they tasted like salty ocean water. And love.

Pure, accepting love.

Like the feeling of meeting each other's gazes across the room and breaking out into helpless, goofy grins over nothing.

When they kissed, Thea memorized next year's Thanksgiving proclamation. *I am thankful for everything that led me to him. Everything, always and forever.*

Epilogue

Four Years Later

"Why did Alec just text me to tell you to stop sending him flowers?" Thea signed to her husband as they sat backstage and waited for his band to be called to the wings for the concert.

Thea had gone along with him on every tour of Medusa's Tears, and he had searched high and low for contacts in different major cities to align makeup gigs for her in each one.

Before each show, Draven kissed Thea's forehead and the back of her hand, and Mallory swooned at how adorable it was. Thea's friends had finally gotten it; they had finally seen how the two were a perfect match.

Funny how all it takes is to see a man on his knees for you and hundreds of love notes to prove to your closest friends that he is serious about you, Thea thought, smiling to herself. Then again, her friends would never let her accept anything less.

Thea asked Draven, *"You've been sending my ex-boyfriend flowers?"*

"Dude," Wren signed, shaking his head from where he sat in the green room with them. Mal sat to his right and grinned. Mal always grinned whenever Draven signed to Thea.

Draven chuckled and signed back, *"I send Thea's ex a 'sorry for your loss' bouquet each year on the day she moved in with me. Just trying to thank him, you know?"*

Mal and Wren laughed, but Thea quirked an eyebrow.

"Thank him for cheating on me?" Thea asked.

"Thank him for letting you go, so I could have you."

Draven palmed her hips from her seat beside him and lifted her with his sexy, bulging biceps. He planted her onto his lap. She wiggled, and he kissed her neck, clearly forgetting that he needed to go on stage in a matter of minutes and that their friends were right there.

"Damn, you guys really can't go without touching each other for more than three minutes, huh?" Mal signed.

"I clocked it this time," Wren signed. *"Three minutes and seven seconds. A new record of self-control."*

"I say we leave before they actively make out and forget we're here like on Christmas—"

"We thought that door was locked!" Draven signed back as Thea giggled and hid her face.

Wren shook his head again, the way he often did when

Draven spoke, but his expression never held the same disapproval it did from years back. Only fondness. Sometimes minor annoyance, but only when Draven deserved it.

"*Okay, we'll leave you two alone to discuss Draven sending your ex roses. At least, I assume roses,*" Wren signed to Draven. "*Cause of the thorns?*"

"*I order extra sharp thorns,*" Draven signed, and Thea playfully slapped his shoulder.

"*See you out there, man.*" Wren nodded and walked with Mal to the door.

Draven yelled something to get Wren's attention back and signed, so Thea and Mal could understand, "*If my wife locks me in here to have her wicked way with me, go ahead and start the show without me.*"

Wren rolled his eyes, this time wearing some annoyance on his face as he replied, "*We can't start without you, bro.*"

Draven shrugged. "*I'm just the drummer.*"

Wren scoffed and signed back, "*And a lyricist. And an arrogant asshole who knows our fans will throw a riot if we try to start without you.*"

"*Fine,*" Draven signed, making no effort to hide his smile. He turned to Thea. "*You're going to have to wait till after the show for your husband to pleasure you till you scream.*"

"*Gross. We're out of here,*" Wren signed.

Mal blew a kiss to them and left with her husband.

In the privacy of the green room, Thea bit back a grin

and asked Draven, *"What kind of flowers do you send Alec?"*

"Sunflowers because you are my sun," he signed.

She rolled her eyes and quirked an eyebrow. *"Really?"*

His chest shook with restrained laughter as he signed, *"Did you know petunias symbolize bitterness?"*

She snorted. *"Stop sending him flowers, Draven. We're married now. You won."*

"Okay, if that's what my WIFE wants," Draven signed but yelled "wife" aloud, because he loved calling her that. She could pick up a tomato in a grocery store, and he would stand beside her, looking so proud as he said, "That's my *wife*," as if she had just cured some disease.

God, I love this man, she thought.

"What song are you guys opening up with tonight?" she signed.

His wicked grin told her before he could reply, *"My favorite. 'Woman in pearls.'"*

Do not blush, she told herself, but even married to this man, her cheeks pinkened. She knew the lyrics well, reading them late at night after the song was released and hit number one on the charts.

"Standing there so prim and proper
Do they know you fuck a rocker?
Wearing pretty pearls like a collar
Do they know that you're a watcher?
Watching my hand stroke up and down
So wet, baby, you could drown."

"Can I veto that song?" she signed, blushing deeply

now as the words ran through her head. Her parents had finally warmed up to Draven, but when that song went viral, her father did not make eye contact with either of them for three months.

"Why would you want to veto the song about you watching me jerk off? It was a pivotal part of our relationship."

She stuck her tongue out at him, and he flicked the pink tip of his against hers, causing a rusty groan to hum in her chest.

His head jerked to the side just when he began kissing her. He pouted, and she knew he was being called to the stage.

"Watch our first song, baby." He pointed to the large screen TV in the green room where they relaxed. *"You'll like it, I promise."*

Suspicious, she watched. When the band took their places on stage, closed captioning ran across the screen, reading *"Audience: Screams."*

She smirked at the way her husband held his drumsticks over his head, preparing for the first song.

After the first lyric appeared on the TV, her lips curled into a tender smile because she knew this song well. Another one Draven wrote about her.

"Thought it'd sound like church bells, but it sounds like silence.

Thought it'd sound like bird chirps, but it sounds like quiet."

She stretched out on the sofa and closed her eyes. If she

focused hard enough, she could almost feel the thrumming vibrations of the speakers from her spot laying down. She knew the lyrics well, not needing to glance at the TV.

"Nothing else sounds like you.
They think I'm not good enough.
Do you agree?
When you dreamed up your perfect man,
he'd never look like me.
They tell me I'll never be enough.
But, baby, I'll be all that you need,
because you sound like love, to me."

THE END

Don't want to miss another M. K. Hale romcom?
Join her newsletter:
http://www.mkhale.com/contact.html
Follow her on Instagram & Facebook: @mkhaleauthor
Join her Facebook Fan Group for Exclusives:
"M. K. Hale's Hotties"
If you enjoyed the story, I would LOVE if you would

be willing to leave a review or help get the word out about this romcom to others who might enjoy it! Thank you for reading!

Leave an Amazon Review
Leave an Apple Books Review
Leave a Goodreads Review
Leave a BookBub Review

Acknowledgments

The characters in this book have a special place in my heart. They really bloomed on the page and fell in love so hard and fast, I was like, "Wait! You two can't get together so quick! We need more drama."

Thank you to my beta readers Atousa and Kiki! Thank you to my parents who champion me to everyone they know—even though my books contain sex scenes. It's appreciated! Thank you to my aunts for believing in me and my uncle who always asks, "What's new with your book?" I cherish being able to respond, "Which one?"

Thank you to my mom—my best friend—who spends countless hours listening to me talk about characters and plots while we walk around the neighborhood, and she pretends to not be bored. The woman, who, after reading THE DRUMMER'S ROOMMATE, asked me, "*Now what's the difference between this and porn?*" She believes there is too much sex in this book.

Thank you to God/Fate/Life for all he has given me and for not smiting me when I write smut.

Finally, THANK YOU, READERS! YOU ARE THE REASON FOR MY EXISTENCE. I hope you enjoyed Thea and Draven's story. If you did, I would LOVE if you would be willing to leave a review or help get the word out about this story to others who might enjoy it!

I'm forgetting to thank somebody; I just know it. So, this is for you! Insert name here: ___________

M. K. Hale writes romance novels starring dirty-talking heroes and the witty women who leave them tongue-tied. She specializes in romantic comedies and has dabbled in comedy for years, including standup, improv, and sketch comedy. She believes laughter is the best medicine, except for, you know, actual medicine.

She obtained her English degree from the University of Maryland and spends her free time reading as many romance novels as humanly possible. If you enjoy paranormal reverse harem romance with an abnormal amount of heat, she also writes under M. K. Kate.

Follow her on social media: **@mkhaleauthor**
Facebook Fan Group: "M. K. Hale's Hotties"
Join her newsletter:
http://www.mkhale.com/contact.html

TIMESHARE BOYFRIEND: Steamy New Adult Beach Romantic Comedy Enemies to Lovers Novel

The love of a lifetime—two weeks at a time.

Reliving the same summer romance at an annual timeshare turns first love into first hate.

Evie Turner and Adam Pierce start off with the perfect summer romance, but when they reunite five years later, he acts like she is wet sand on the bottom of his expensive shoes. Hurt and embarrassed, Evie dedicates her two weeks at the timeshare each year to making him regret his decision. Throughout their young adult years, she tortures him—in a bikini.

After his words sting like jellyfish, she wants him on his knees, begging for forgiveness. Begging for her.

The girl in love with love. The boy who watches mob movies to remind himself that trust means betrayal. A clock of two weeks ticks away until they spend another three hundred and fifty-one days trying to forget each other. Until next year.

As the passion between them rises with the summer temperature, Evie can't help but feel his embraces are like a sunset: beautiful and temporary.

Above all, Evie must not forget one very important lesson: If he is hot, he can burn you.

Better get the aloe.

HATING HIM: A Steamy New Adult Sports Romantic Comedy

Accidentally seducing the wrong guy has never been so right.

Mandy has a plan to move on from her cheating ex by seducing her best friend's brother. Instead, she mistakenly seduces a stranger with a body from an erotic fairy tale. For Mandy, an art major who only paints in black and white, Brandon adds a dangerous splash of color to her life.

Brandon Gage is used to getting what he wants, so he won't give up his pursuit of her despite her telling him she's been in love with his roommate Jake since high school. After a sports injury, he becomes her patient at the health clinic where she works and hatches his own plan to make Mandy forget about Jake and fall for him.

He soon learns that pretending to date her only makes him want her more. Who will be the winner in "Operation Mandy"?